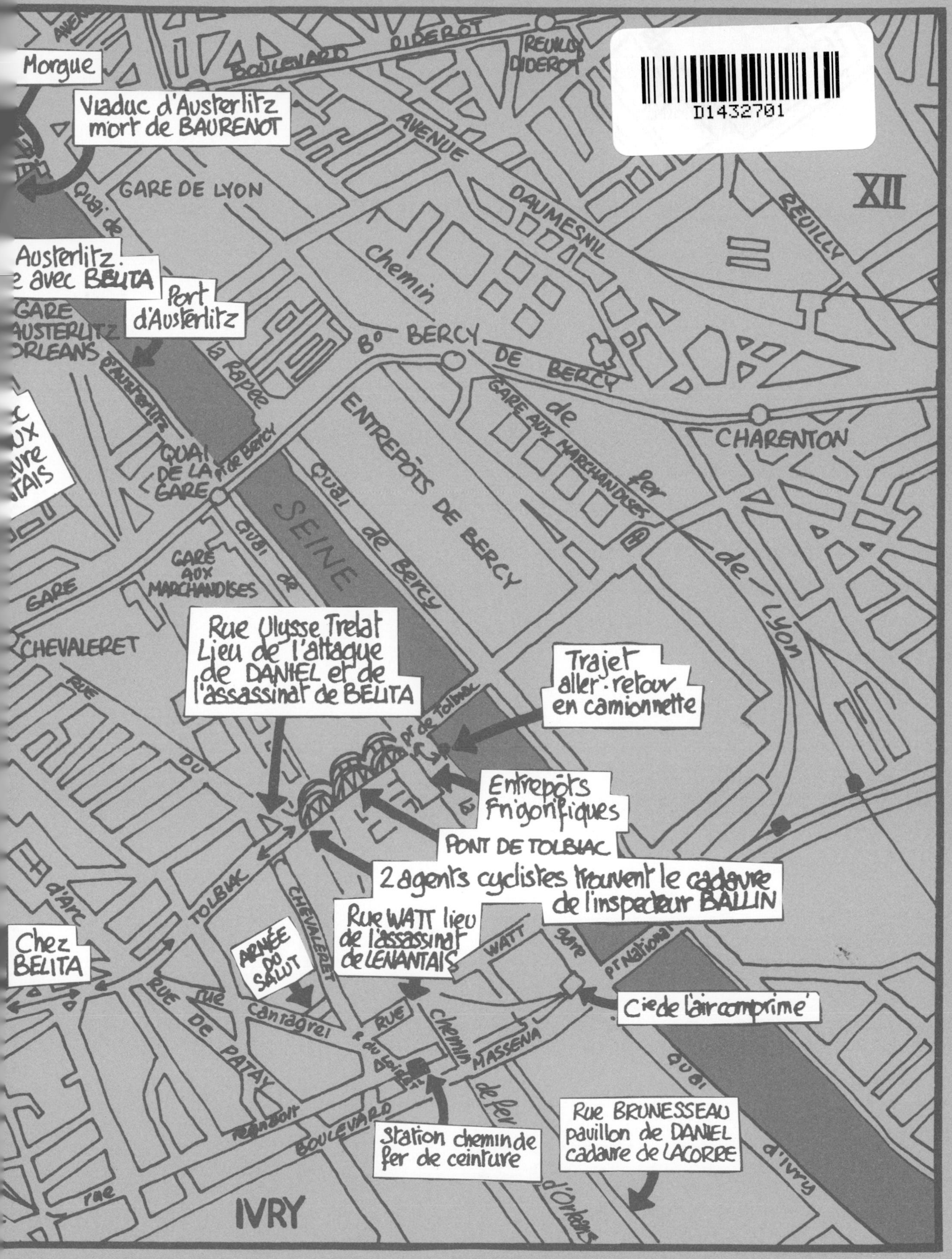

Morgue
Viaduc d'Austerlitz mort de BAURENOT
Austerlitz. avec BELITA
Port d'Austerlitz
GARE AUSTERLITZ ORLEANS
Rue Ulysse Trelat Lieu de l'attaque de DANIEL et de l'assassinat de BELITA
Trajet aller-retour en camionnette
Entrepôts Frigorifiques
PONT DE TOLBIAC
2 agents cyclistes trouvent le cadavre de l'inspecteur BALLIN
Rue WATT lieu de l'assassinat de LENANTAIS
Chez BELITA
ARMÉE DU SALUT
Cie de l'air comprimé
Station chemin de fer de ceinture
Rue BRUNESSEAU pavillon de DANIEL cadavre de LACORRE
BOULEVARD DIDEROT
REUILLY DIDEROT
AVENUE DAUMESNIL
REUILLY
XII
GARE DE LYON
Quai de la Rapée
Chemin de fer de Lyon
Bd BERCY
DE BERCY
GARE AUX MARCHANDISES
CHARENTON
ENTREPÔTS DE BERCY
Quai de Bercy
SEINE
QUAI DE LA GARE
Pt de Bercy
Quai de la gare
GARE AUX MARCHANDISES
GARE
CHEVALERET
RUE DU
Pt de Tolbiac
TOLBIAC
CHEVALERET
d'Arc
RUE DE PATAY
rue Cantagrel
RUE
r. du Loiret
Chemin de fer d'Orléans
MASSENA
WATT
gare
Pt National
Quai d'Ivry
BOULEVARD
rue
IVRY

TARDI & LÉO MALET A NESTOR BURMA MYSTERY

FOG OVER TOLBIAC BRIDGE

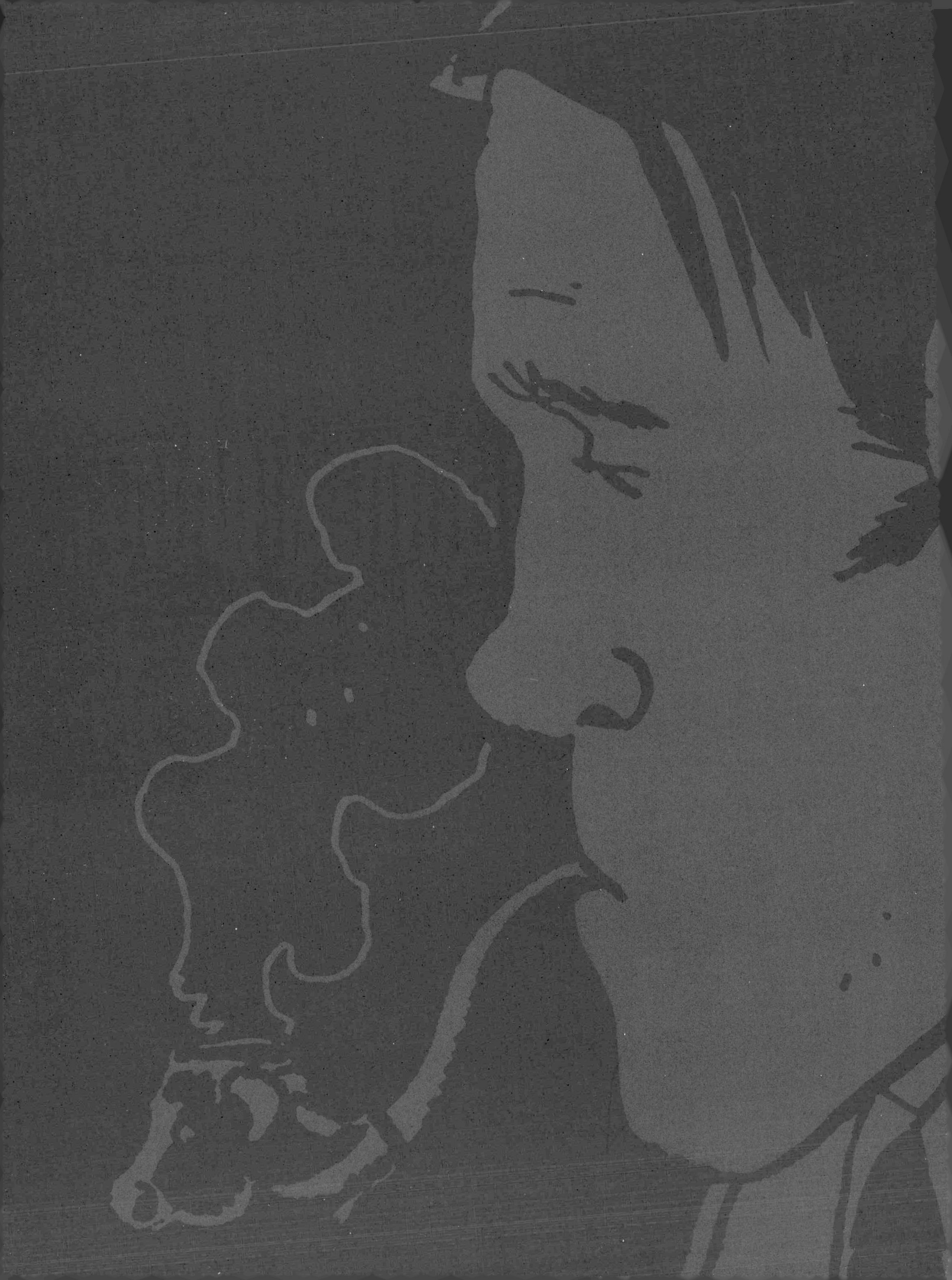

ADAPTED BY TARDI FROM THE NOVEL BY LEO MALET PUBLISHED BY FANTAGRAPHICS

FOG OVER TOLBIAC BRIDGE

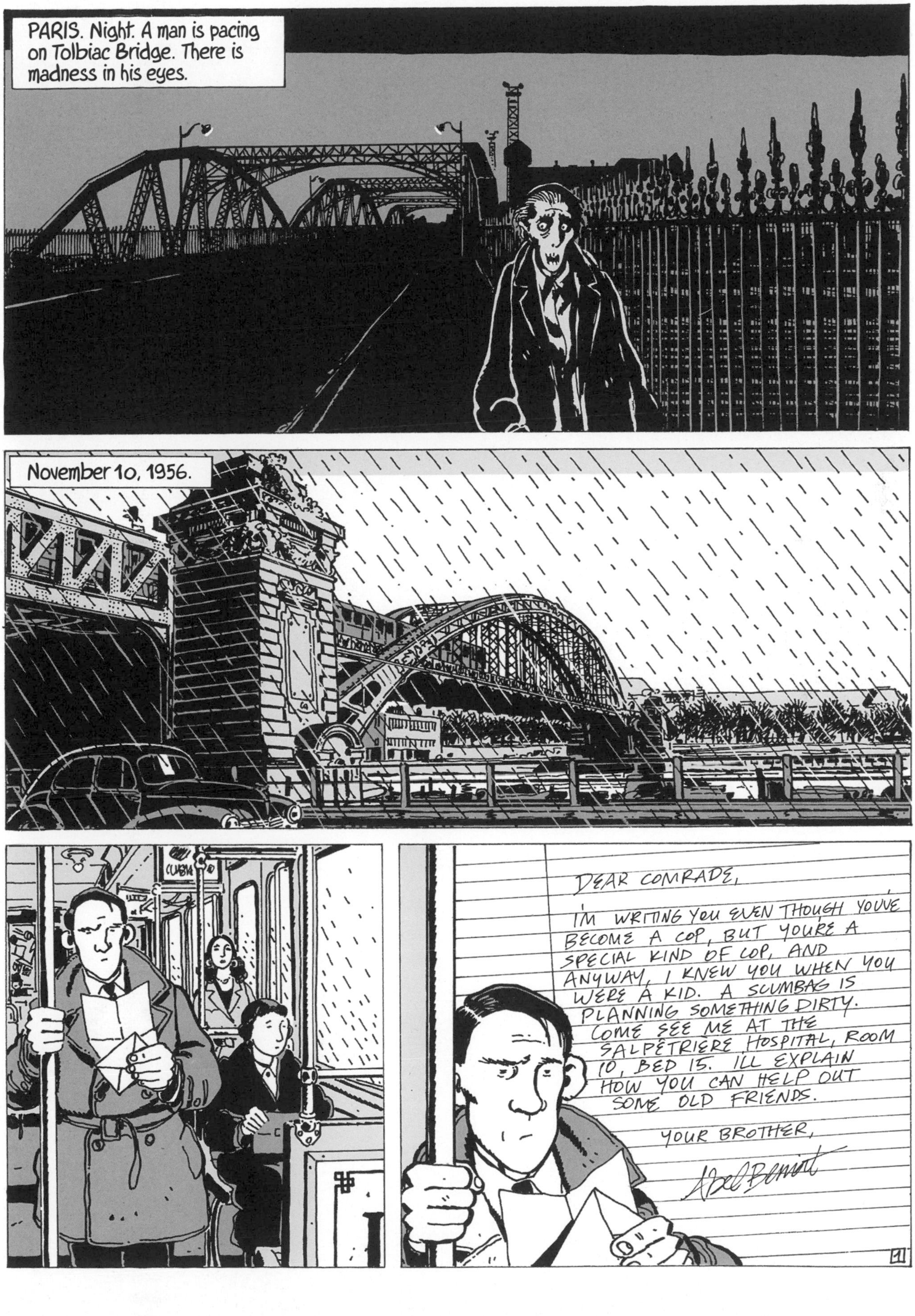

PARIS. Night. A man is pacing on Tolbiac Bridge. There is madness in his eyes.
November 10, 1956.
DEAR COMRADE,
I'M WRITING YOU EVEN THOUGH YOU'VE BECOME A COP, BUT YOU'RE A SPECIAL KIND OF COP, AND ANYWAY, I KNEW YOU WHEN YOU WERE A KID. A SCUMBAG IS PLANNING SOMETHING DIRTY. COME SEE ME AT THE SALPÊTRIÈRE HOSPITAL, ROOM 10, BED 15. I'LL EXPLAIN HOW YOU CAN HELP OUT SOME OLD FRIENDS.
YOUR BROTHER,
Abel Benoit

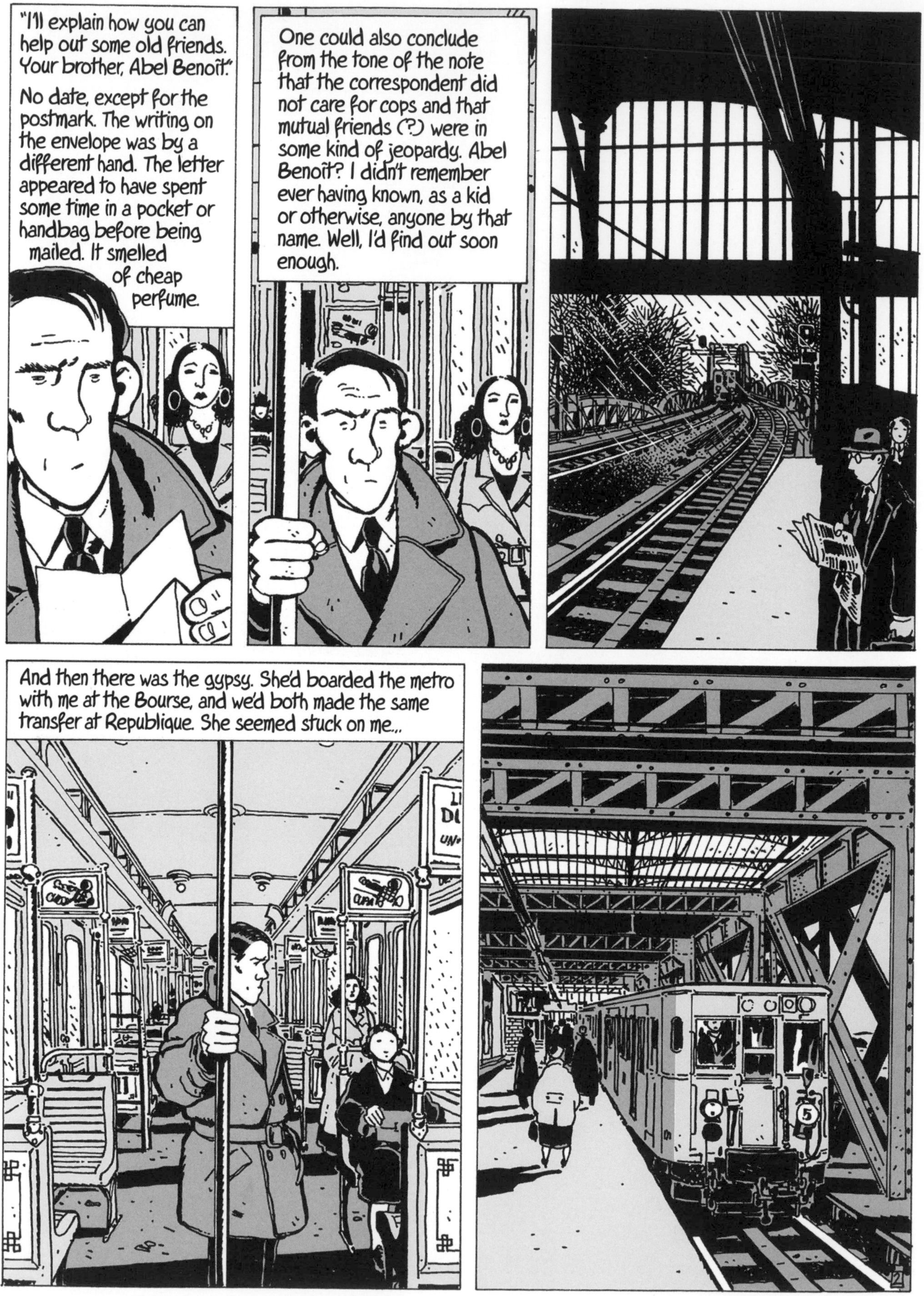
"I'll explain how you can help out some old friends. Your brother, Abel Benoît."
No date, except for the postmark. The writing on the envelope was by a different hand. The letter appeared to have spent some time in a pocket or handbag before being mailed. It smelled of cheap perfume.
One could also conclude from the tone of the note that the correspondent did not care for cops and that mutual friends (?) were in some kind of jeopardy. Abel Benoît? I didn't remember ever having known, as a kid or otherwise, anyone by that name. Well, I'd find out soon enough.
And then there was the gypsy. She'd boarded the metro with me at the Bourse, and we'd both made the same transfer at Republique. She seemed stuck on me...

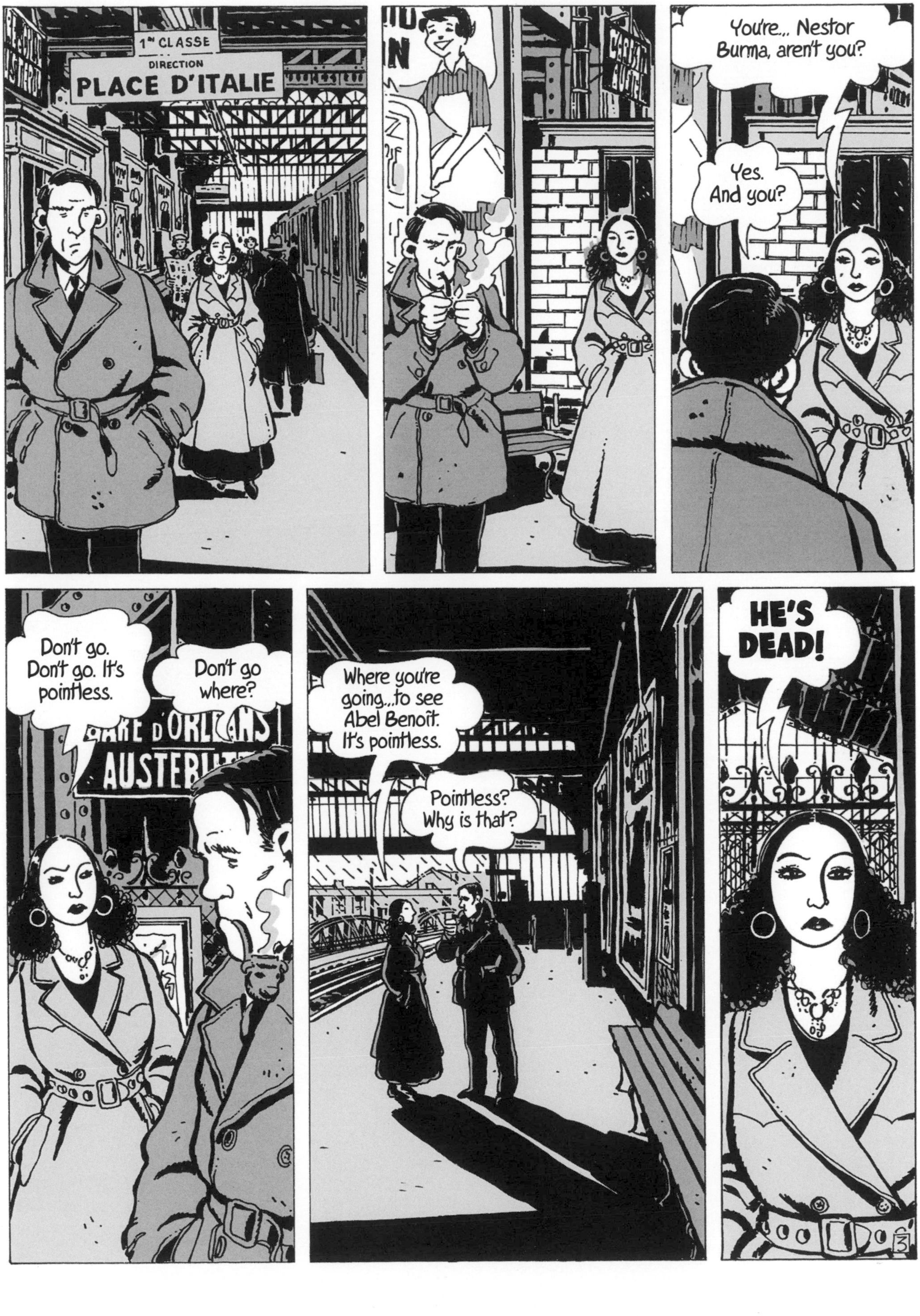
1re CLASSE
DIRECTION
PLACE D'ITALIE
You're... Nestor Burma, aren't you?
Yes. And you?
Don't go. Don't go. It's pointless.
Don't go where?
GARE D'ORLÉANS AUSTERLITZ
Where you're going...to see Abel Benoît. It's pointless.
Pointless? Why is that?
HE'S DEAD!
3

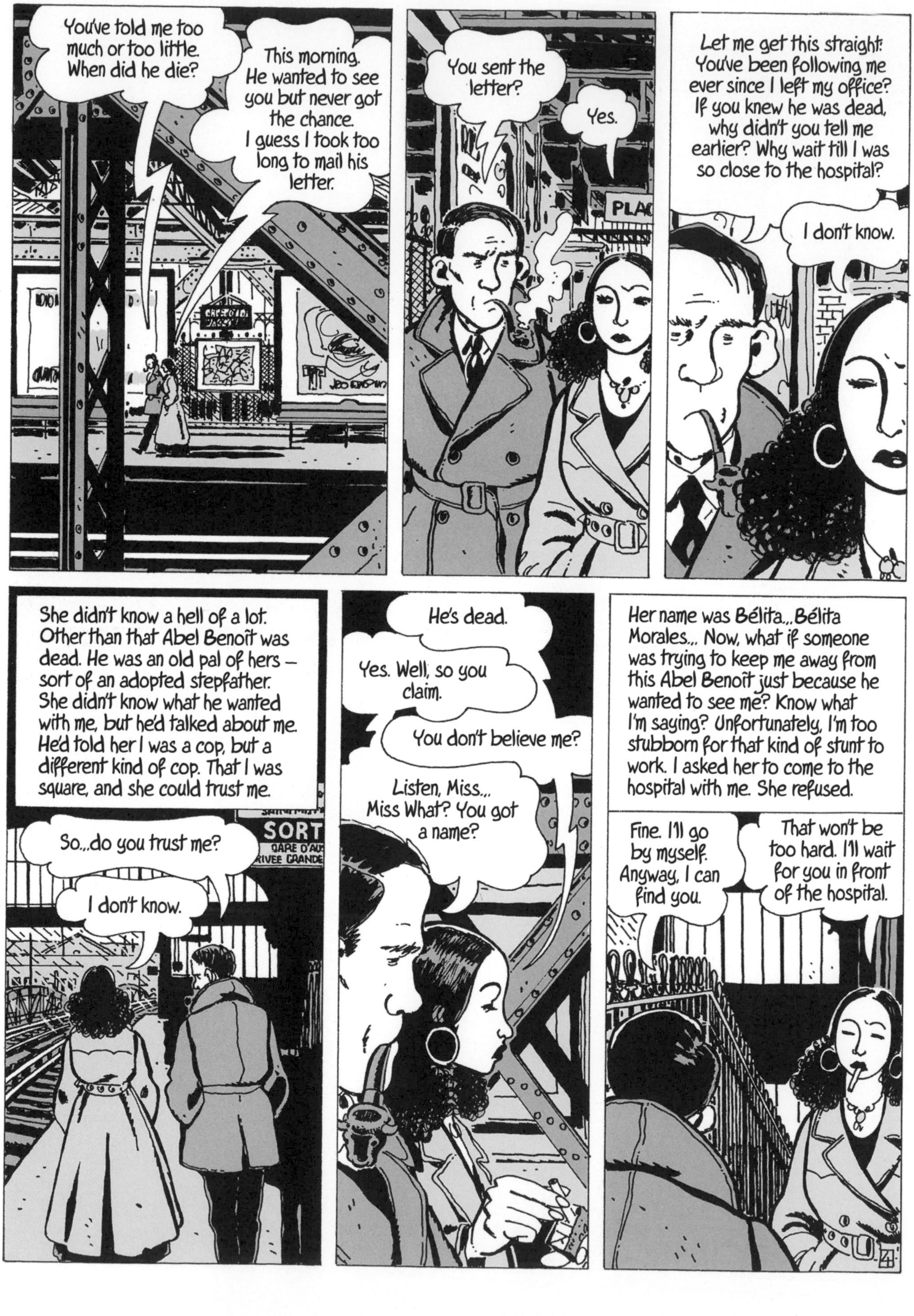

You've told me too much or too little. When did he die?
This morning. He wanted to see you but never got the chance. I guess I took too long to mail his letter.
You sent the letter?
Yes.
PLAC
Let me get this straight: You've been following me ever since I left my office? If you knew he was dead, why didn't you tell me earlier? Why wait till I was so close to the hospital?
I don't know.
She didn't know a hell of a lot. Other than that Abel Benoît was dead. He was an old pal of hers – sort of an adopted stepfather. She didn't know what he wanted with me, but he'd talked about me. He'd told her I was a cop, but a different kind of cop. That I was square, and she could trust me.
SORT
So... do you trust me?
I don't know.
He's dead.
Yes. Well, so you claim.
You don't believe me?
Listen, Miss... Miss What? You got a name?
Her name was Bélita... Bélita Morales... Now, what if someone was trying to keep me away from this Abel Benoît just because he wanted to see me? Know what I'm saying? Unfortunately, I'm too stubborn for that kind of stunt to work. I asked her to come to the hospital with me. She refused.
Fine. I'll go by myself. Anyway, I can find you.
That won't be too hard. I'll wait for you in front of the hospital.
4

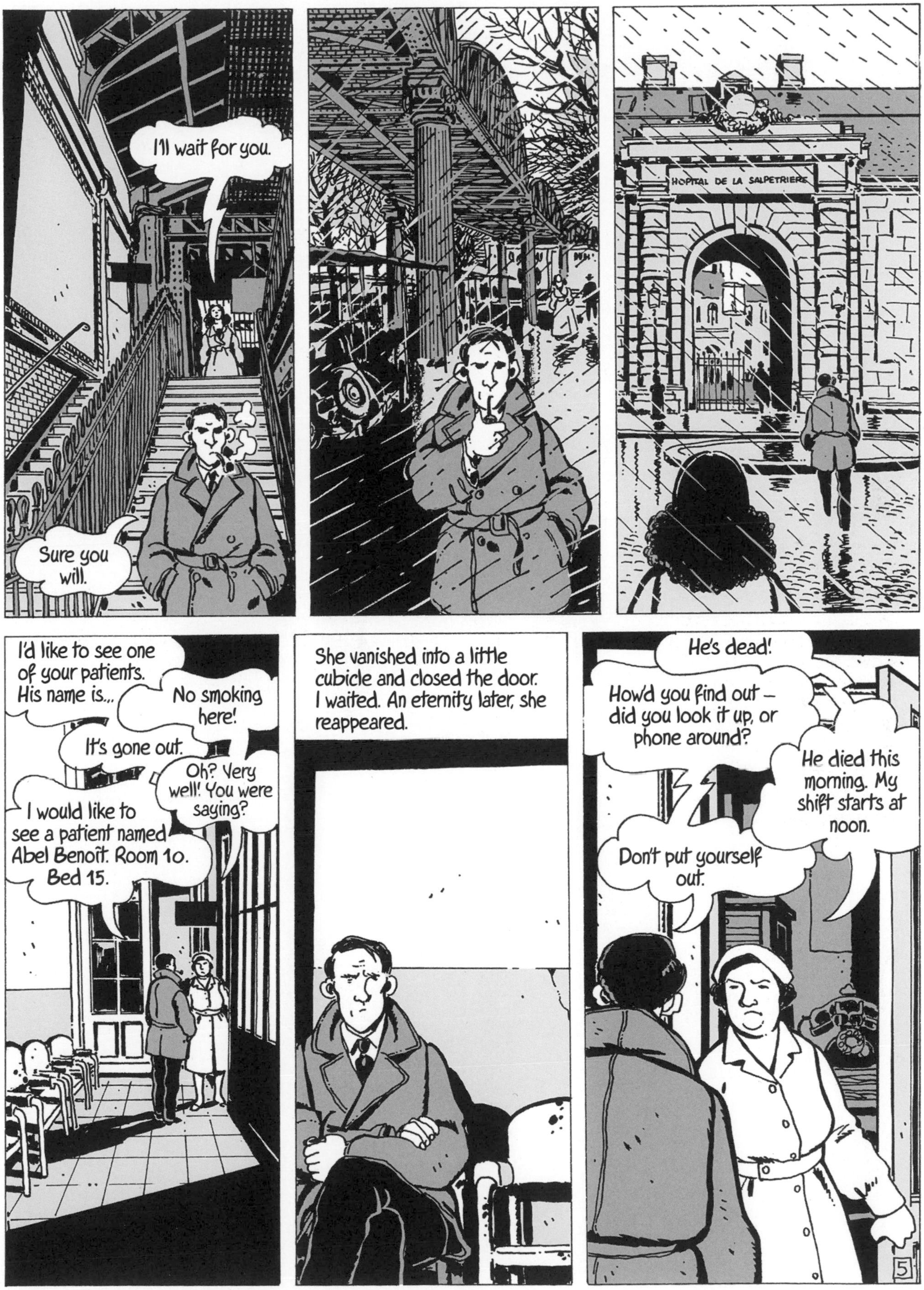
I'll wait for you.
Sure you will.
HOPITAL DE LA SALPETRIERE
I'd like to see one of your patients. His name is...
No smoking here!
It's gone out.
Oh? Very well! You were saying?
I would like to see a patient named Abel Benoît. Room 10. Bed 15.
She vanished into a little cubicle and closed the door. I waited. An eternity later, she reappeared.
He's dead!
How'd you find out – did you look it up, or phone around?
He died this morning. My shift starts at noon.
Don't put yourself out.
5

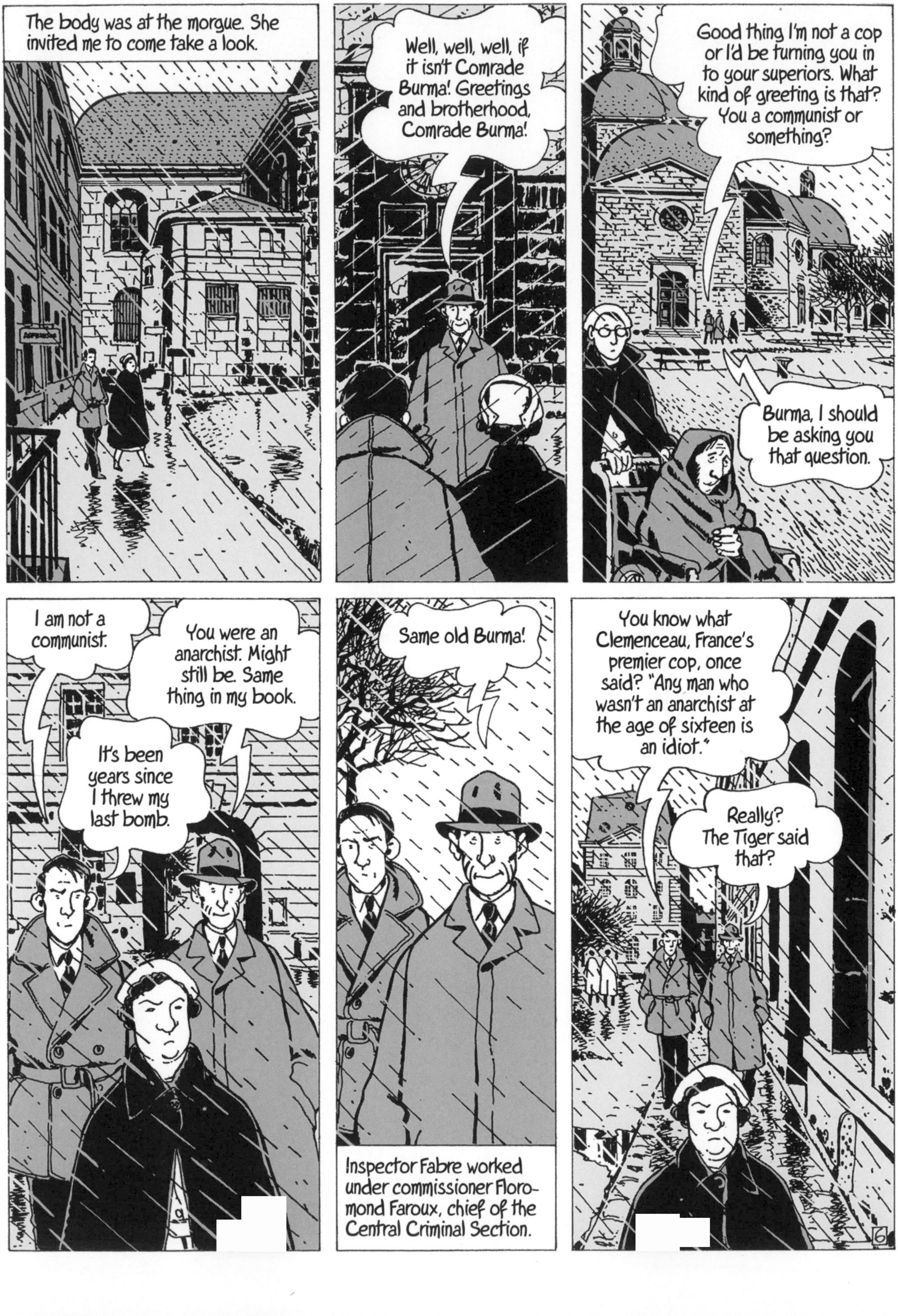
The body was at the morgue. She invited me to come take a look.
Well, well, well, if it isn't Comrade Burma! Greetings and brotherhood, Comrade Burma!
Good thing I'm not a cop or I'd be turning you in to your superiors. What kind of greeting is that? You a communist or something?
Burma, I should be asking you that question.
I am not a communist.
You were an anarchist. Might still be. Same thing in my book.
It's been years since I threw my last bomb.
Same old Burma!
Inspector Fabre worked under commissioner Floromond Faroux, chief of the Central Criminal Section.
You know what Clemenceau, France's premier cop, once said? "Any man who wasn't an anarchist at the age of sixteen is an idiot."
Really? The Tiger said that?
6

But he didn't add: "He's an even bigger idiot, however, if he's still an anarchist at the age of forty."

Clemenceau's sayings are a mixed bag. A lot of 'em leave me cold.

You came to see Abel Benoît?

Judging from your cheerful disposition, this may be complicated, but not too serious—except for the stiff, of course.

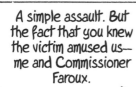

Thank you, Ma'am. You're free to go.

A simple assault. But the fact that you knew the victim amused us—me and Commissioner Faroux.

I've got a better punch line: I didn't know this Abel Benoît.

Why, then, were you asking about him?

Because he wrote and asked to see me. But I don't know him.

He knew you, though. We found a bunch of press clippings on the deceased, and some old magazines with reports of your various cases.

Oh?

Do you have his letter?

No. Left it at the office.

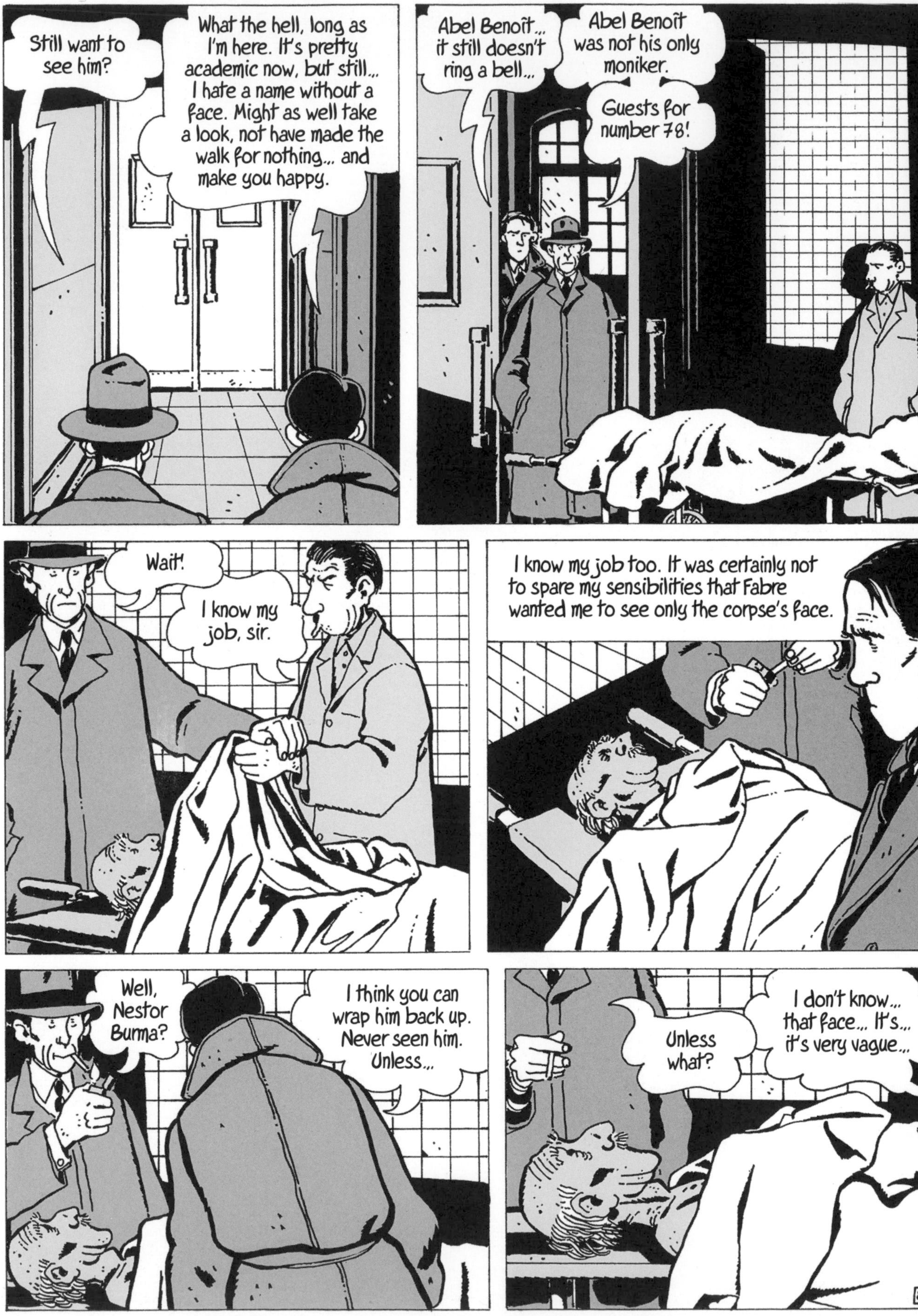
Still want to see him?
What the hell, long as I'm here. It's pretty academic now, but still... I hate a name without a face. Might as well take a look, not have made the walk for nothing... and make you happy.
Abel Benoît... it still doesn't ring a bell...
Abel Benoît was not his only moniker.
Guests for number 78!
Wait!
I know my job, sir.
I know my job too. It was certainly not to spare my sensibilities that Fabre wanted me to see only the corpse's face.
Well, Nestor Burma?
I think you can wrap him back up. Never seen him. Unless...
Unless what?
I don't know... that face... It's... it's very vague...
8

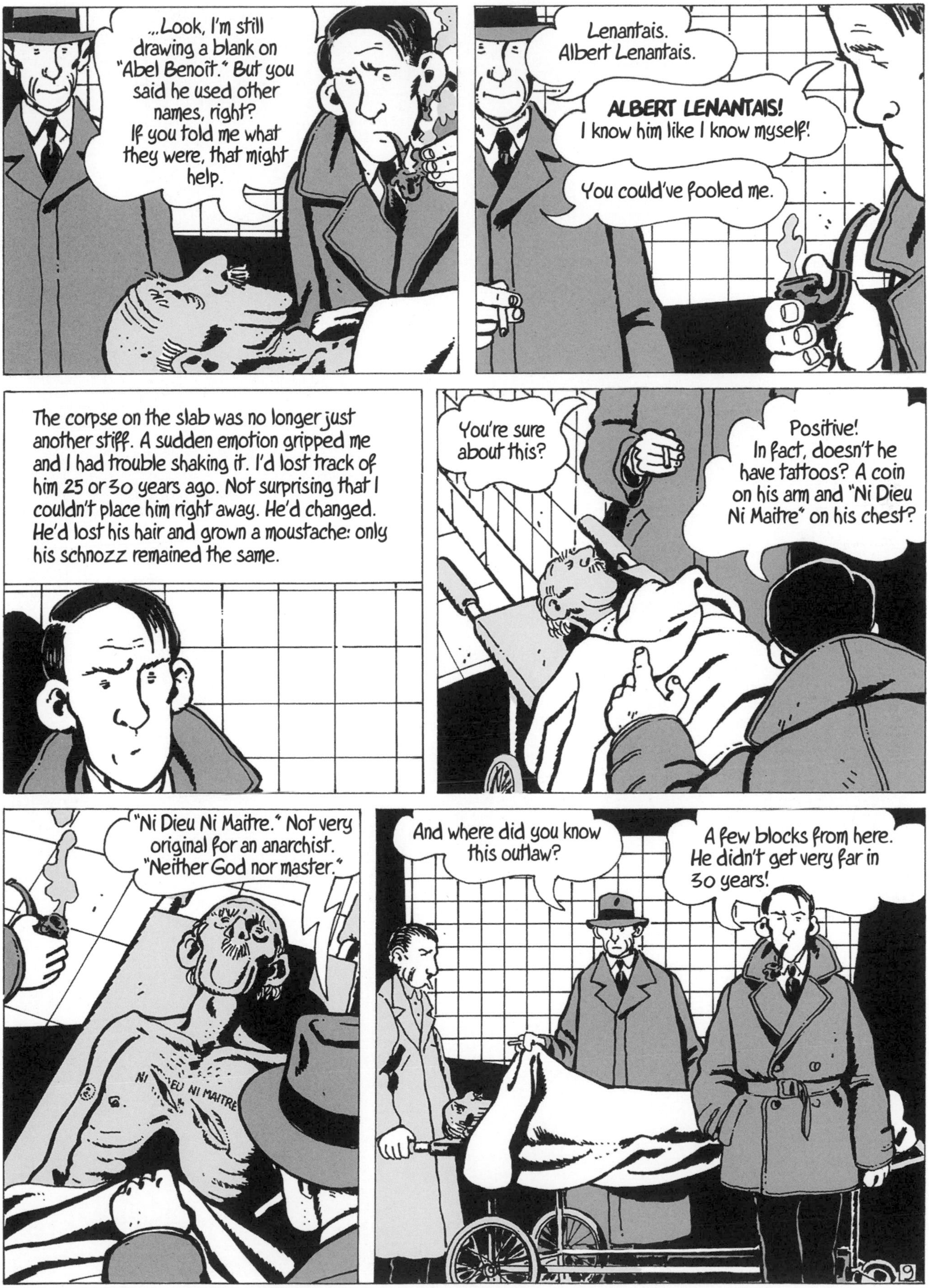
...Look, I'm still drawing a blank on "Abel Benoît." But you said he used other names, right? If you told me what they were, that might help.
Lenantais. Albert Lenantais.
ALBERT LENANTAIS! I know him like I know myself!
You could've fooled me.
The corpse on the slab was no longer just another stiff. A sudden emotion gripped me and I had trouble shaking it. I'd lost track of him 25 or 30 years ago. Not surprising that I couldn't place him right away. He'd changed. He'd lost his hair and grown a moustache: only his schnozz remained the same.
You're sure about this?
Positive! In fact, doesn't he have tattoos? A coin on his arm and "Ni Dieu Ni Maitre" on his chest?
"Ni Dieu Ni Maitre." Not very original for an anarchist. "Neither God nor master."
And where did you know this outlaw?
A few blocks from here. He didn't get very far in 30 years!
9

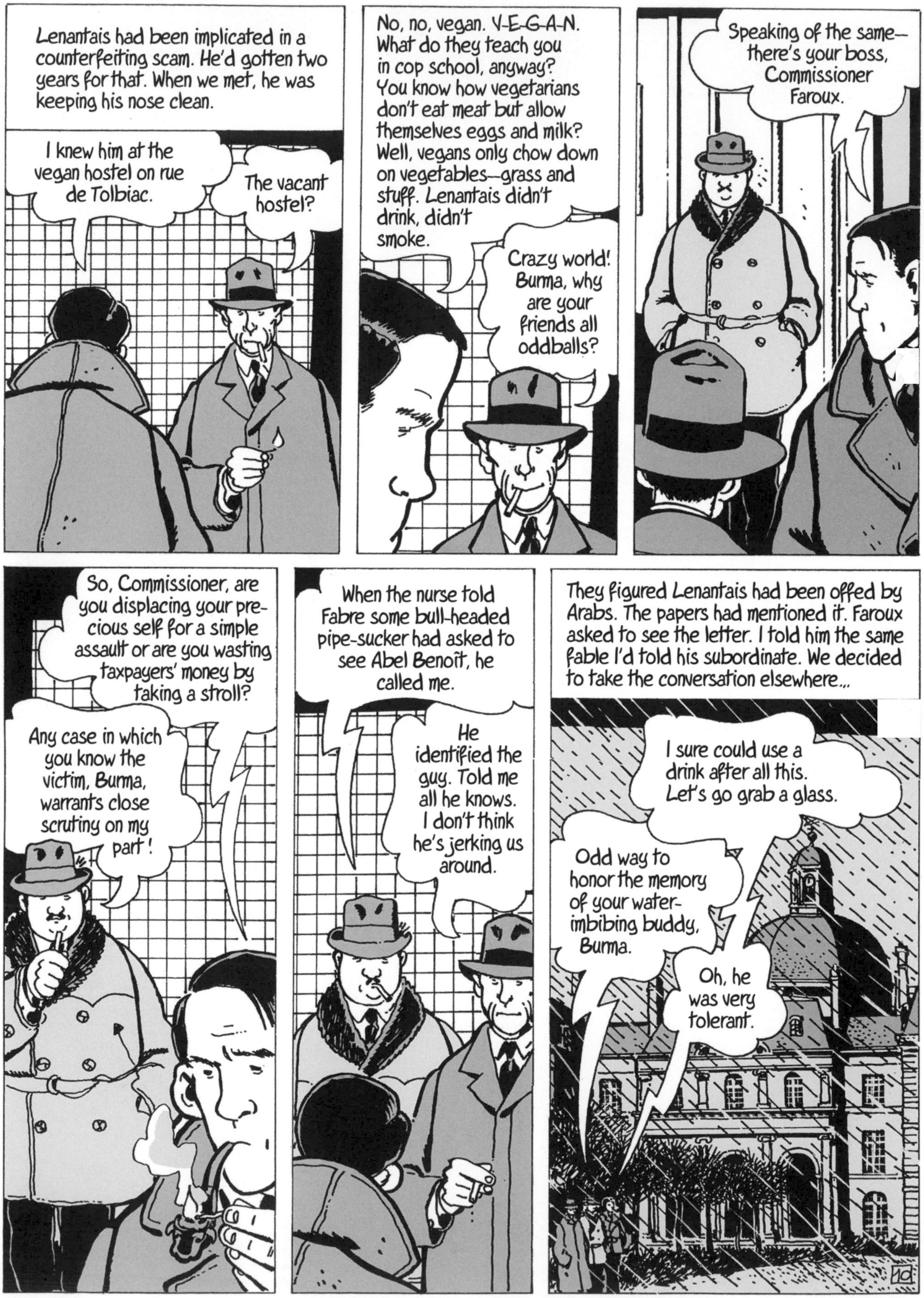
Lenantais had been implicated in a counterfeiting scam. He'd gotten two years for that. When we met, he was keeping his nose clean.
I knew him at the vegan hostel on rue de Tolbiac.
The vacant hostel?
No, no, vegan. V-E-G-A-N. What do they teach you in cop school, anyway? You know how vegetarians don't eat meat but allow themselves eggs and milk? Well, vegans only chow down on vegetables--grass and stuff. Lenantais didn't drink, didn't smoke.
Crazy world! Burma, why are your friends all oddballs?
Speaking of the same-- there's your boss, Commissioner Faroux.
So, Commissioner, are you displacing your precious self for a simple assault or are you wasting taxpayers' money by taking a stroll?
Any case in which you know the victim, Burma, warrants close scrutiny on my part!
When the nurse told Fabre some bull-headed pipe-sucker had asked to see Abel Benoît, he called me.
He identified the guy. Told me all he knows. I don't think he's jerking us around.
They figured Lenantais had been offed by Arabs. The papers had mentioned it. Faroux asked to see the letter. I told him the same fable I'd told his subordinate. We decided to take the conversation elsewhere...
I sure could use a drink after all this. Let's go grab a glass.
Odd way to honor the memory of your water-imbibing buddy, Burma.
Oh, he was very tolerant.
10

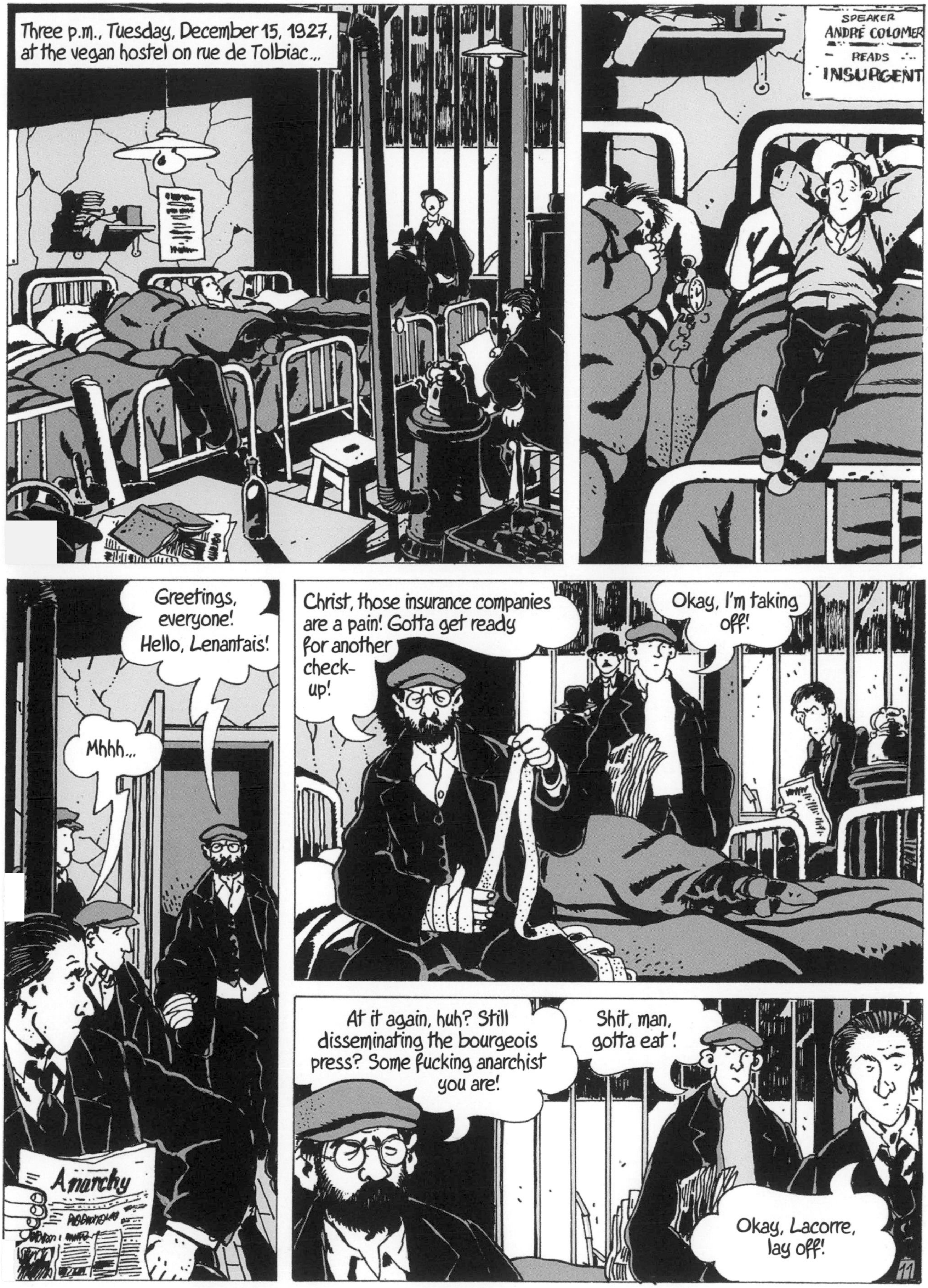

Three p.m., Tuesday, December 15, 1927, at the vegan hostel on rue de Tolbiac...
SPEAKER
ANDRÉ COLOMER
READS
INSURGENT
Greetings, everyone! Hello, Lenantais!
Mhhh...
Anarchy
Christ, those insurance companies are a pain! Gotta get ready for another check-up!
Okay, I'm taking off!
At it again, huh? Still disseminating the bourgeois press? Some fucking anarchist you are!
Shit, man, gotta eat!
Okay, Lacorre, lay off!

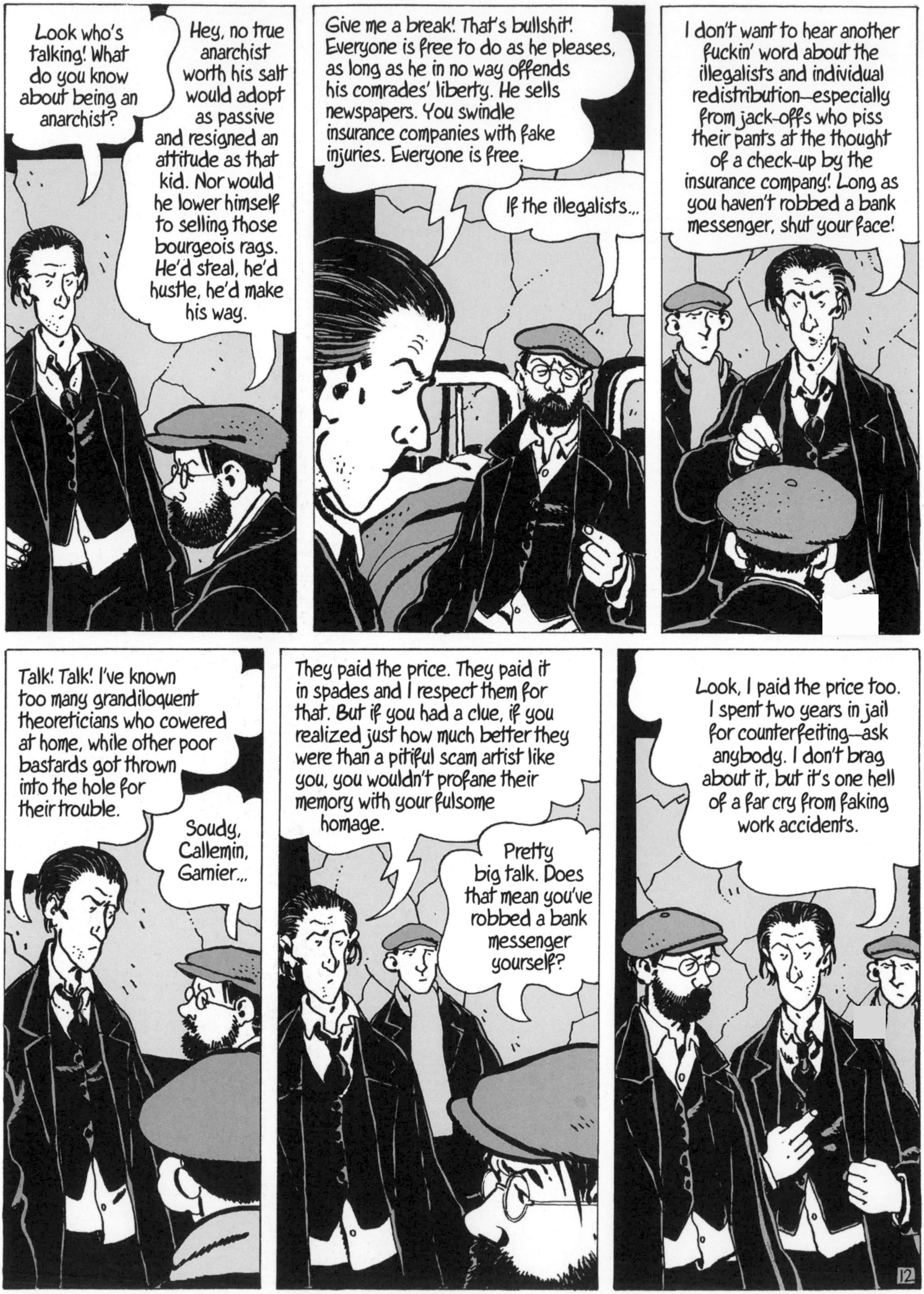
Look who's talking! What do you know about being an anarchist?
Hey, no true anarchist worth his salt would adopt as passive and resigned an attitude as that kid. Nor would he lower himself to selling those bourgeois rags. He'd steal, he'd hustle, he'd make his way.
Give me a break! That's bullshit! Everyone is free to do as he pleases, as long as he in no way offends his comrades' liberty. He sells newspapers. You swindle insurance companies with fake injuries. Everyone is free.
If the illegalists...
I don't want to hear another fuckin' word about the illegalists and individual redistribution—especially from jack-offs who piss their pants at the thought of a check-up by the insurance company! Long as you haven't robbed a bank messenger, shut your face!
Talk! Talk! I've known too many grandiloquent theoreticians who cowered at home, while other poor bastards got thrown into the hole for their trouble.
Soudy, Callemin, Garnier...
They paid the price. They paid it in spades and I respect them for that. But if you had a clue, if you realized just how much better they were than a pitiful scam artist like you, you wouldn't profane their memory with your fulsome homage.
Pretty big talk. Does that mean you've robbed a bank messenger yourself?
Look, I paid the price too. I spent two years in jail for counterfeiting—ask anybody. I don't brag about it, but it's one hell of a far cry from faking work accidents.

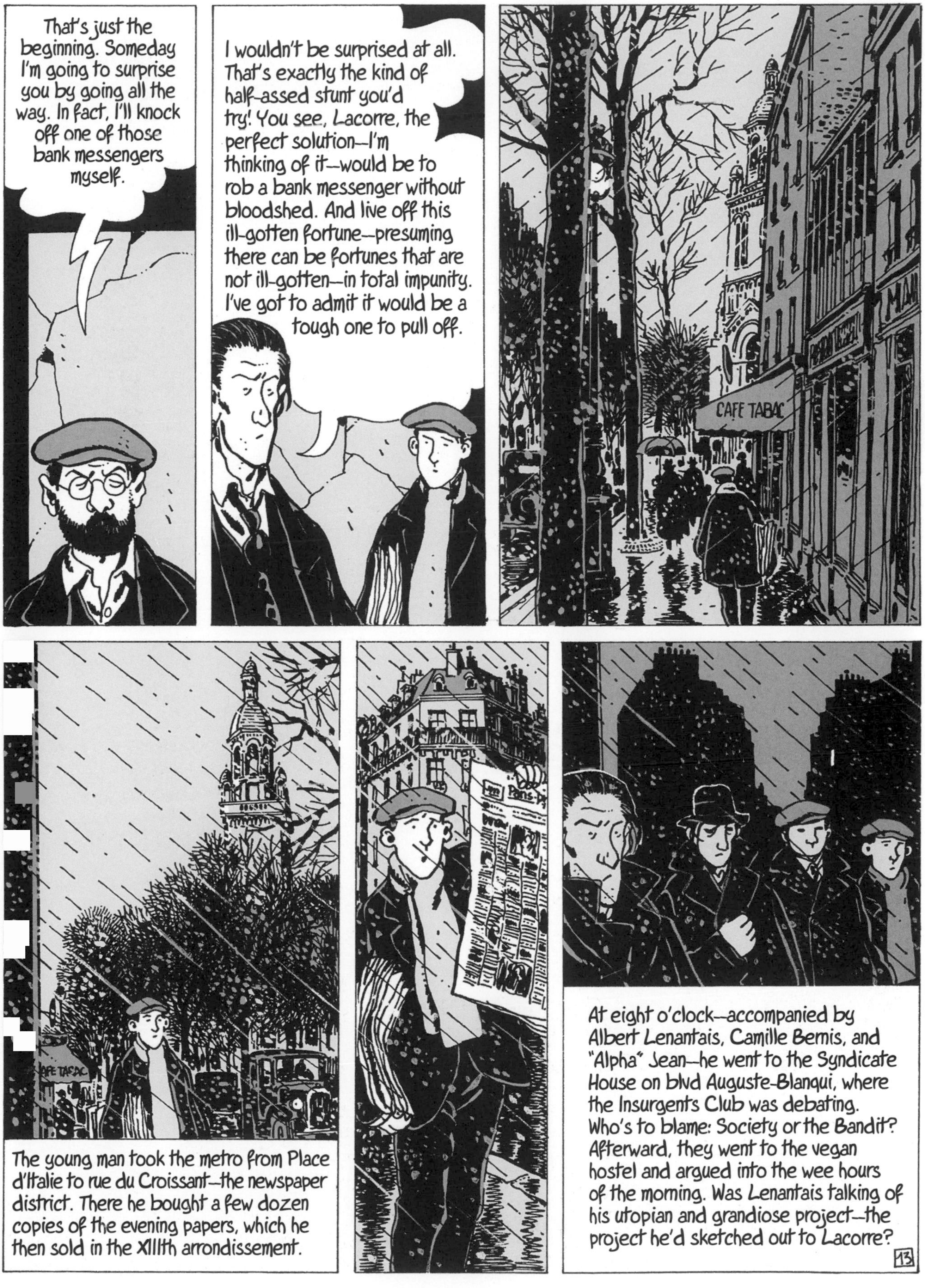
That's just the beginning. Someday I'm going to surprise you by going all the way. In fact, I'll knock off one of those bank messengers myself.
I wouldn't be surprised at all. That's exactly the kind of half-assed stunt you'd try! You see, Lacorre, the perfect solution—I'm thinking of it—would be to rob a bank messenger without bloodshed. And live off this ill-gotten fortune—presuming there can be fortunes that are not ill-gotten—in total impunity. I've got to admit it would be a tough one to pull off.
CAFE TABAC
The young man took the metro from Place d'Italie to rue du Croissant—the newspaper district. There he bought a few dozen copies of the evening papers, which he then sold in the XIIIth arrondissement.
At eight o'clock—accompanied by Albert Lenantais, Camille Bernis, and "Alpha" Jean—he went to the Syndicate House on blvd Auguste-Blanqui, where the Insurgents Club was debating. Who's to blame: Society or the Bandit? Afterward, they went to the vegan hostel and argued into the wee hours of the morning. Was Lenantais talking of his utopian and grandiose project—the project he'd sketched out to Lacorre?

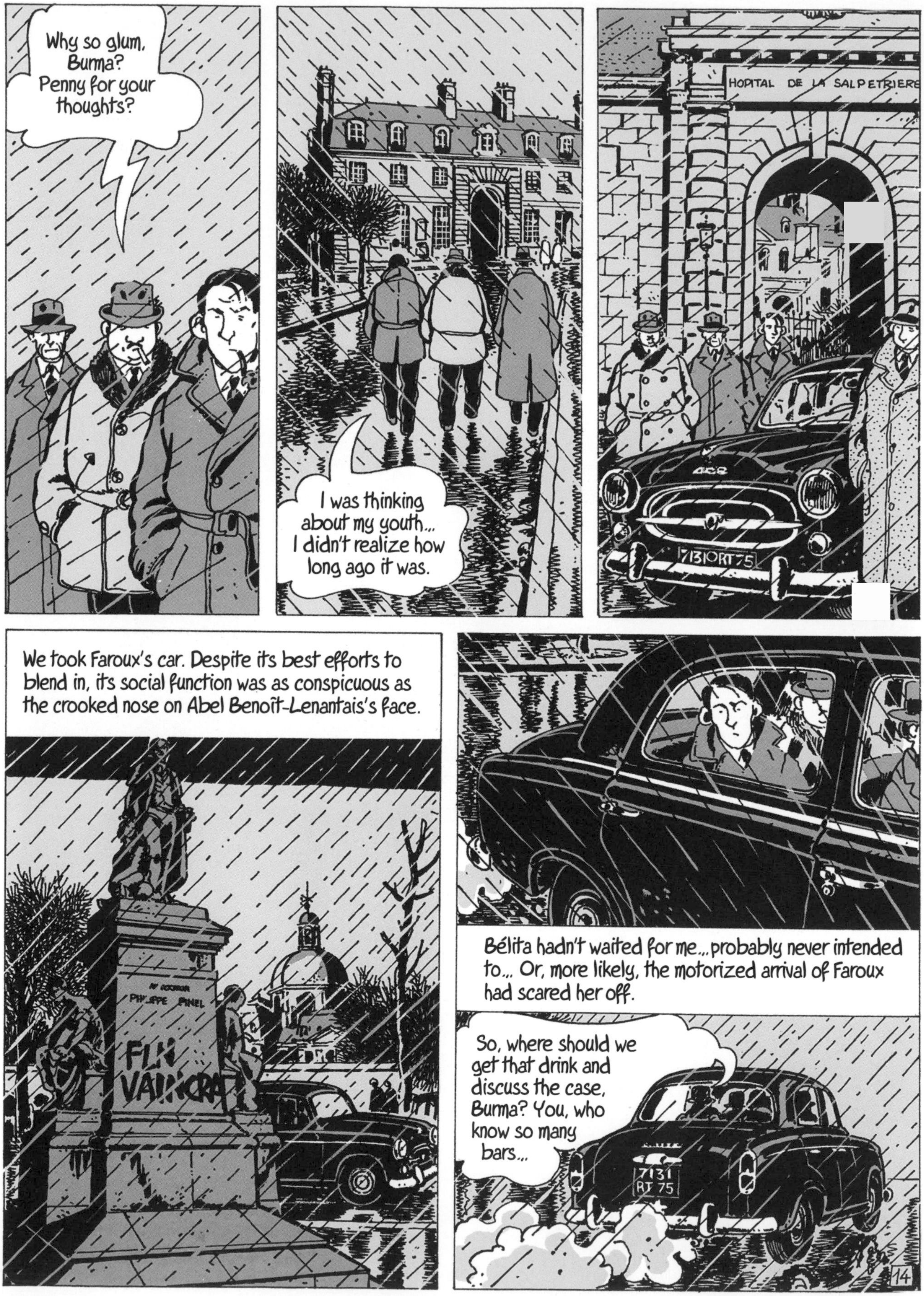
Why so glum, Burma? Penny for your thoughts?
HOPITAL DE LA SALPETRIERE
I was thinking about my youth... I didn't realize how long ago it was.
We took Faroux's car. Despite its best efforts to blend in, its social function was as conspicuous as the crooked nose on Abel Benoît-Lenantais's face.
PHILIPPE PINEL
FLN VAINCRA
Bélita hadn't waited for me... probably never intended to... Or, more likely, the motorized arrival of Faroux had scared her off.
So, where should we get that drink and discuss the case, Burma? You, who know so many bars...
14

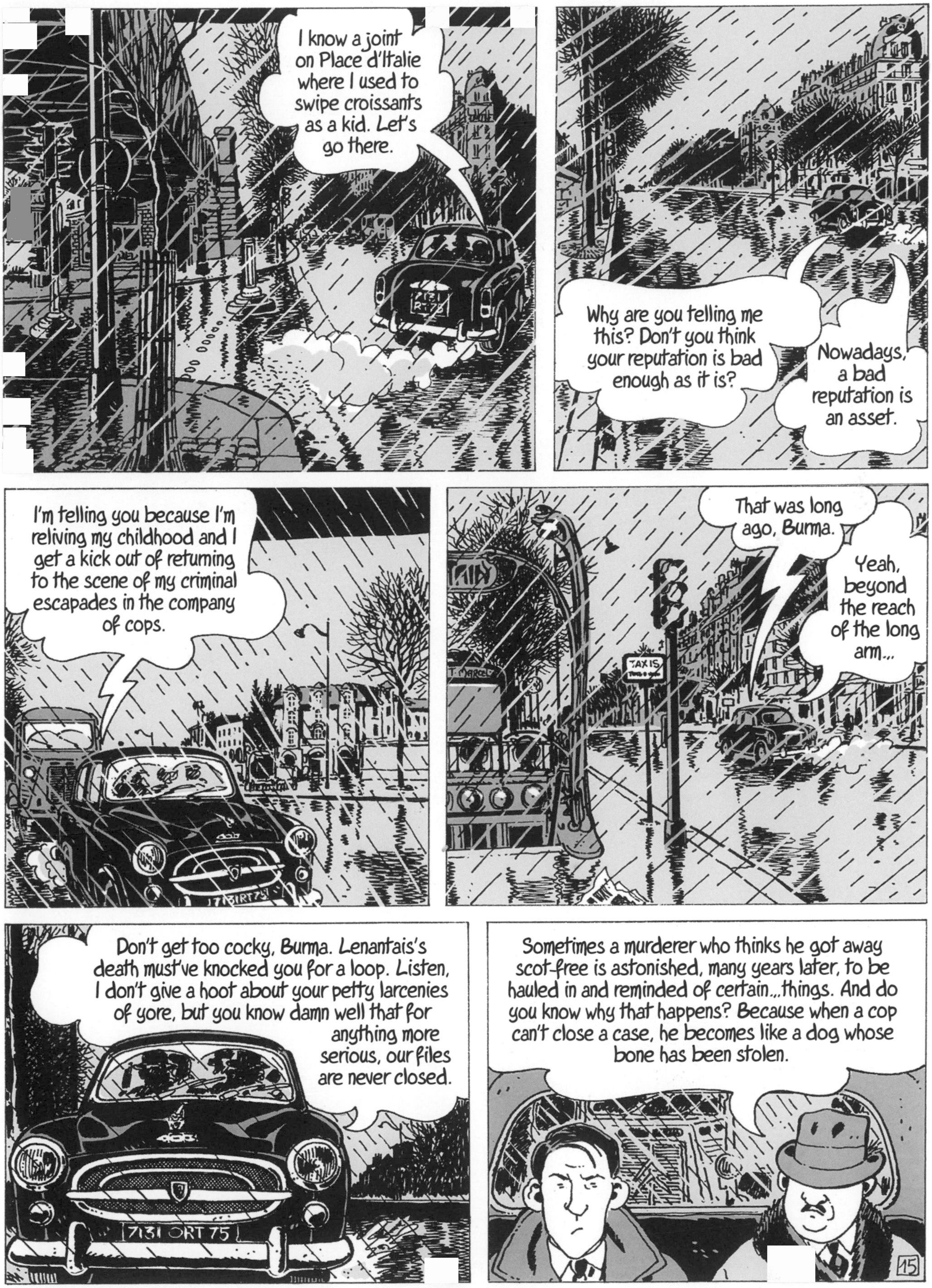

I know a joint on Place d'Italie where I used to swipe croissants as a kid. Let's go there.
Why are you telling me this? Don't you think your reputation is bad enough as it is?
Nowadays, a bad reputation is an asset.
I'm telling you because I'm reliving my childhood and I get a kick out of returning to the scene of my criminal escapades in the company of cops.
That was long ago, Burma.
Yeah, beyond the reach of the long arm...
TAXIS
Don't get too cocky, Burma. Lenantais's death must've knocked you for a loop. Listen, I don't give a hoot about your petty larcenies of yore, but you know damn well that for anything more serious, our files are never closed.
7131 ORT 75
Sometimes a murderer who thinks he got away scot-free is astonished, many years later, to be hauled in and reminded of certain... things. And do you know why that happens? Because when a cop can't close a case, he becomes like a dog whose bone has been stolen.

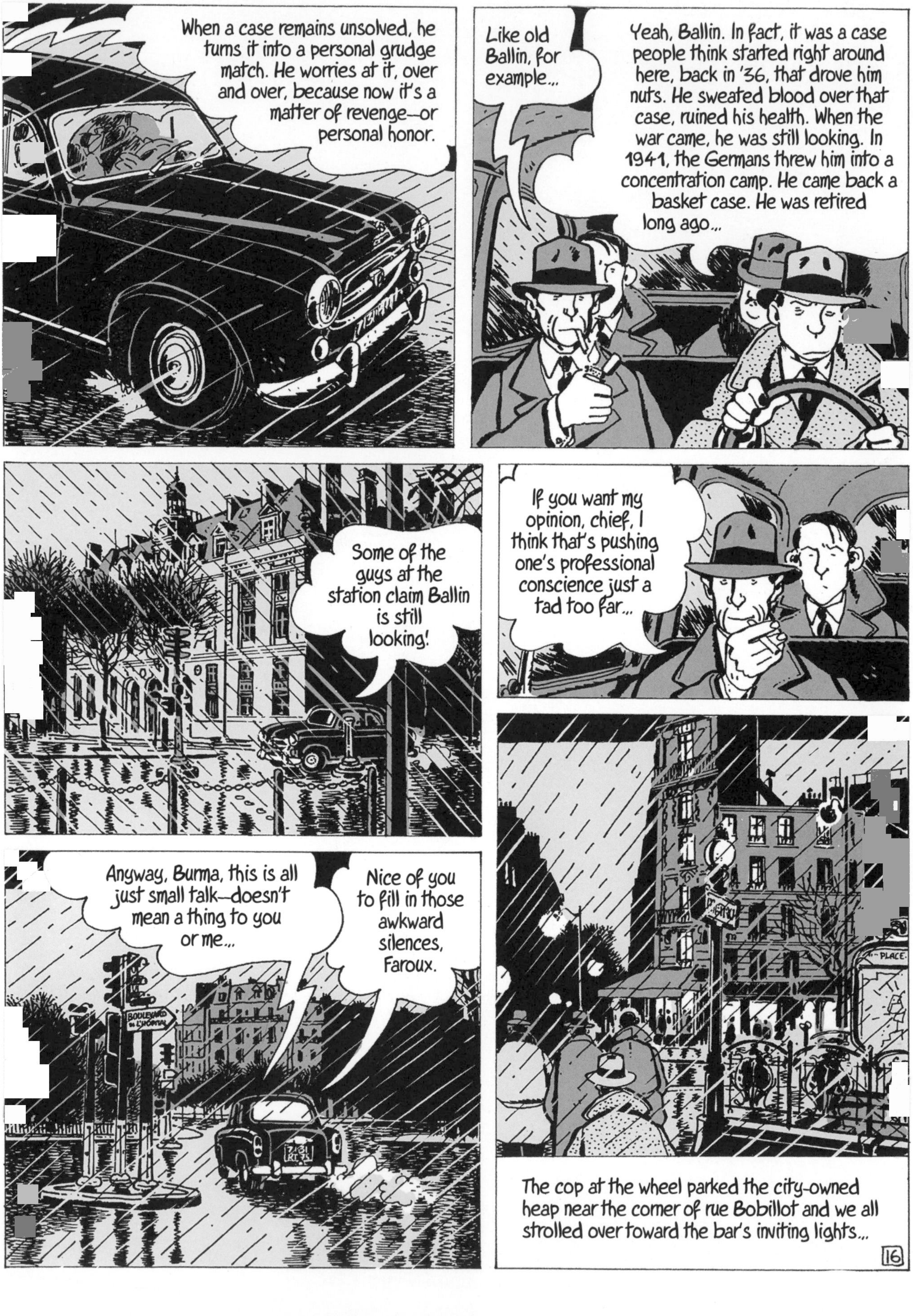
When a case remains unsolved, he turns it into a personal grudge match. He worries at it, over and over, because now it's a matter of revenge--or personal honor.
Like old Ballin, for example...
Yeah, Ballin. In fact, it was a case people think started right around here, back in '36, that drove him nuts. He sweated blood over that case, ruined his health. When the war came, he was still looking. In 1941, the Germans threw him into a concentration camp. He came back a basket case. He was retired long ago...
Some of the guys at the station claim Ballin is still looking!
If you want my opinion, chief, I think that's pushing one's professional conscience just a tad too far...
Anyway, Burma, this is all just small talk--doesn't mean a thing to you or me...
Nice of you to fill in those awkward silences, Faroux.
BOULEVARD DE L'HÔPITAL
PLACE
The cop at the wheel parked the city-owned heap near the corner of rue Bobillot and we all strolled over toward the bar's inviting lights...

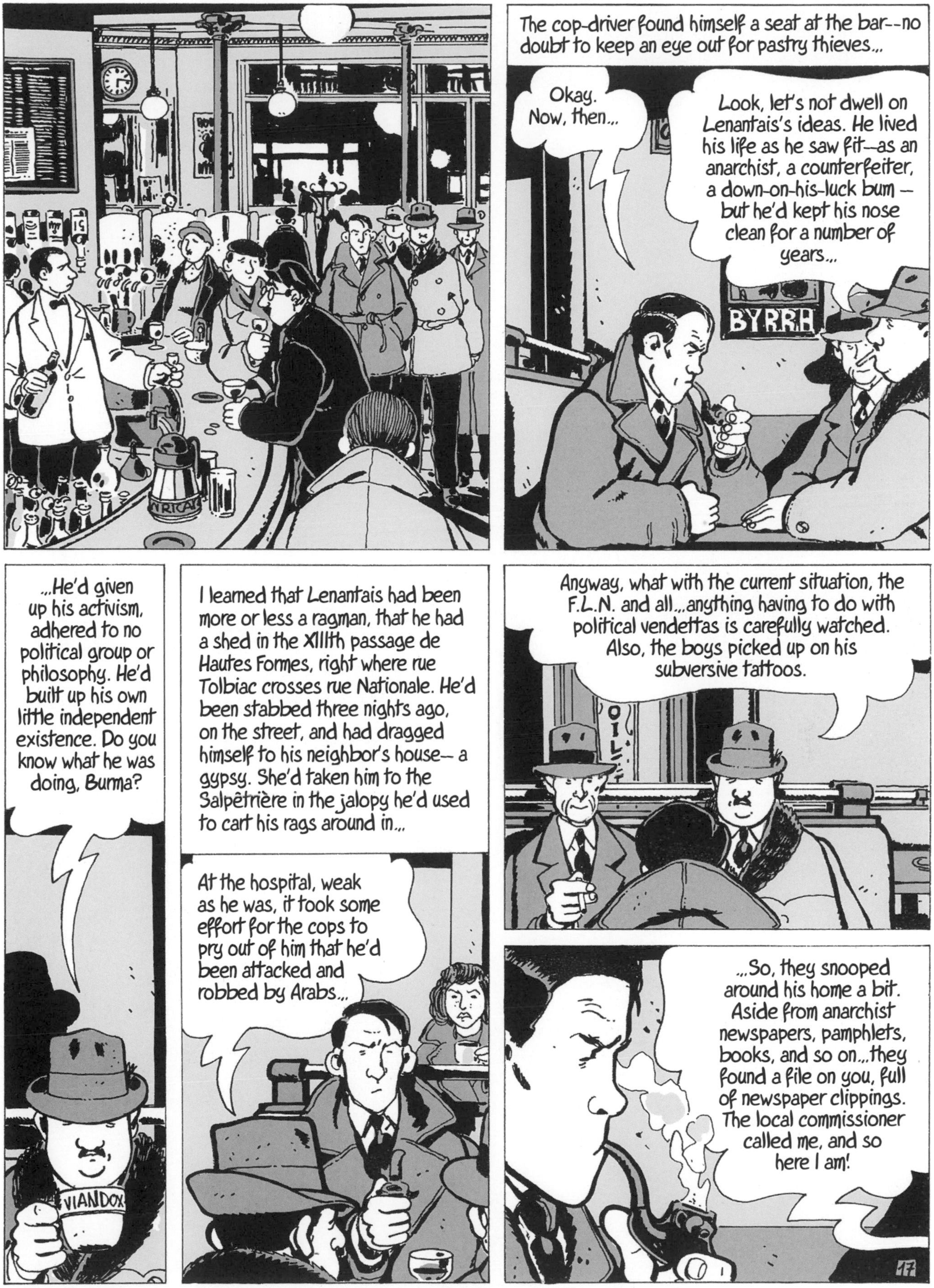

The cop-driver found himself a seat at the bar--no doubt to keep an eye out for pastry thieves...
Okay. Now, then...
Look, let's not dwell on Lenantais's ideas. He lived his life as he saw fit--as an anarchist, a counterfeiter, a down-on-his-luck bum -- but he'd kept his nose clean for a number of years...
BYRRH
...He'd given up his activism, adhered to no political group or philosophy. He'd built up his own little independent existence. Do you know what he was doing, Burma?
VIANDOX
I learned that Lenantais had been more or less a ragman, that he had a shed in the XIIIth passage de Hautes Formes, right where rue Tolbiac crosses rue Nationale. He'd been stabbed three nights ago, on the street, and had dragged himself to his neighbor's house-- a gypsy. She'd taken him to the Salpêtrière in the jalopy he'd used to cart his rags around in...
At the hospital, weak as he was, it took some effort for the cops to pry out of him that he'd been attacked and robbed by Arabs...
Anyway, what with the current situation, the F.L.N. and all... anything having to do with political vendettas is carefully watched. Also, the boys picked up on his subversive tattoos.
...So, they snooped around his home a bit. Aside from anarchist newspapers, pamphlets, books, and so on... they found a file on you, full of newspaper clippings. The local commissioner called me, and so here I am!

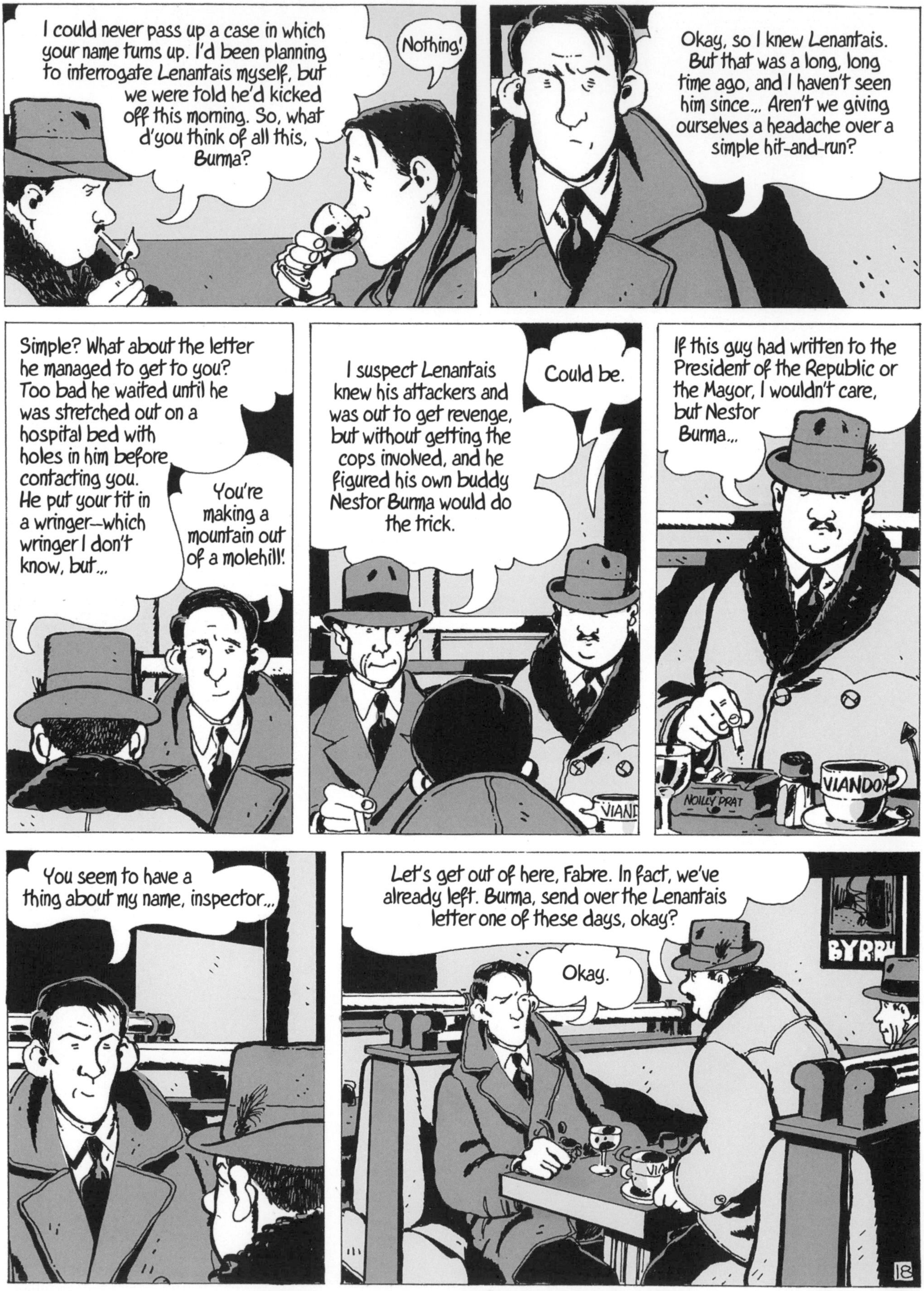

I could never pass up a case in which your name turns up. I'd been planning to interrogate Lenantais myself, but we were told he'd kicked off this morning. So, what d'you think of all this, Burma?
Nothing!
Okay, so I knew Lenantais. But that was a long, long time ago, and I haven't seen him since... Aren't we giving ourselves a headache over a simple hit-and-run?
Simple? What about the letter he managed to get to you? Too bad he waited until he was stretched out on a hospital bed with holes in him before contacting you. He put your tit in a wringer—which wringer I don't know, but...
You're making a mountain out of a molehill!
I suspect Lenantais knew his attackers and was out to get revenge, but without getting the cops involved, and he figured his own buddy Nestor Burma would do the trick.
Could be.
VIAND
If this guy had written to the President of the Republic or the Mayor, I wouldn't care, but Nestor Burma...
NOILLY PRAT
VIANDOX
You seem to have a thing about my name, inspector...
Let's get out of here, Fabre. In fact, we've already left. Burma, send over the Lenantais letter one of these days, okay?
Okay.
BYRR

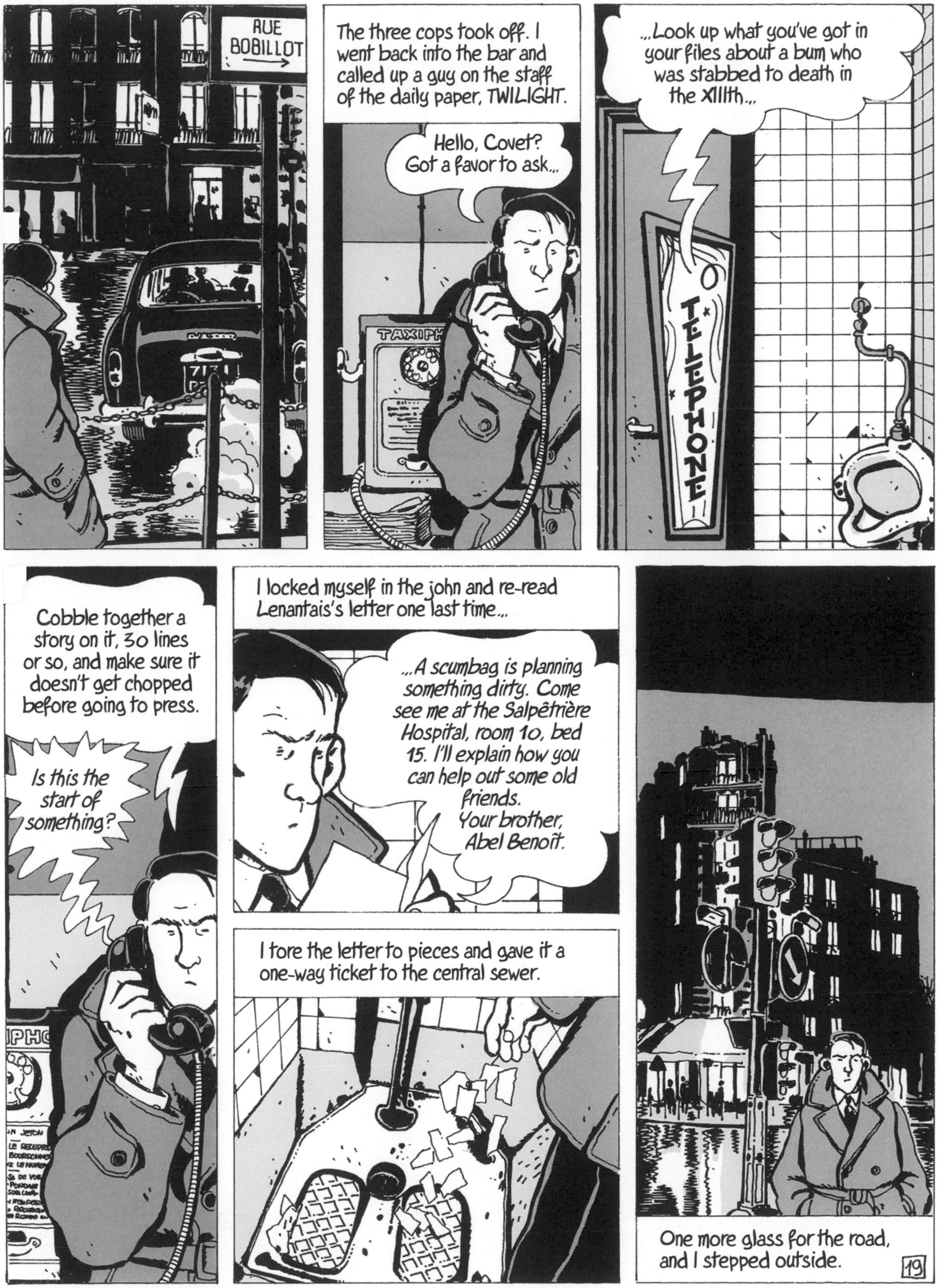
RUE BOBILLOT
The three cops took off. I went back into the bar and called up a guy on the staff of the daily paper, TWILIGHT.
Hello, Covet? Got a favor to ask...
TAXIPH
...Look up what you've got in your files about a bum who was stabbed to death in the XIIIth...
TELEPHONE
Cobble together a story on it, 30 lines or so, and make sure it doesn't get chopped before going to press.
Is this the start of something?
I locked myself in the john and re-read Lenantais's letter one last time...
...A scumbag is planning something dirty. Come see me at the Salpêtrière Hospital, room 10, bed 15. I'll explain how you can help out some old friends. Your brother, Abel Benoît.
I tore the letter to pieces and gave it a one-way ticket to the central sewer.
One more glass for the road, and I stepped outside.

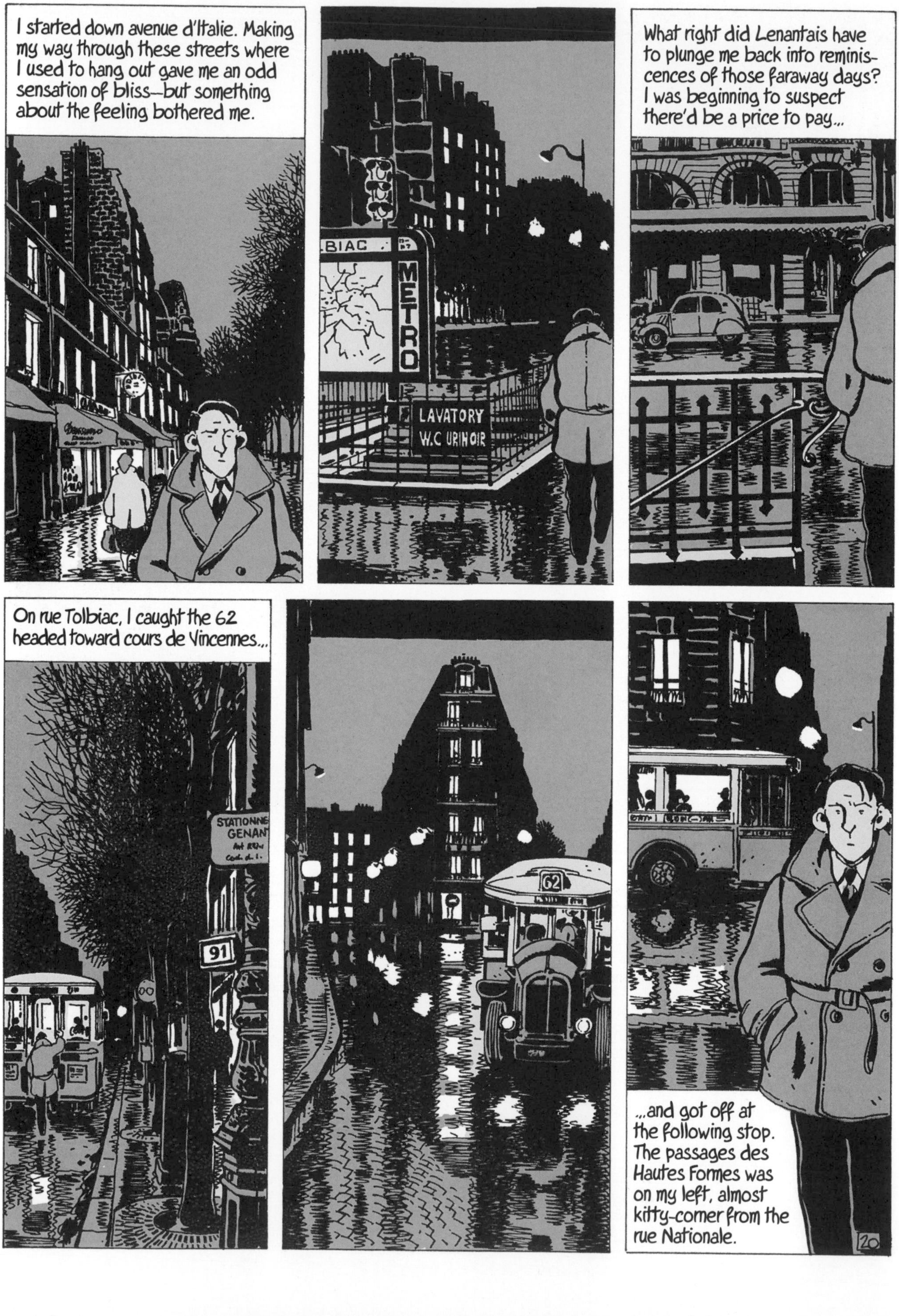
I started down avenue d'Italie. Making my way through these streets where I used to hang out gave me an odd sensation of bliss—but something about the feeling bothered me.
BIAC
METRO
LAVATORY
W.C URINOIR
What right did Lenantais have to plunge me back into reminiscences of those faraway days? I was beginning to suspect there'd be a price to pay...
On rue Tolbiac, I caught the 62 headed toward cours de Vincennes...
STATIONNE
GENANT
91
62
...and got off at the following stop. The passages des Hautes Formes was on my left, almost kitty-corner from the rue Nationale.
20

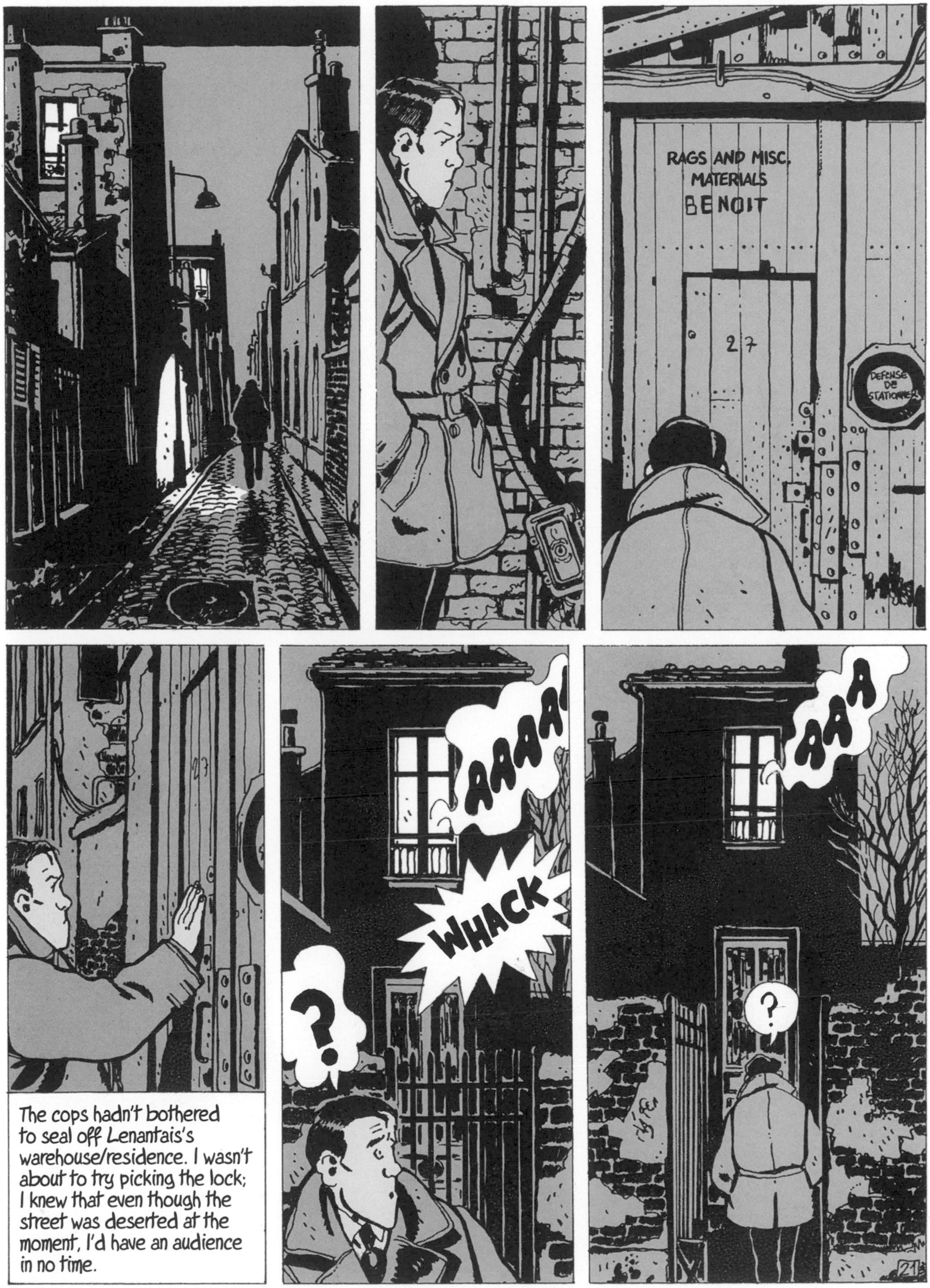
RAGS AND MISC. MATERIALS
BENOIT
27
DEFENSE DE STATIONNER
The cops hadn't bothered to seal off Lenantais's warehouse/residence. I wasn't about to try picking the lock; I knew that even though the street was deserted at the moment, I'd have an audience in no time.
AAAAA
WHACK
?
AAA
?

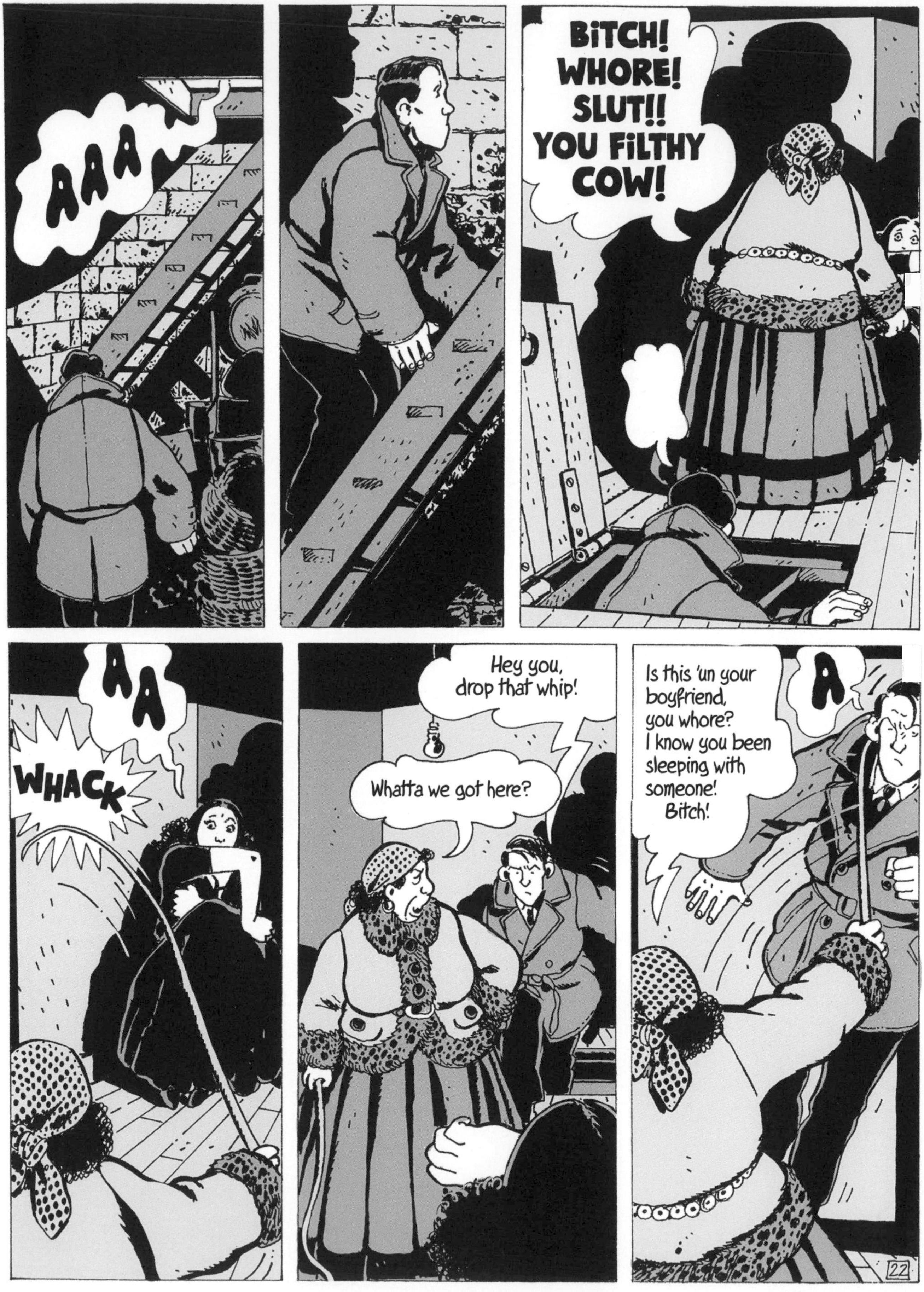
AAA
BITCH! WHORE! SLUT!! YOU FILTHY COW!
AA
WHACK
Hey you, drop that whip!
Whatta we got here?
Is this 'un your boyfriend, you whore? I know you been sleeping with someone! Bitch!
A
22

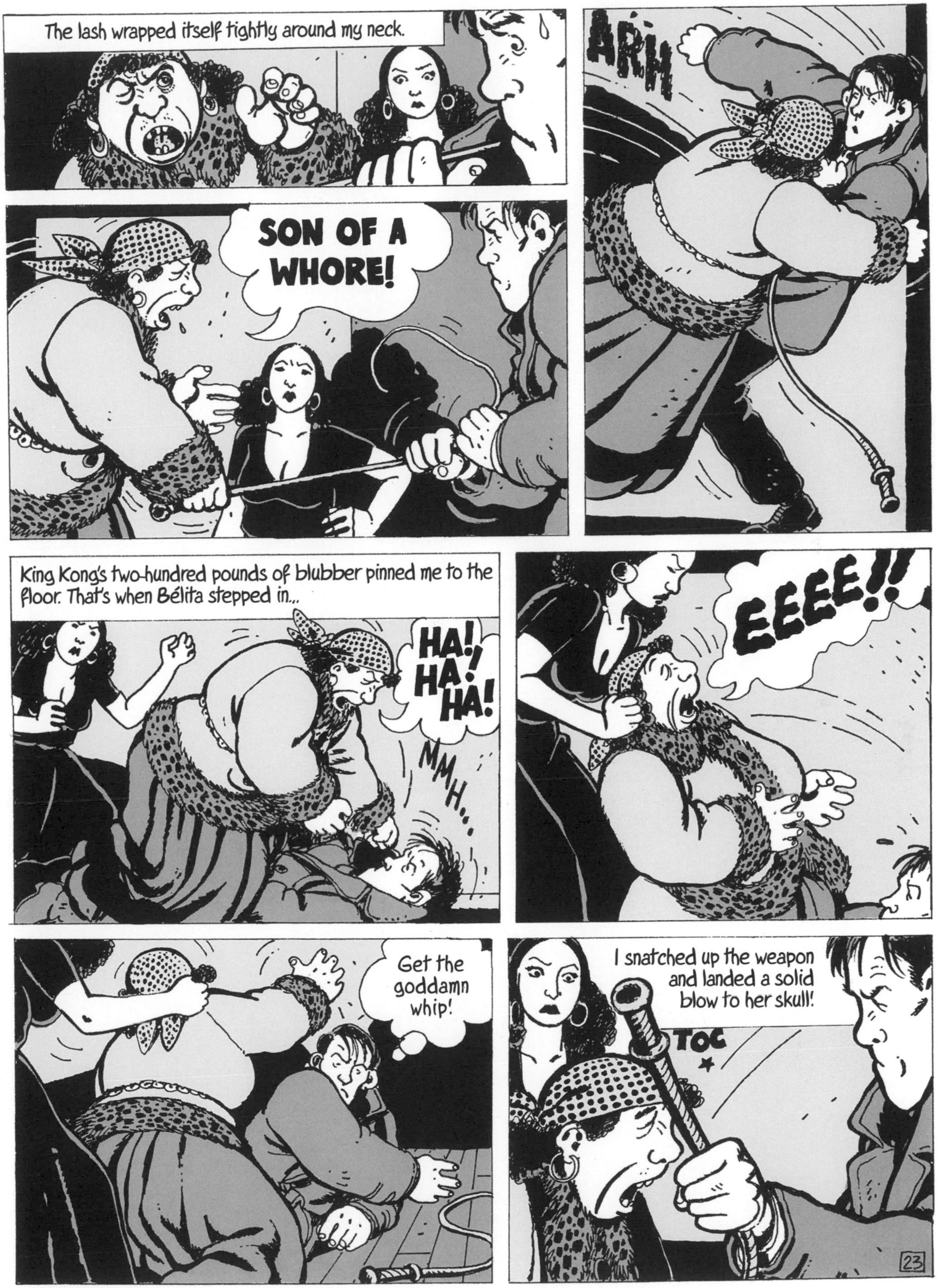

The lash wrapped itself tightly around my neck.
ARH
SON OF A WHORE!
King Kong's two-hundred pounds of blubber pinned me to the floor. That's when Bélita stepped in...
HA! HA! HA!
MMH...
EEEE!!
Get the goddamn whip!
I snatched up the weapon and landed a solid blow to her skull!
TOC
23

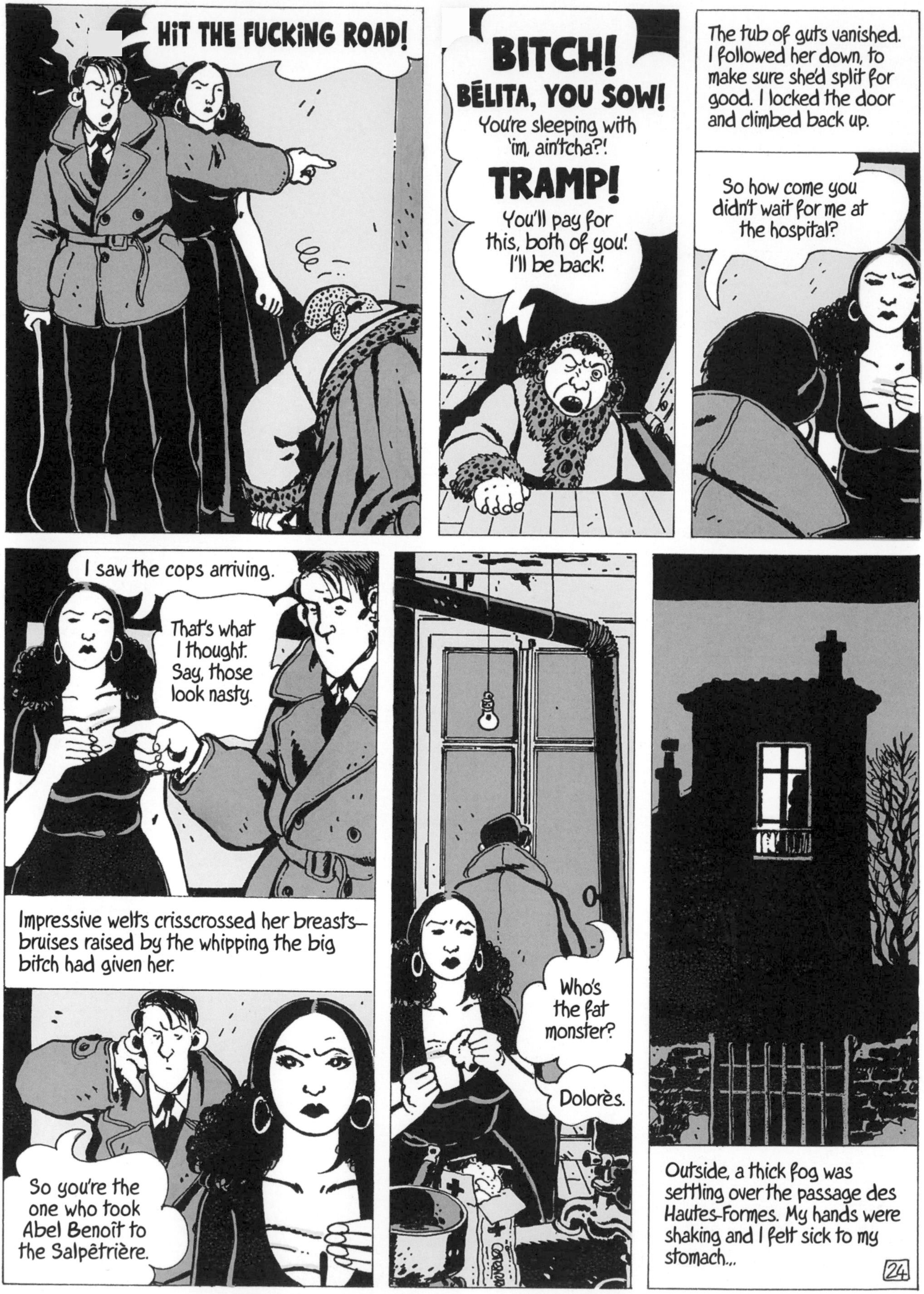
HiT THE FUCKiNG ROAD!
BITCH!
BÉLITA, YOU SOW!
You're sleeping with 'im, ain'tcha?!
TRAMP!
You'll pay for this, both of you! I'll be back!
The tub of guts vanished. I followed her down, to make sure she'd split for good. I locked the door and climbed back up.
So how come you didn't wait for me at the hospital?
I saw the cops arriving.
That's what I thought. Say, those look nasty.
Impressive welts crisscrossed her breasts—bruises raised by the whipping the big bitch had given her.
So you're the one who took Abel Benoît to the Salpêtrière.
Who's the fat monster?
Dolorès.
Outside, a thick fog was settling over the passage des Hautes-Formes. My hands were shaking and I felt sick to my stomach...

Bélita had known Lenantais only under the name Abel Benoît. He'd met her four years ago, as a result of the wanderings necessitated by his chosen trade, in an empty lot in Ivry where she'd been living with some distant relatives.

For some reason, Dolorès—her stepmother, the one with the whip—had taken to using her as a punching bag.

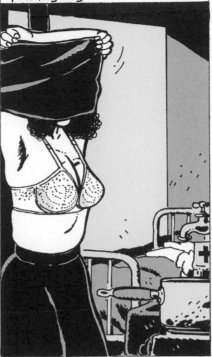

Lenantais had interceded, stood up to the gypsies, and one day, Bélita had shown up on the old anarchist's doorstep. He'd taken her under his wing and taught her to read and write.

He'd set her up across the way. She earned her living by selling flowers on the street, and everything'd been jake till Lenantais got himself killed.

The old guy struck some sort of deal with Dolorès and the others. He bought me.

Bought you?

He paid them to leave me alone. Dolorès and the others wanted me back. They resented that I'd dropped them because Abel Benoît had told me to.

His real name was Lenantais Albert.

Dolorès must have got wind that the old guy wouldn't be able to keep up the payments, and she came to try to get me back.

It wasn't Arabs that attacked and robbed Abel Benoît. He told me to say that, because it was all the cops needed to know. Here's his wallet!

25

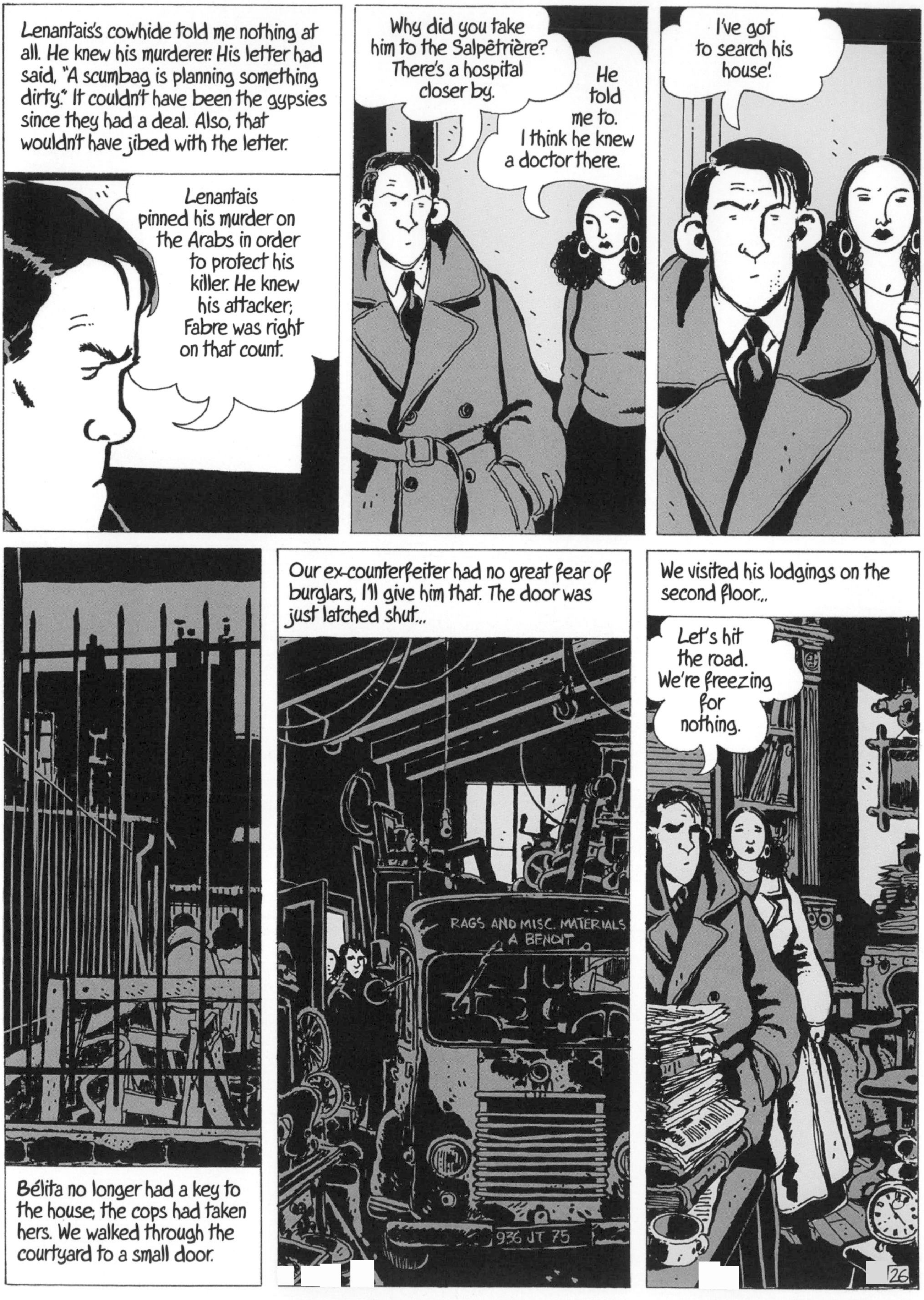
Lenantais's cowhide told me nothing at all. He knew his murderer. His letter had said, "A scumbag is planning something dirty." It couldn't have been the gypsies since they had a deal. Also, that wouldn't have jibed with the letter.
Lenantais pinned his murder on the Arabs in order to protect his killer. He knew his attacker; Fabre was right on that count.
Why did you take him to the Salpêtrière? There's a hospital closer by.
He told me to. I think he knew a doctor there.
I've got to search his house!
Bélita no longer had a key to the house; the cops had taken hers. We walked through the courtyard to a small door.
Our ex-counterfeiter had no great fear of burglars, I'll give him that. The door was just latched shut...
RAGS AND MISC. MATERIALS
A. BENOIT
936 JT 75
We visited his lodgings on the second floor...
Let's hit the road. We're freezing for nothing.

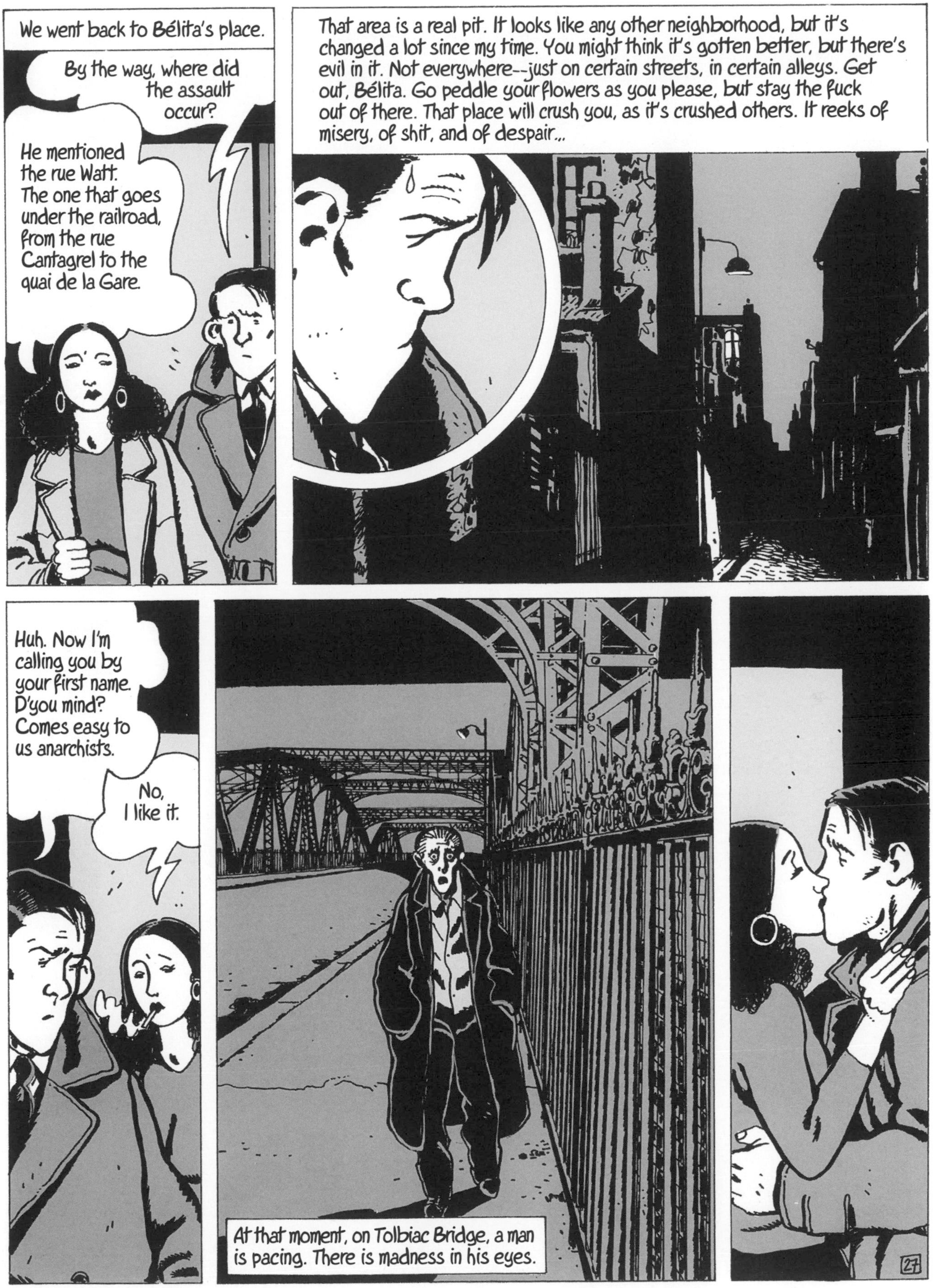
We went back to Bélita's place.
By the way, where did the assault occur?
He mentioned the rue Watt. The one that goes under the railroad, from the rue Cantagrel to the quai de la Gare.
That area is a real pit. It looks like any other neighborhood, but it's changed a lot since my time. You might think it's gotten better, but there's evil in it. Not everywhere--just on certain streets, in certain alleys. Get out, Bélita. Go peddle your flowers as you please, but stay the fuck out of there. That place will crush you, as it's crushed others. It reeks of misery, of shit, and of despair...
Huh. Now I'm calling you by your first name. D'you mind? Comes easy to us anarchists.
No, I like it.
At that moment, on Tolbiac Bridge, a man is pacing. There is madness in his eyes.

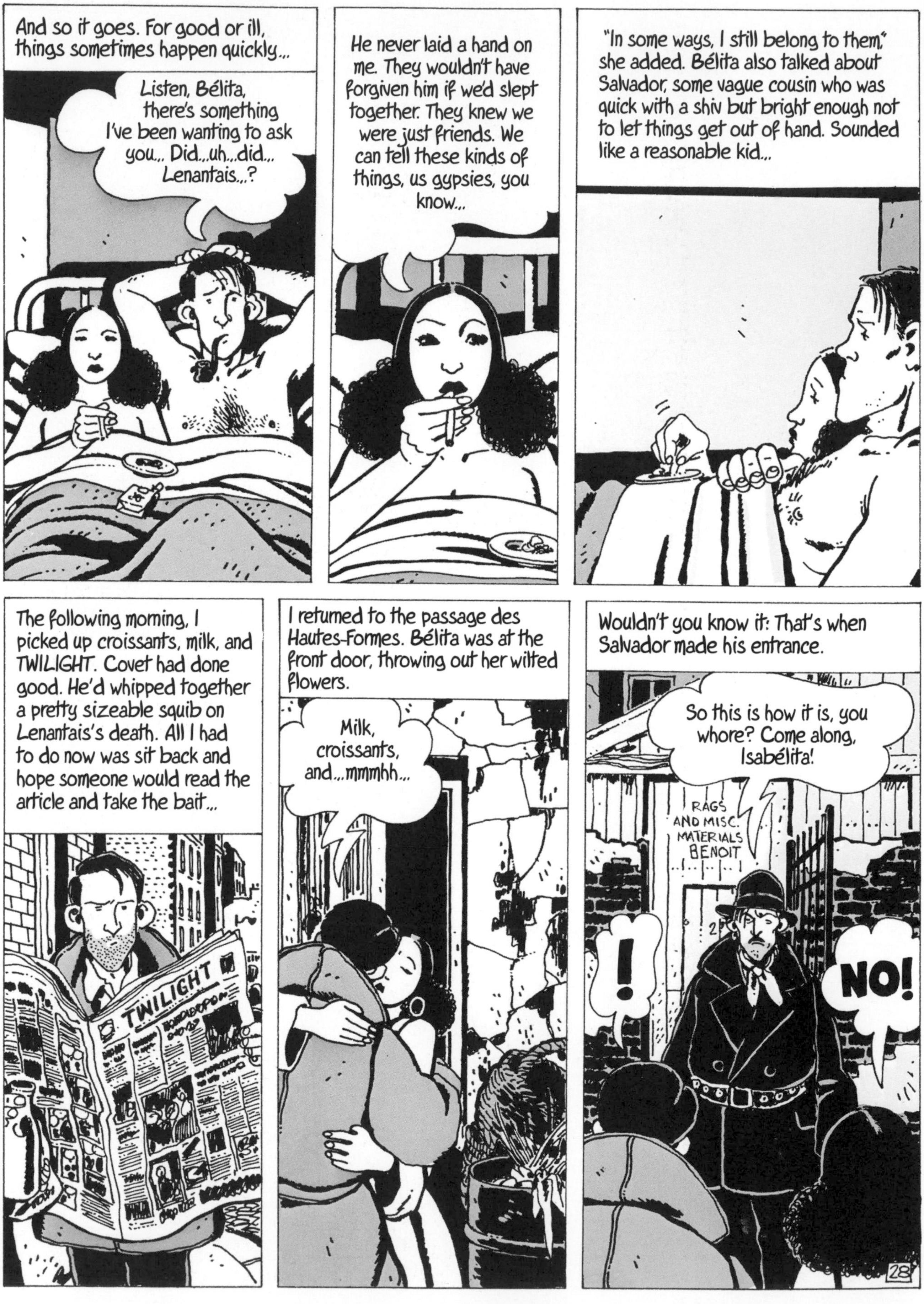
And so it goes. For good or ill, things sometimes happen quickly...
Listen, Bélita, there's something I've been wanting to ask you... Did...uh...did... Lenantais...?
He never laid a hand on me. They wouldn't have forgiven him if we'd slept together. They knew we were just friends. We can tell these kinds of things, us gypsies, you know...
"In some ways, I still belong to them," she added. Bélita also talked about Salvador, some vague cousin who was quick with a shiv but bright enough not to let things get out of hand. Sounded like a reasonable kid...
The following morning, I picked up croissants, milk, and TWILIGHT. Covet had done good. He'd whipped together a pretty sizeable squib on Lenantais's death. All I had to do now was sit back and hope someone would read the article and take the bait...
TWILIGHT
I returned to the passage des Hautes-Formes. Bélita was at the front door, throwing out her wilted flowers.
Milk, croissants, and...mmmhh...
Wouldn't you know it: That's when Salvador made his entrance.
So this is how it is, you whore? Come along, Isabélita!
RAGS AND MISC. MATERIALS BENOIT
!
NO!

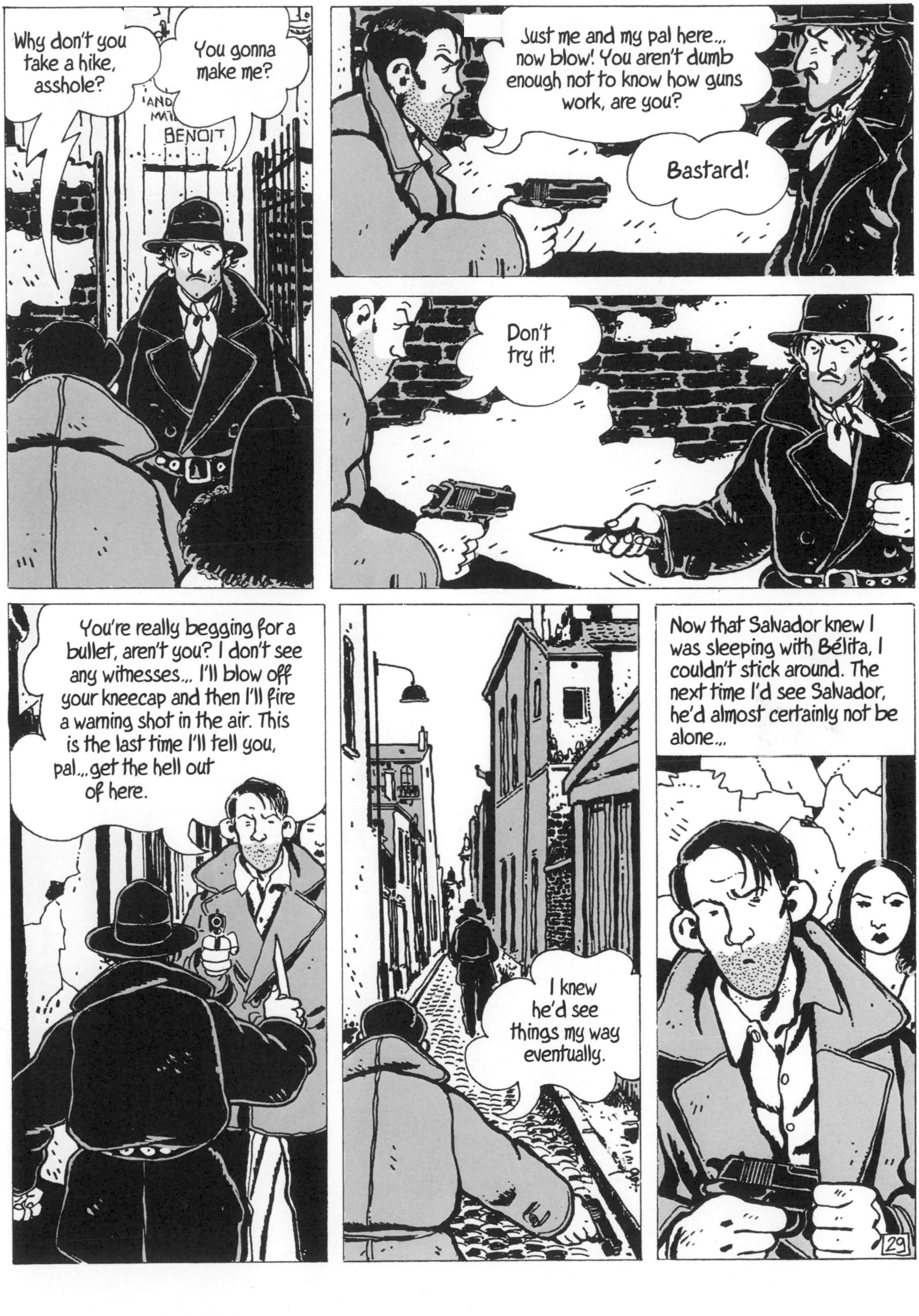
Why don't you take a hike, asshole?
You gonna make me?
AND
MA
BENOIT
Just me and my pal here... now blow! You aren't dumb enough not to know how guns work, are you?
Bastard!
Don't try it!
You're really begging for a bullet, aren't you? I don't see any witnesses... I'll blow off your kneecap and then I'll fire a warning shot in the air. This is the last time I'll tell you, pal... get the hell out of here.
I knew he'd see things my way eventually.
Now that Salvador knew I was sleeping with Bélita, I couldn't stick around. The next time I'd see Salvador, he'd almost certainly not be alone...
29

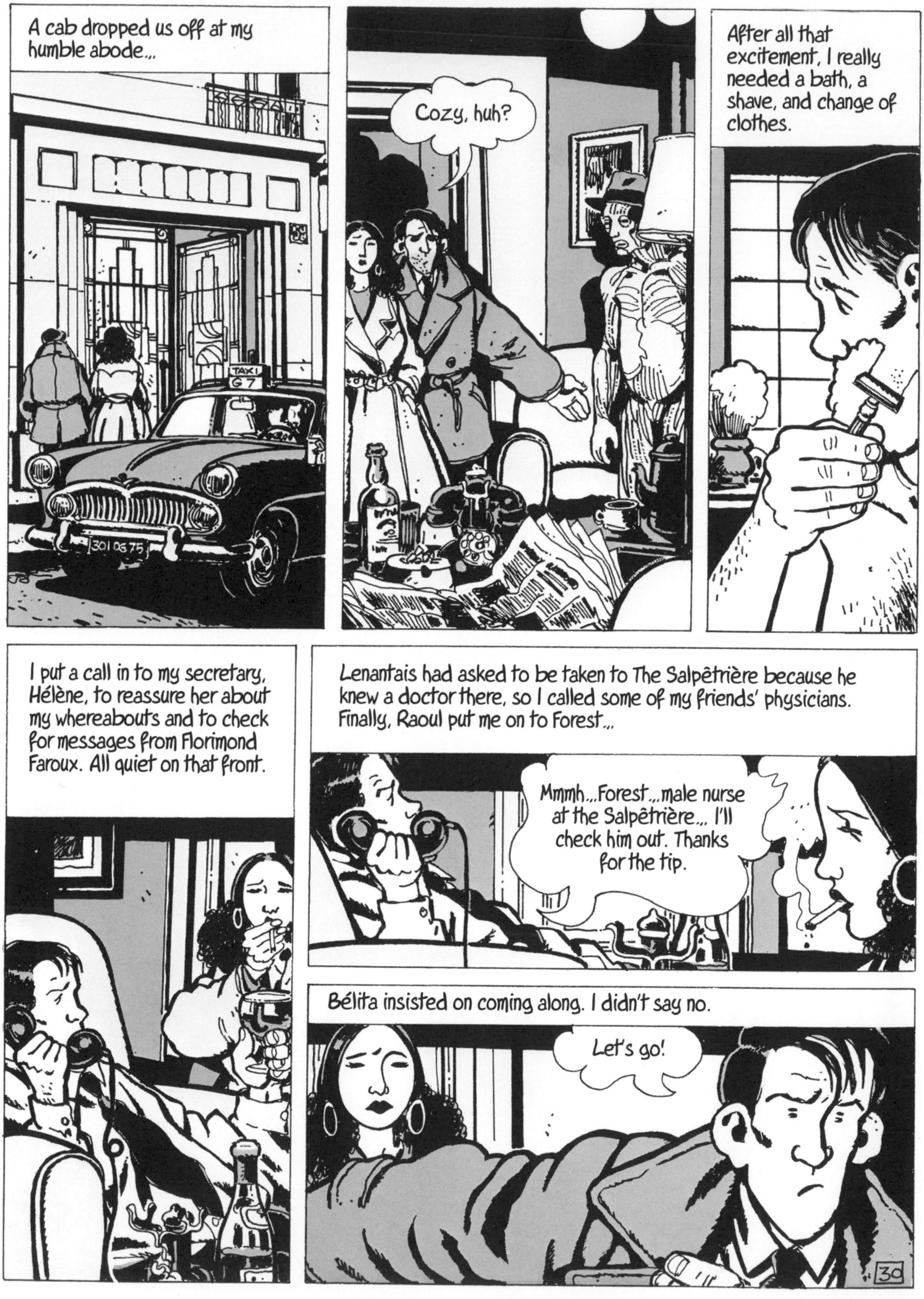

A cab dropped us off at my humble abode...
TAXI G7
301 DG 75
Cozy, huh?
After all that excitement, I really needed a bath, a shave, and change of clothes.
I put a call in to my secretary, Hélène, to reassure her about my whereabouts and to check for messages from Florimond Faroux. All quiet on that front.
Lenantais had asked to be taken to The Salpêtrière because he knew a doctor there, so I called some of my friends' physicians. Finally, Raoul put me on to Forest...
Mmmh... Forest... male nurse at the Salpêtrière... I'll check him out. Thanks for the tip.
Bélita insisted on coming along. I didn't say no.
Let's go!
30

We began with the Salpêtrière. Bélita decided to wait outside.

I asked to see Forest. He wore that solemn expression so characteristic of those who are wrestling with the idea of historical materialism. A point in his favor: I decided to be straight with him.

My name is Nestor Burma. I'm a private eye. Raoul sent me. I need some info. About Benoît, the ragman who died here, yesterday.

Right, the anarchist.

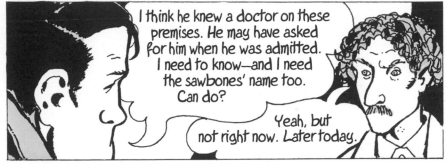

I think he knew a doctor on these premises. He may have asked for him when he was admitted. I need to know—and I need the sawbones' name too. Can do?

Yeah, but not right now. Later today.

I wrote down my office number for him. I met up with Bélita and we moved on to rue de l'Interne Loeb, where an erstwhile ragman colleague of Lenantais's lived...

Bélita knew Old Man Anselme; she'd often seen him in the company of Lenantais.

The old geezer was no help at all. We continued our journey.

31

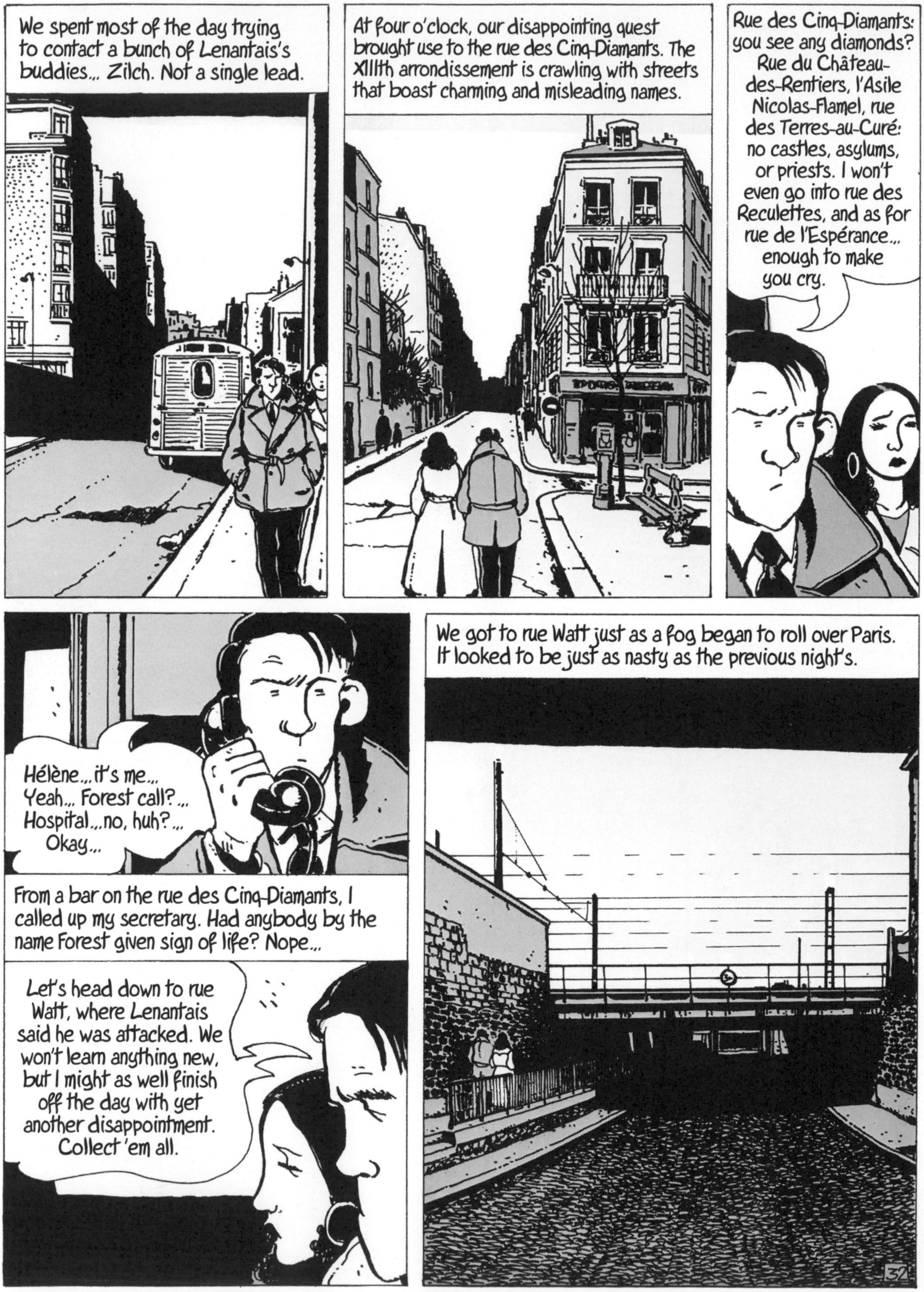
We spent most of the day trying to contact a bunch of Lenantais's buddies... Zilch. Not a single lead.
At four o'clock, our disappointing quest brought use to the rue des Cinq-Diamants. The XIIIth arrondissement is crawling with streets that boast charming and misleading names.
Rue des Cinq-Diamants: you see any diamonds? Rue du Château-des-Rentiers, l'Asile Nicolas-Flamel, rue des Terres-au-Curé: no castles, asylums, or priests. I won't even go into rue des Reculettes, and as for rue de l'Espérance... enough to make you cry.
Hélène... it's me... Yeah... Forest call?... Hospital... no, huh?... Okay...
From a bar on the rue des Cinq-Diamants, I called up my secretary. Had anybody by the name Forest given sign of life? Nope...
Let's head down to rue Watt, where Lenantais said he was attacked. We won't learn anything new, but I might as well finish off the day with yet another disappointment. Collect 'em all.
We got to rue Watt just as a fog began to roll over Paris. It looked to be just as nasty as the previous night's.

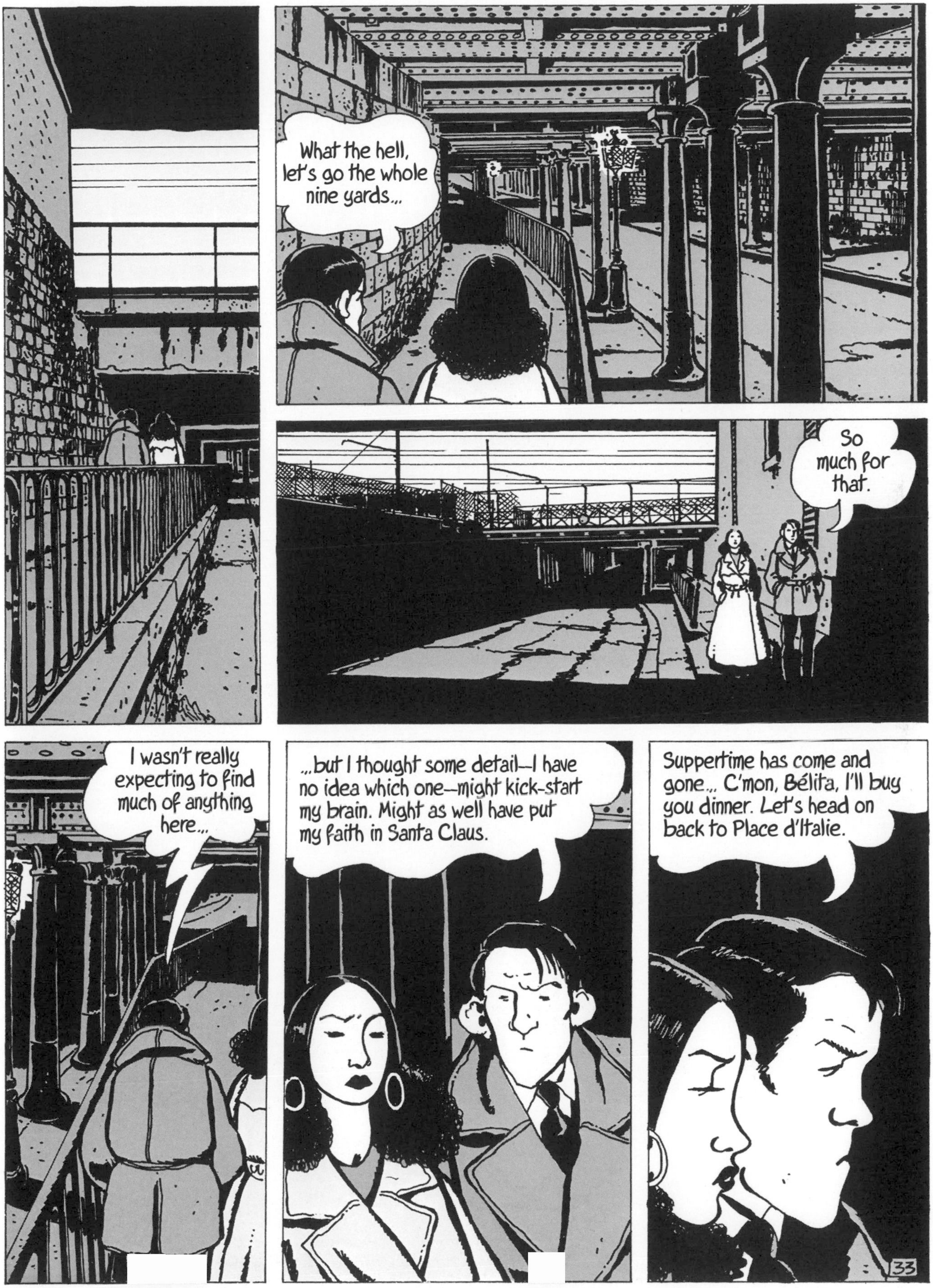
What the hell, let's go the whole nine yards...
So much for that.
I wasn't really expecting to find much of anything here...
...but I thought some detail—I have no idea which one—might kick-start my brain. Might as well have put my faith in Santa Claus.
Suppertime has come and gone... C'mon, Bélita, I'll buy you dinner. Let's head on back to Place d'Italie.
33

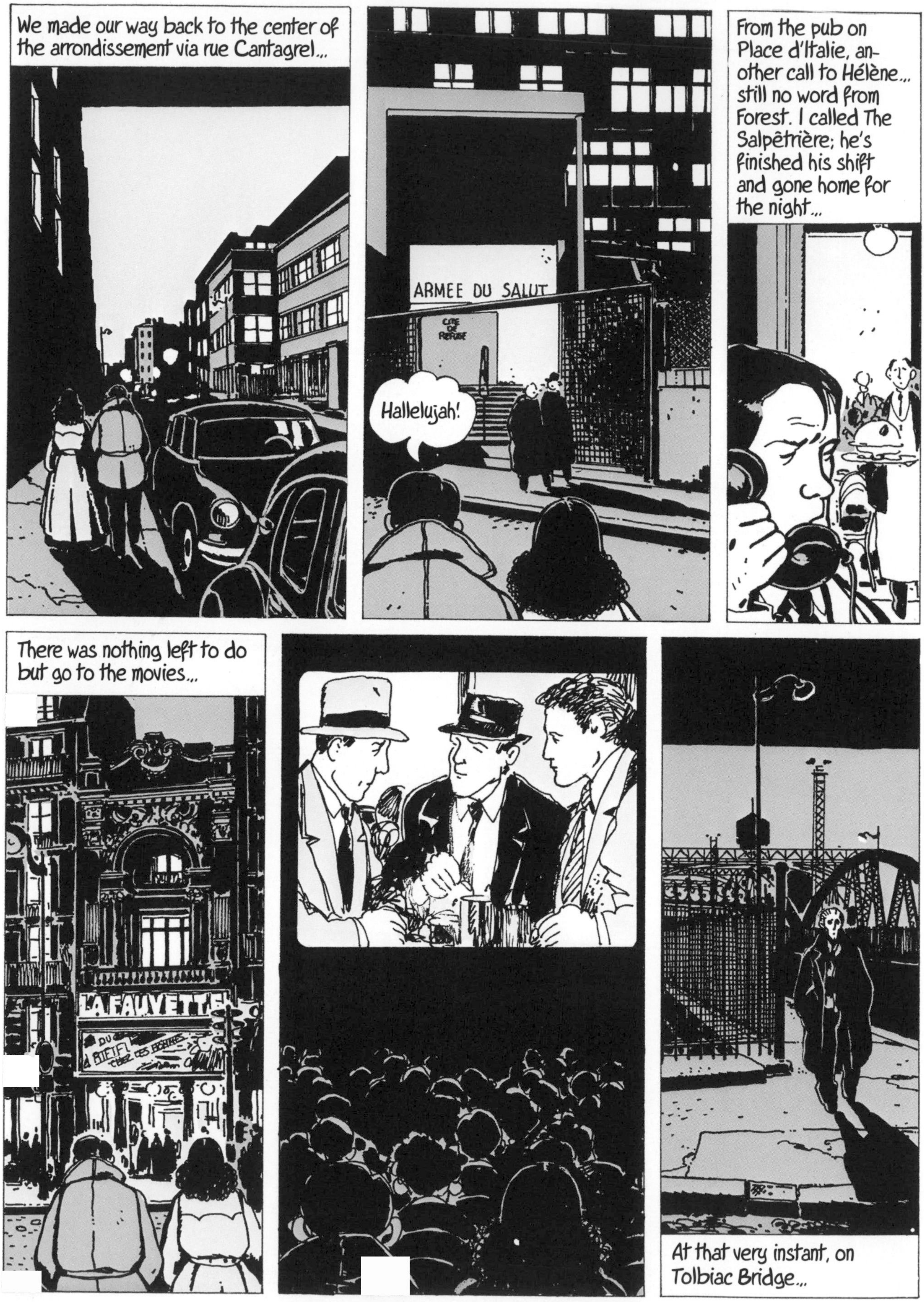
We made our way back to the center of the arrondissement via rue Cantagrel...
ARMEE DU SALUT
Hallelujah!
From the pub on Place d'Italie, another call to Hélène... still no word from Forest. I called The Salpêtrière; he's finished his shift and gone home for the night...
There was nothing left to do but go to the movies...
LA FAUVETTE
At that very instant, on Tolbiac Bridge...

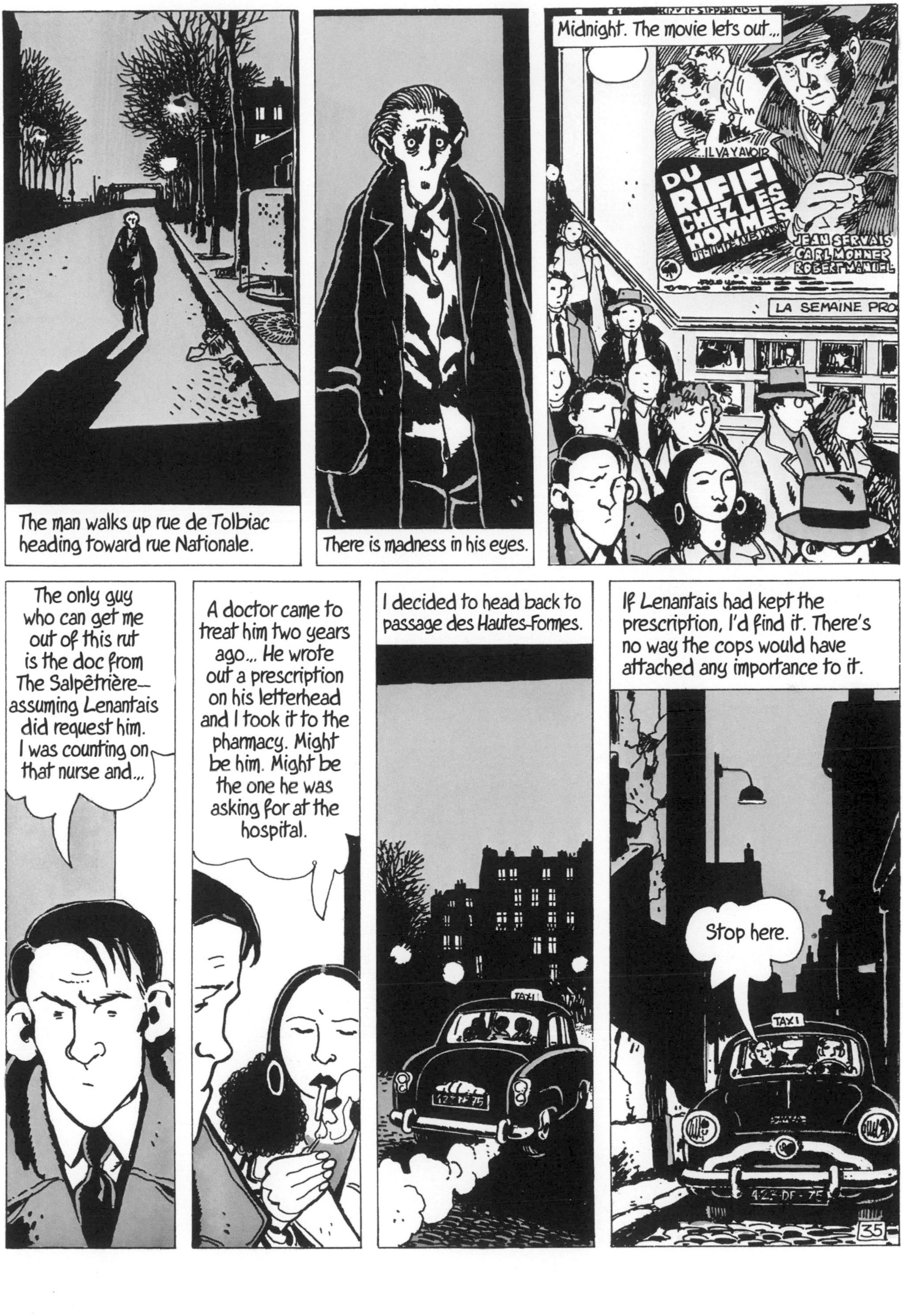
The man walks up rue de Tolbiac heading toward rue Nationale.
There is madness in his eyes.
Midnight. The movie lets out...
...IL VA Y AVOIR
DU RIFIFI CHEZ LES HOMMES
JEAN SERVAIS
CARL MOHNER
ROBERT MANUEL
LA SEMAINE PRO
The only guy who can get me out of this rut is the doc from The Salpêtrière— assuming Lenantais did request him. I was counting on that nurse and...
A doctor came to treat him two years ago... He wrote out a prescription on his letterhead and I took it to the pharmacy. Might be him. Might be the one he was asking for at the hospital.
I decided to head back to passage des Hautes-Formes.
If Lenantais had kept the prescription, I'd find it. There's no way the cops would have attached any importance to it.
TAXI
Stop here.
TAXI
35

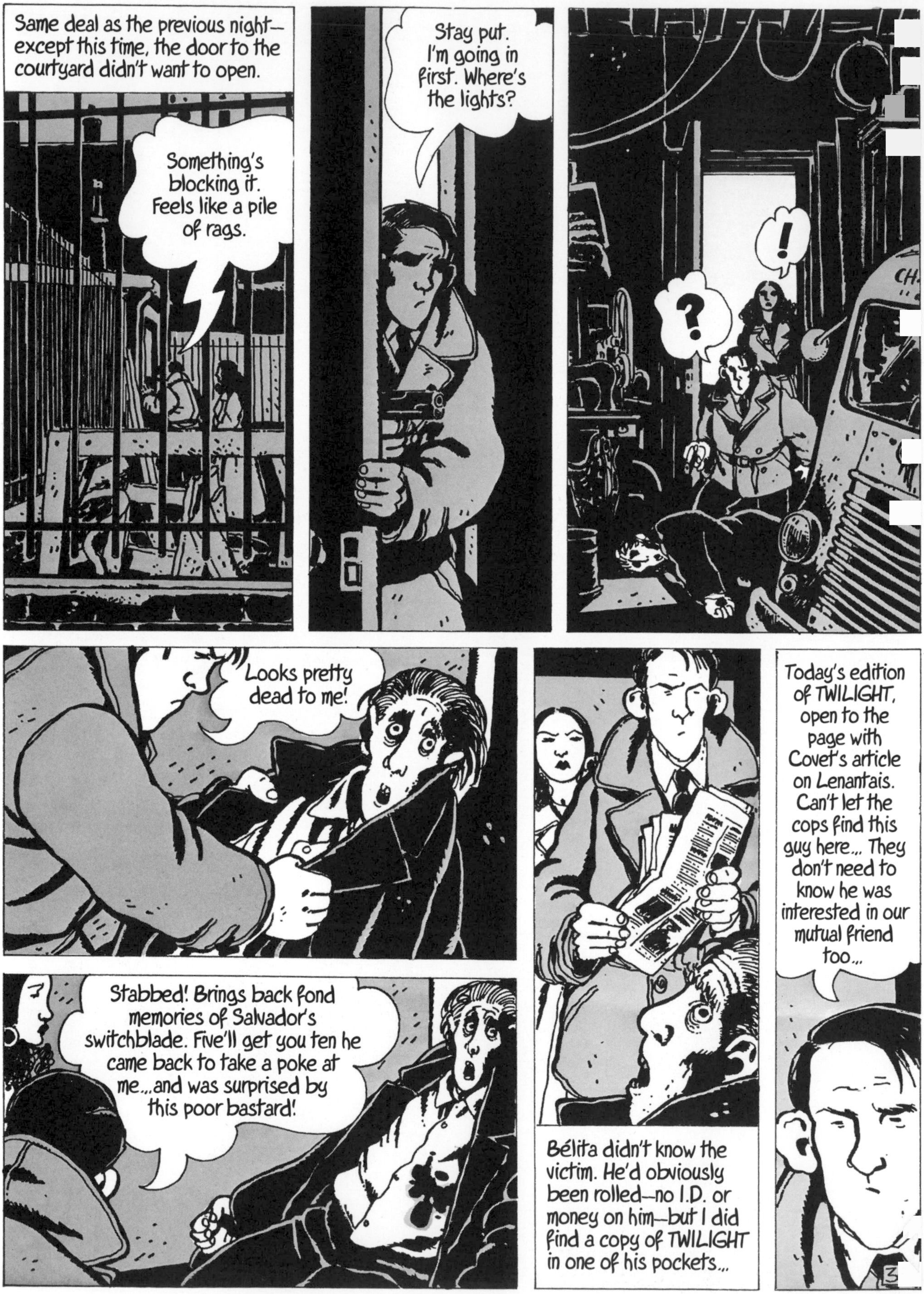
Same deal as the previous night— except this time, the door to the courtyard didn't want to open.
Something's blocking it. Feels like a pile of rags.
Stay put. I'm going in first. Where's the lights?
?
!
Looks pretty dead to me!
Stabbed! Brings back fond memories of Salvador's switchblade. Five'll get you ten he came back to take a poke at me...and was surprised by this poor bastard!
Bélita didn't know the victim. He'd obviously been rolled—no I.D. or money on him—but I did find a copy of TWILIGHT in one of his pockets...
Today's edition of TWILIGHT, open to the page with Covet's article on Lenantais. Can't let the cops find this guy here... They don't need to know he was interested in our mutual friend too...

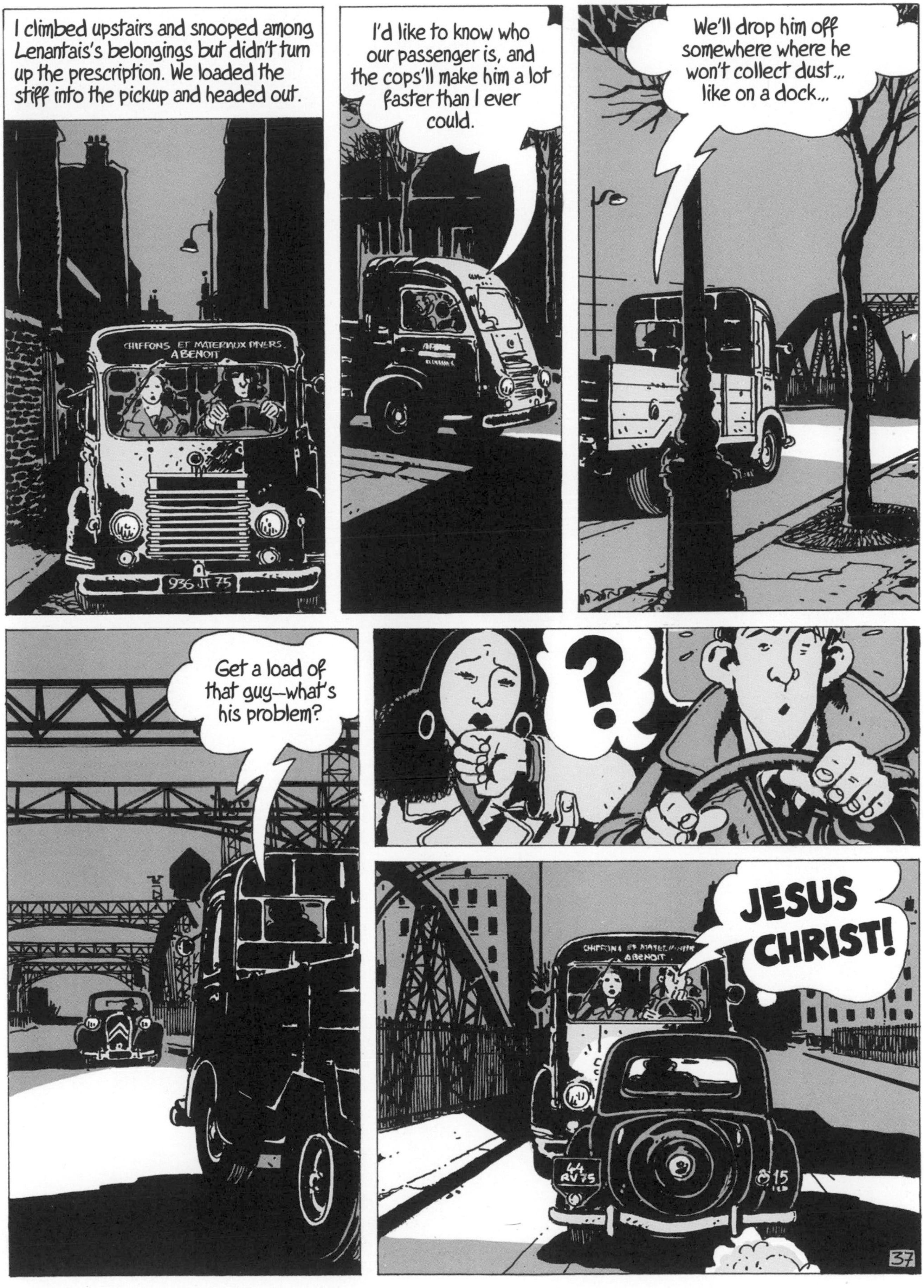

I climbed upstairs and snooped among Lenantais's belongings but didn't turn up the prescription. We loaded the stiff into the pickup and headed out.
CHIFFONS ET MATERIAUX DIVERS
A BENOIT
936 JT 75
I'd like to know who our passenger is, and the cops'll make him a lot faster than I ever could.
We'll drop him off somewhere where he won't collect dust... like on a dock...
Get a load of that guy--what's his problem?
?
JESUS CHRIST!
RV 75

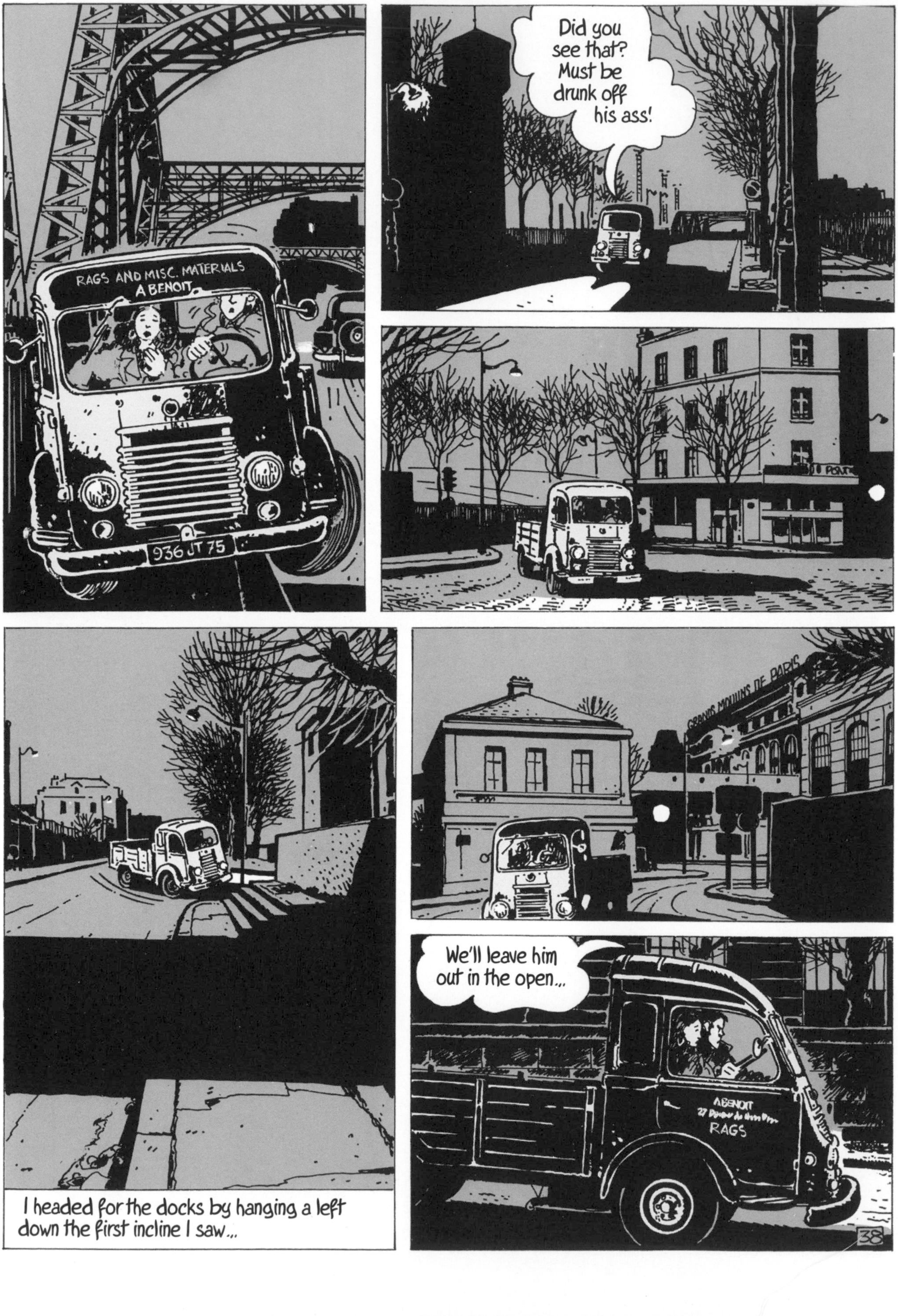
RAGS AND MISC. MATERIALS
A BENOIT
936 JT 75
Did you see that? Must be drunk off his ass!
I headed for the docks by hanging a left down the first incline I saw...
GRANDS MOULINS DE PARIS
We'll leave him out in the open...
A BENOIT
RAGS

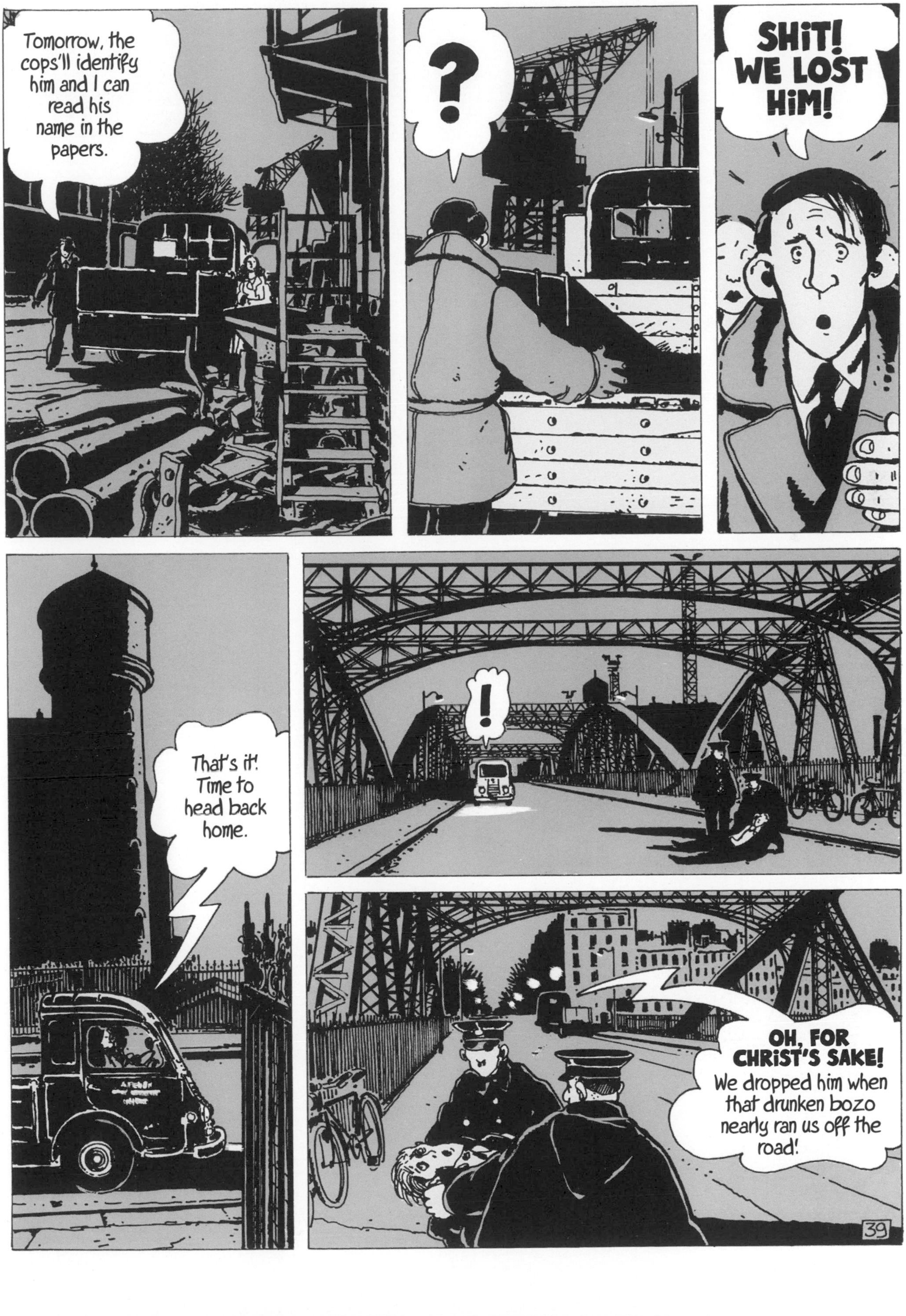
Tomorrow, the cops'll identify him and I can read his name in the papers.
?
SHIT! WE LOST HIM!
That's it! Time to head back home.
!
OH, FOR CHRIST'S SAKE! We dropped him when that drunken bozo nearly ran us off the road!

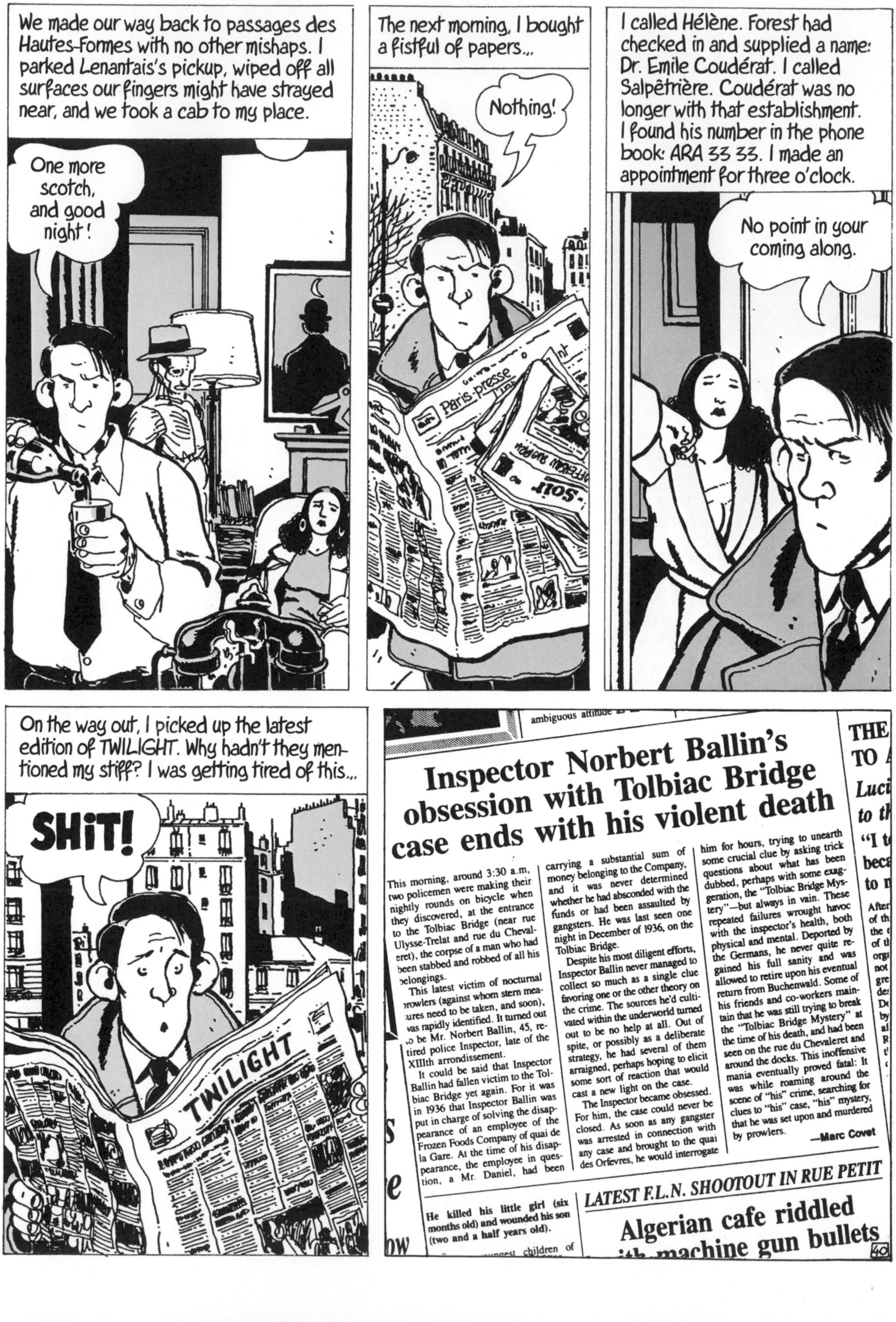
We made our way back to passages des Hautes-Formes with no other mishaps. I parked Lenantais's pickup, wiped off all surfaces our fingers might have strayed near, and we took a cab to my place.
One more scotch, and good night!
The next morning, I bought a fistful of papers...
Nothing!
Paris-presse
I called Hélène. Forest had checked in and supplied a name: Dr. Emile Coudérat. I called Salpêtrière. Coudérat was no longer with that establishment. I found his number in the phone book: ARA 33 33. I made an appointment for three o'clock.
No point in your coming along.
On the way out, I picked up the latest edition of TWILIGHT. Why hadn't they mentioned my stiff? I was getting tired of this...
SHIT!
TWILIGHT
ambiguous attitude as
Inspector Norbert Ballin's obsession with Tolbiac Bridge case ends with his violent death
This morning, around 3:30 a.m, two policemen were making their nightly rounds on bicycle when they discovered, at the entrance to the Tolbiac Bridge (near rue Ulysse-Trelat and rue du Chevaleret), the corpse of a man who had been stabbed and robbed of all his belongings.
This latest victim of nocturnal prowlers (against whom stern measures need to be taken, and soon), was rapidly identified. It turned out to be Mr. Norbert Ballin, 45, retired police Inspector, late of the XIIIth arrondissement.
It could be said that Inspector Ballin had fallen victim to the Tolbiac Bridge yet again. For it was in 1936 that Inspector Ballin was put in charge of solving the disappearance of an employee of the Frozen Foods Company of quai de la Gare. At the time of his disappearance, the employee in question, a Mr. Daniel, had been carrying a substantial sum of money belonging to the Company, and it was never determined whether he had absconded with the funds or had been assaulted by gangsters. He was last seen one night in December of 1936, on the Tolbiac Bridge.
Despite his most diligent efforts, Inspector Ballin never managed to collect so much as a single clue favoring one or the other theory on the crime. The sources he'd cultivated within the underworld turned out to be no help at all. Out of spite, or possibly as a deliberate strategy, he had several of them arraigned, perhaps hoping to elicit some sort of reaction that would cast a new light on the case.
The Inspector became obsessed. For him, the case could never be closed. As soon as any gangster was arrested in connection with any case and brought to the quai des Orfevres, he would interrogate him for hours, trying to unearth some crucial clue by asking trick questions about what has been dubbed, perhaps with some exaggeration, the "Tolbiac Bridge Mystery"—but always in vain. These repeated failures wrought havoc with the inspector's health, both physical and mental. Deported by the Germans, he never quite regained his full sanity and was allowed to retire upon his eventual return from Buchenwald. Some of his friends and co-workers maintain that he was still trying to break the "Tolbiac Bridge Mystery" at the time of his death, and had been seen on the rue du Chevaleret and around the docks. This inoffensive mania eventually proved fatal: It was while roaming around the scene of "his" crime, searching for clues to "his" case, "his" mystery, that he was set upon and murdered by prowlers.
—Marc Covet
LATEST F.L.N. SHOOTOUT IN RUE PETIT
Algerian cafe riddled with machine gun bullets
He killed his little girl (six months old) and wounded his son (two and a half years old).
40

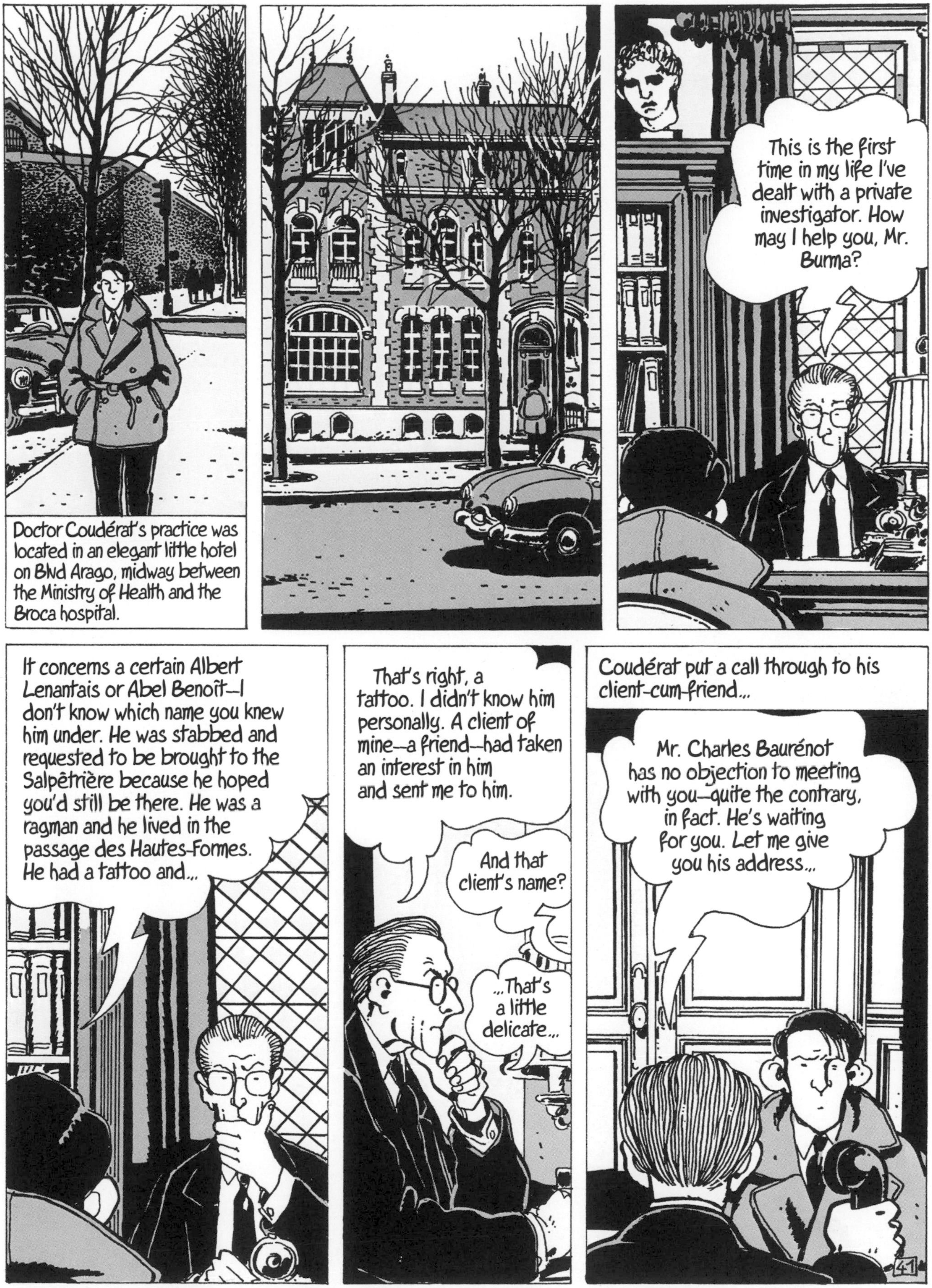
Doctor Coudérat's practice was located in an elegant little hotel on Blvd Arago, midway between the Ministry of Health and the Broca hospital.
This is the first time in my life I've dealt with a private investigator. How may I help you, Mr. Burma?
It concerns a certain Albert Lenantais or Abel Benoît—I don't know which name you knew him under. He was stabbed and requested to be brought to the Salpêtrière because he hoped you'd still be there. He was a ragman and he lived in the passage des Hautes-Formes. He had a tattoo and...
That's right, a tattoo. I didn't know him personally. A client of mine—a friend—had taken an interest in him and sent me to him.
And that client's name?
...That's a little delicate...
Coudérat put a call through to his client-cum-friend...
Mr. Charles Baurénot has no objection to meeting with you—quite the contrary, in fact. He's waiting for you. Let me give you his address...
41

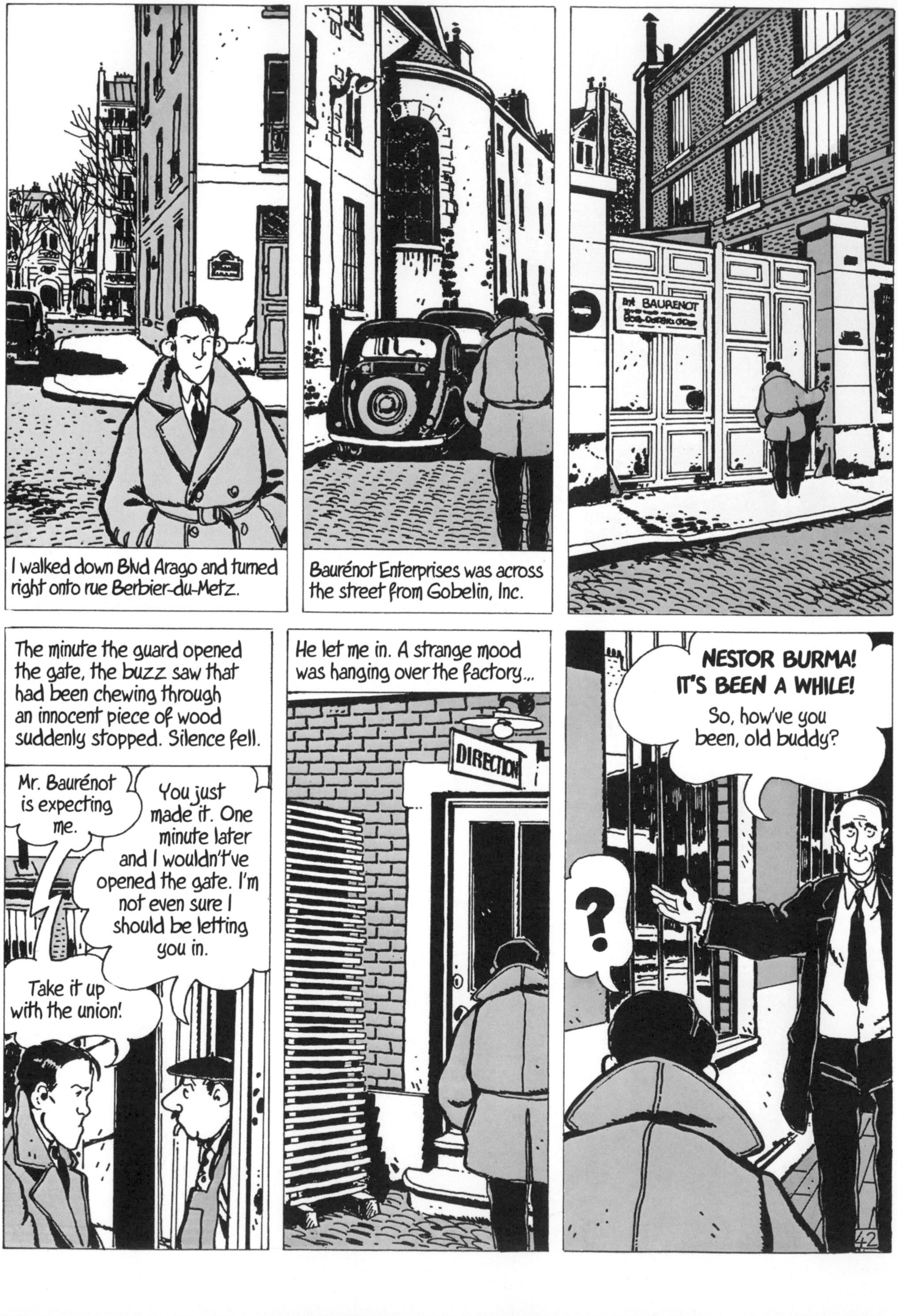
I walked down Blvd Arago and turned right onto rue Berbier-du-Metz.
Baurénot Enterprises was across the street from Gobelin, Inc.
BAURENOT
The minute the guard opened the gate, the buzz saw that had been chewing through an innocent piece of wood suddenly stopped. Silence fell.
Mr. Baurénot is expecting me.
You just made it. One minute later and I wouldn't've opened the gate. I'm not even sure I should be letting you in.
Take it up with the union!
He let me in. A strange mood was hanging over the factory...
DIRECTION
NESTOR BURMA! IT'S BEEN A WHILE!
So, how've you been, old buddy?
?

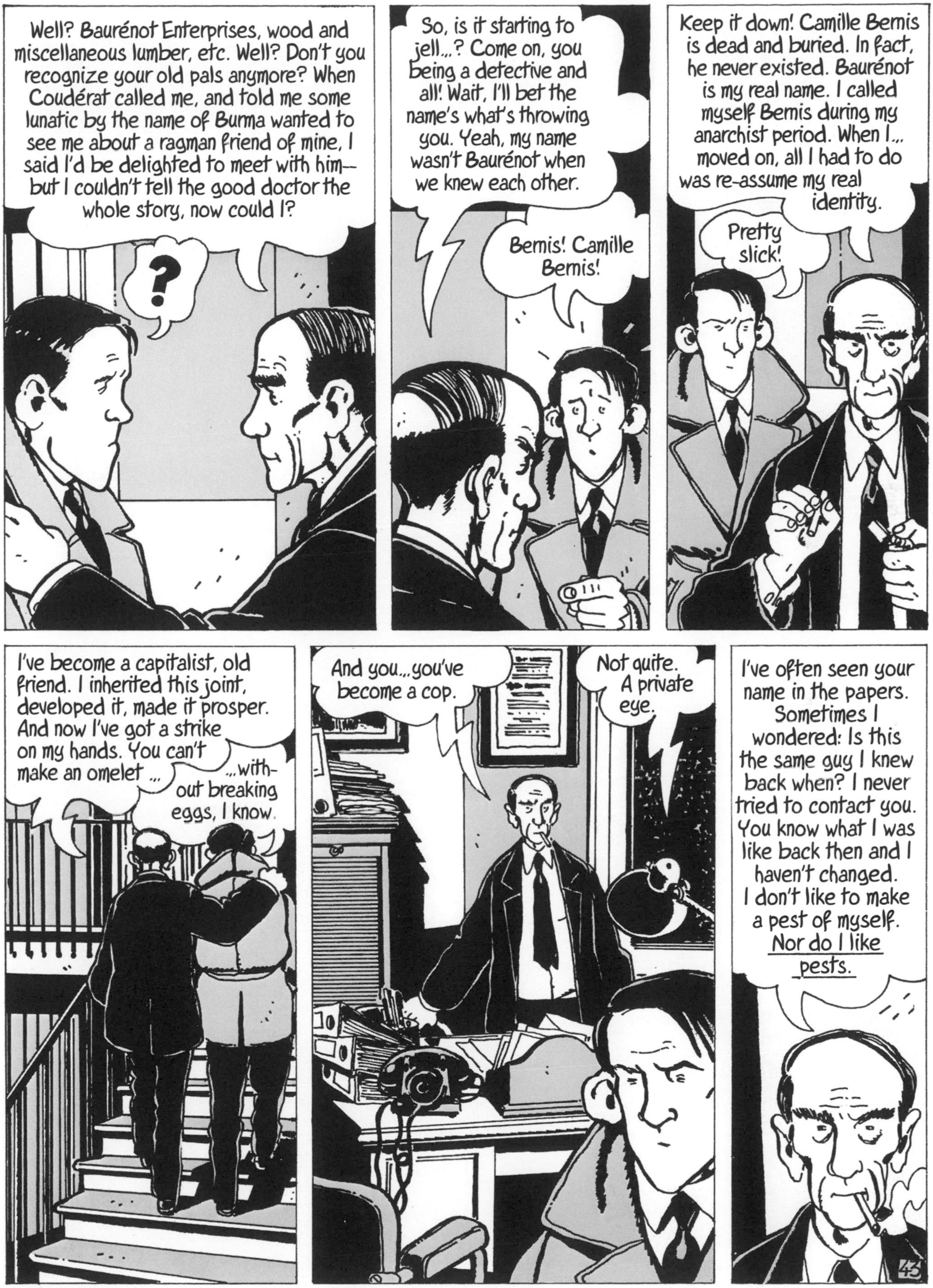
Well? Bauránot Enterprises, wood and miscellaneous lumber, etc. Well? Don't you recognize your old pals anymore? When Coudérat called me, and told me some lunatic by the name of Burma wanted to see me about a ragman friend of mine, I said I'd be delighted to meet with him-- but I couldn't tell the good doctor the whole story, now could I?
?
So, is it starting to jell...? Come on, you being a detective and all! Wait, I'll bet the name's what's throwing you. Yeah, my name wasn't Bauránot when we knew each other.
Bernis! Camille Bernis!
Keep it down! Camille Bernis is dead and buried. In fact, he never existed. Bauránot is my real name. I called myself Bernis during my anarchist period. When I... moved on, all I had to do was re-assume my real identity.
Pretty slick!
I've become a capitalist, old friend. I inherited this joint, developed it, made it prosper. And now I've got a strike on my hands. You can't make an omelet ...
...without breaking eggs, I know.
And you... you've become a cop.
Not quite. A private eye.
I've often seen your name in the papers. Sometimes I wondered: Is this the same guy I knew back when? I never tried to contact you. You know what I was like back then and I haven't changed. I don't like to make a pest of myself. Nor do I like pests.
43

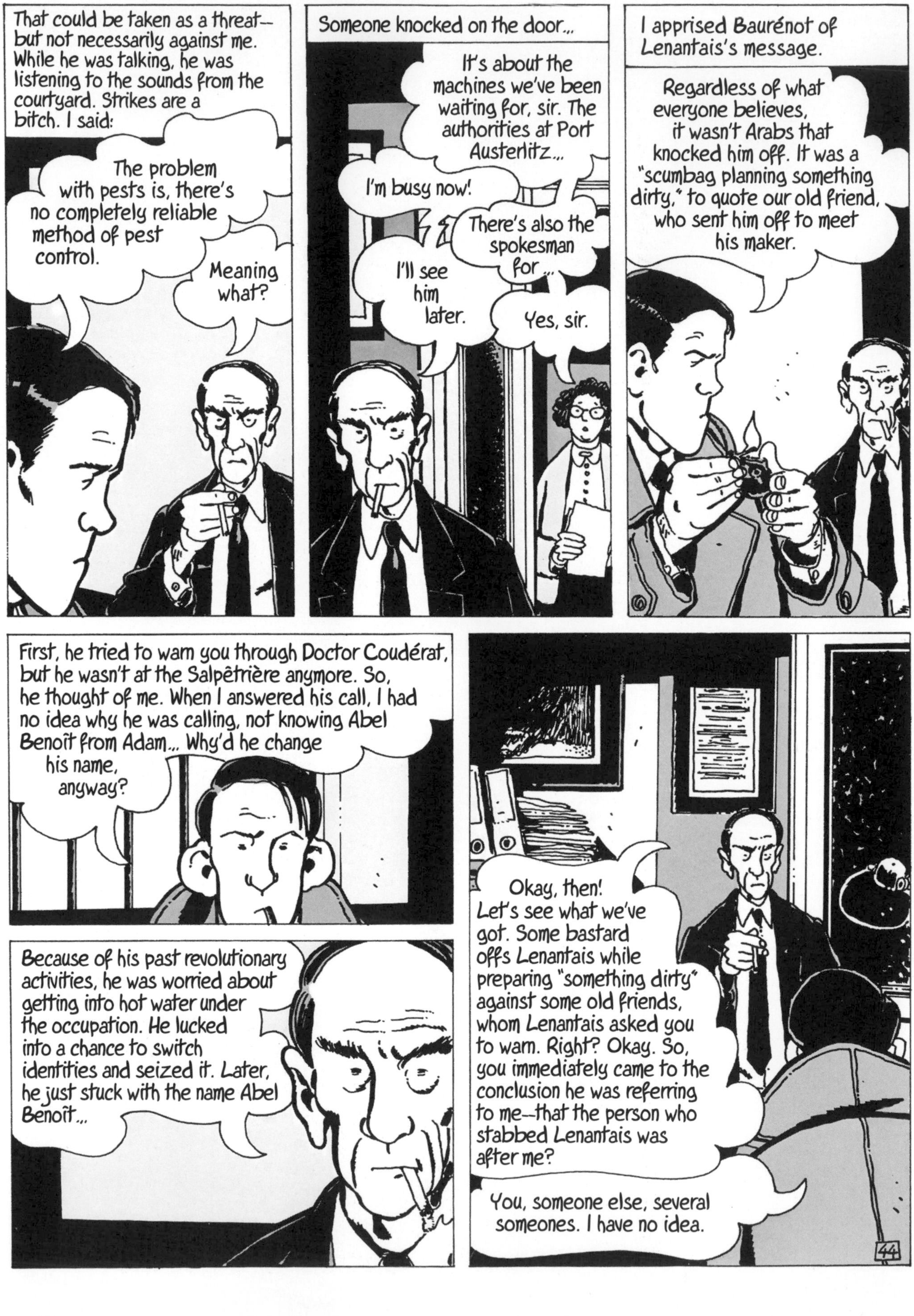
That could be taken as a threat-- but not necessarily against me. While he was talking, he was listening to the sounds from the courtyard. Strikes are a bitch. I said:
The problem with pests is, there's no completely reliable method of pest control.
Meaning what?
Someone knocked on the door...
It's about the machines we've been waiting for, sir. The authorities at Port Austerlitz...
I'm busy now!
There's also the spokesman for...
I'll see him later.
Yes, sir.
I apprised Baurénot of Lenantais's message.
Regardless of what everyone believes, it wasn't Arabs that knocked him off. It was a "scumbag planning something dirty," to quote our old friend, who sent him off to meet his maker.
First, he tried to warn you through Doctor Coudérat, but he wasn't at the Salpêtrière anymore. So, he thought of me. When I answered his call, I had no idea why he was calling, not knowing Abel Benoît from Adam... Why'd he change his name, anyway?
Because of his past revolutionary activities, he was worried about getting into hot water under the occupation. He lucked into a chance to switch identities and seized it. Later, he just stuck with the name Abel Benoît...
Okay, then! Let's see what we've got. Some bastard offs Lenantais while preparing "something dirty" against some old friends, whom Lenantais asked you to warn. Right? Okay. So, you immediately came to the conclusion he was referring to me--that the person who stabbed Lenantais was after me?
You, someone else, several someones. I have no idea.
44

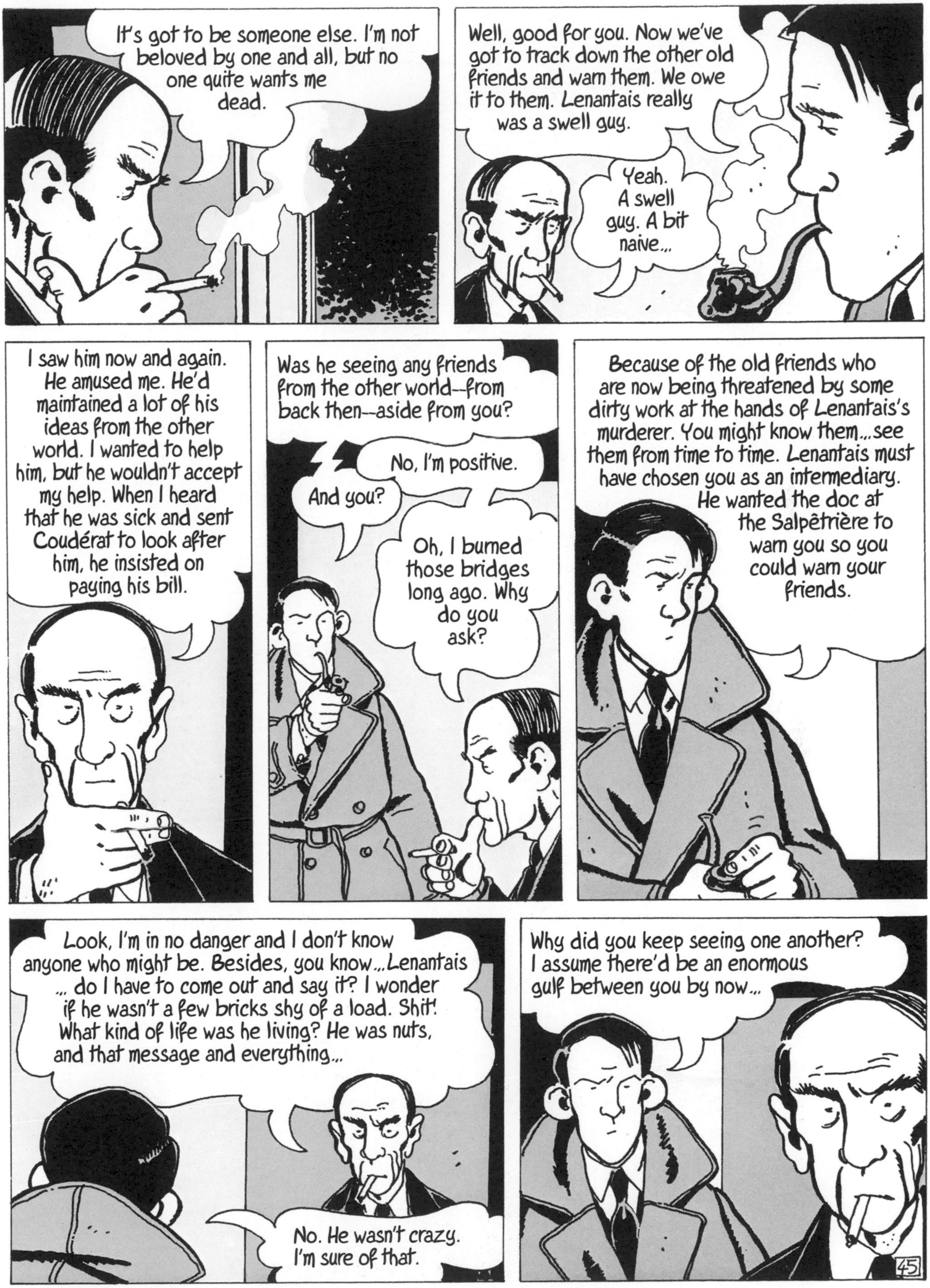
It's got to be someone else. I'm not beloved by one and all, but no one quite wants me dead.
Well, good for you. Now we've got to track down the other old friends and warn them. We owe it to them. Lenantais really was a swell guy.
Yeah. A swell guy. A bit naive...
I saw him now and again. He amused me. He'd maintained a lot of his ideas from the other world. I wanted to help him, but he wouldn't accept my help. When I heard that he was sick and sent Coudérat to look after him, he insisted on paying his bill.
Was he seeing any friends from the other world--from back then--aside from you?
No, I'm positive.
And you?
Oh, I burned those bridges long ago. Why do you ask?
Because of the old friends who are now being threatened by some dirty work at the hands of Lenantais's murderer. You might know them... see them from time to time. Lenantais must have chosen you as an intermediary. He wanted the doc at the Salpêtrière to warn you so you could warn your friends.
Look, I'm in no danger and I don't know anyone who might be. Besides, you know... Lenantais ... do I have to come out and say it? I wonder if he wasn't a few bricks shy of a load. Shit! What kind of life was he living? He was nuts, and that message and everything...
No. He wasn't crazy. I'm sure of that.
Why did you keep seeing one another? I assume there'd be an enormous gulf between you by now...
45

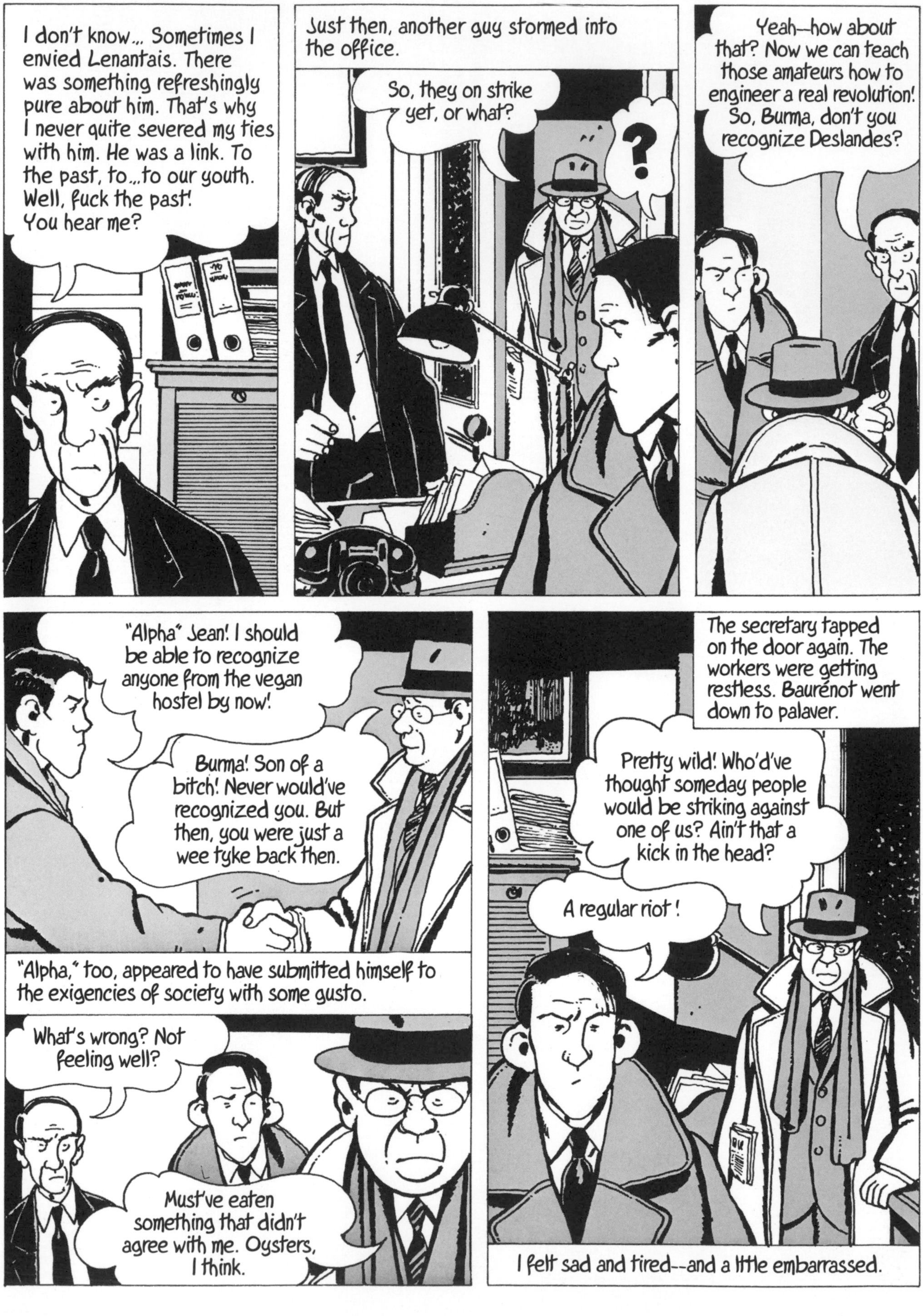
I don't know... Sometimes I envied Lenantais. There was something refreshingly pure about him. That's why I never quite severed my ties with him. He was a link. To the past, to...to our youth. Well, fuck the past! You hear me?
Just then, another guy stormed into the office.
So, they on strike yet, or what?
?
Yeah--how about that? Now we can teach those amateurs how to engineer a real revolution! So, Burma, don't you recognize Deslandes?
"Alpha" Jean! I should be able to recognize anyone from the vegan hostel by now!
Burma! Son of a bitch! Never would've recognized you. But then, you were just a wee tyke back then.
"Alpha," too, appeared to have submitted himself to the exigencies of society with some gusto.
What's wrong? Not feeling well?
Must've eaten something that didn't agree with me. Oysters, I think.
The secretary tapped on the door again. The workers were getting restless. Baurénot went down to palaver.
Pretty wild! Who'd've thought someday people would be striking against one of us? Ain't that a kick in the head?
A regular riot!
I felt sad and tired--and a little embarrassed.

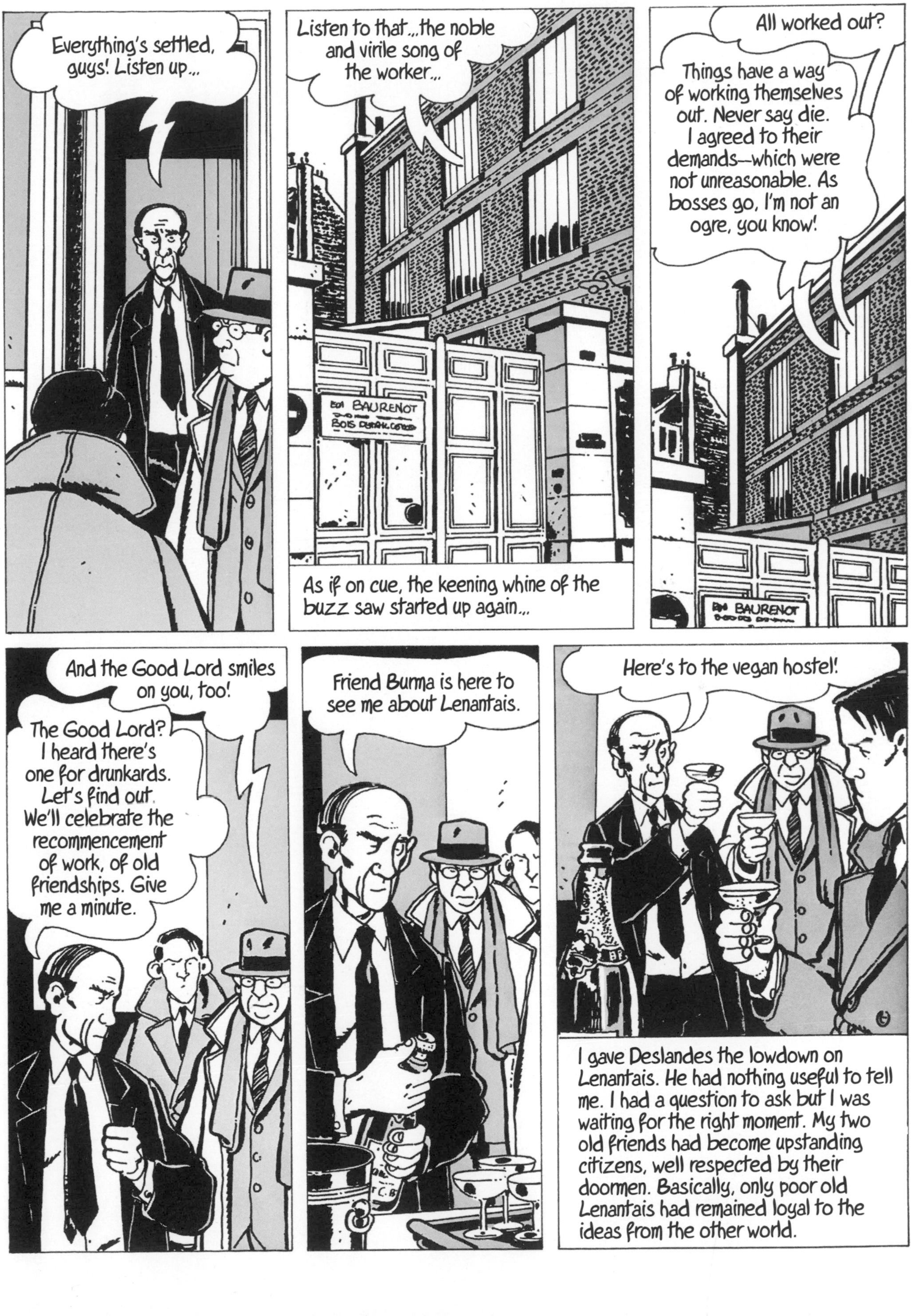
Everything's settled, guys! Listen up...
Listen to that... the noble and virile song of the worker...
BAURENOT
As if on cue, the keening whine of the buzz saw started up again...
All worked out?
Things have a way of working themselves out. Never say die. I agreed to their demands—which were not unreasonable. As bosses go, I'm not an ogre, you know!
BAURENOT
And the Good Lord smiles on you, too!
The Good Lord? I heard there's one for drunkards. Let's find out. We'll celebrate the recommencement of work, of old friendships. Give me a minute.
Friend Burma is here to see me about Lenantais.
Here's to the vegan hostel!
I gave Deslandes the lowdown on Lenantais. He had nothing useful to tell me. I had a question to ask but I was waiting for the right moment. My two old friends had become upstanding citizens, well respected by their doormen. Basically, only poor old Lenantais had remained loyal to the ideas from the other world.

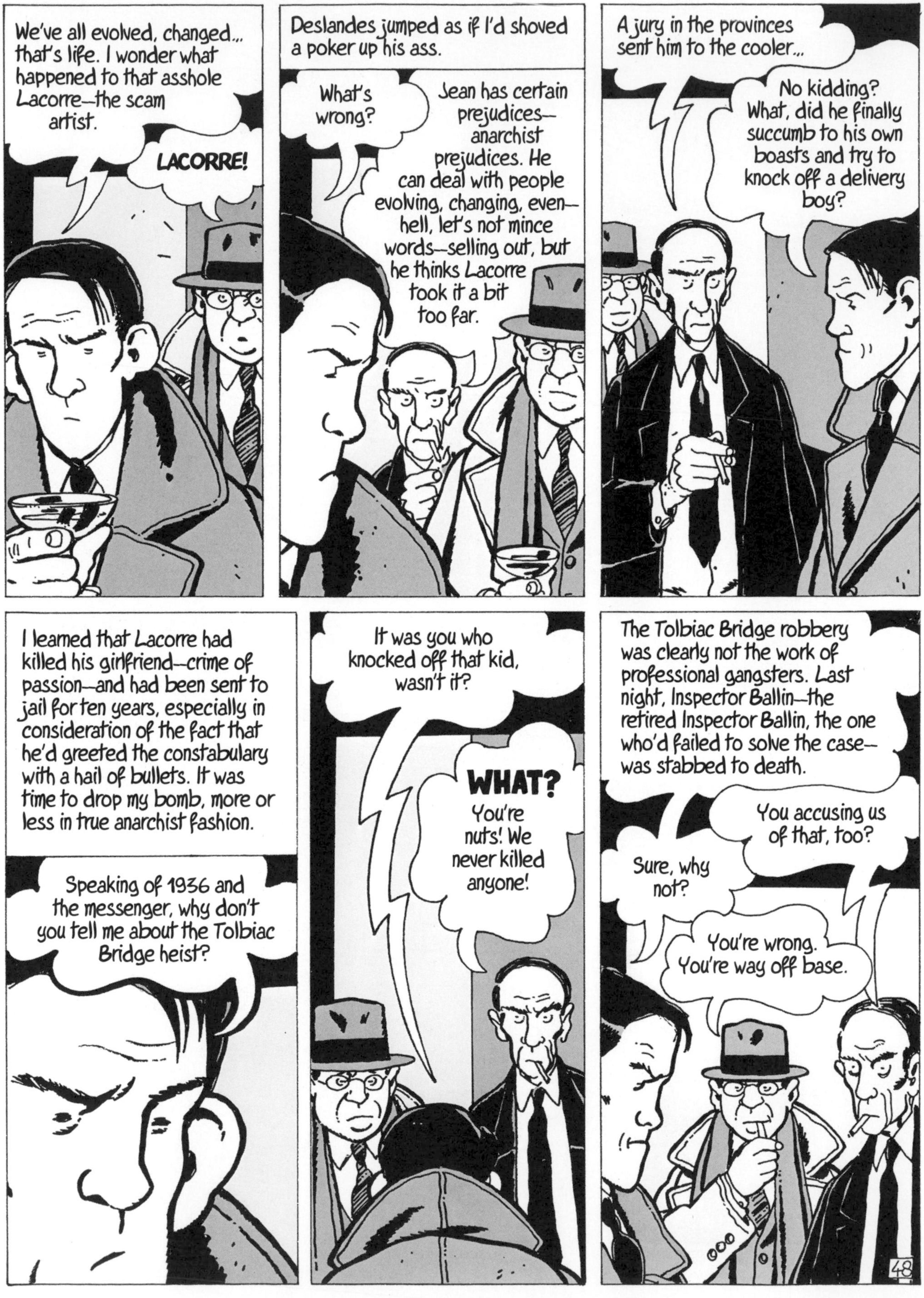
We've all evolved, changed... that's life. I wonder what happened to that asshole Lacorre—the scam artist.
LACORRE!
Deslandes jumped as if I'd shoved a poker up his ass.
What's wrong?
Jean has certain prejudices—anarchist prejudices. He can deal with people evolving, changing, even—hell, let's not mince words—selling out, but he thinks Lacorre took it a bit too far.
A jury in the provinces sent him to the cooler...
No kidding? What, did he finally succumb to his own boasts and try to knock off a delivery boy?
I learned that Lacorre had killed his girlfriend—crime of passion—and had been sent to jail for ten years, especially in consideration of the fact that he'd greeted the constabulary with a hail of bullets. It was time to drop my bomb, more or less in true anarchist fashion.
Speaking of 1936 and the messenger, why don't you tell me about the Tolbiac Bridge heist?
It was you who knocked off that kid, wasn't it?
WHAT?
You're nuts! We never killed anyone!
The Tolbiac Bridge robbery was clearly not the work of professional gangsters. Last night, Inspector Ballin—the retired Inspector Ballin, the one who'd failed to solve the case—was stabbed to death.
You accusing us of that, too?
Sure, why not?
You're wrong. You're way off base.
48

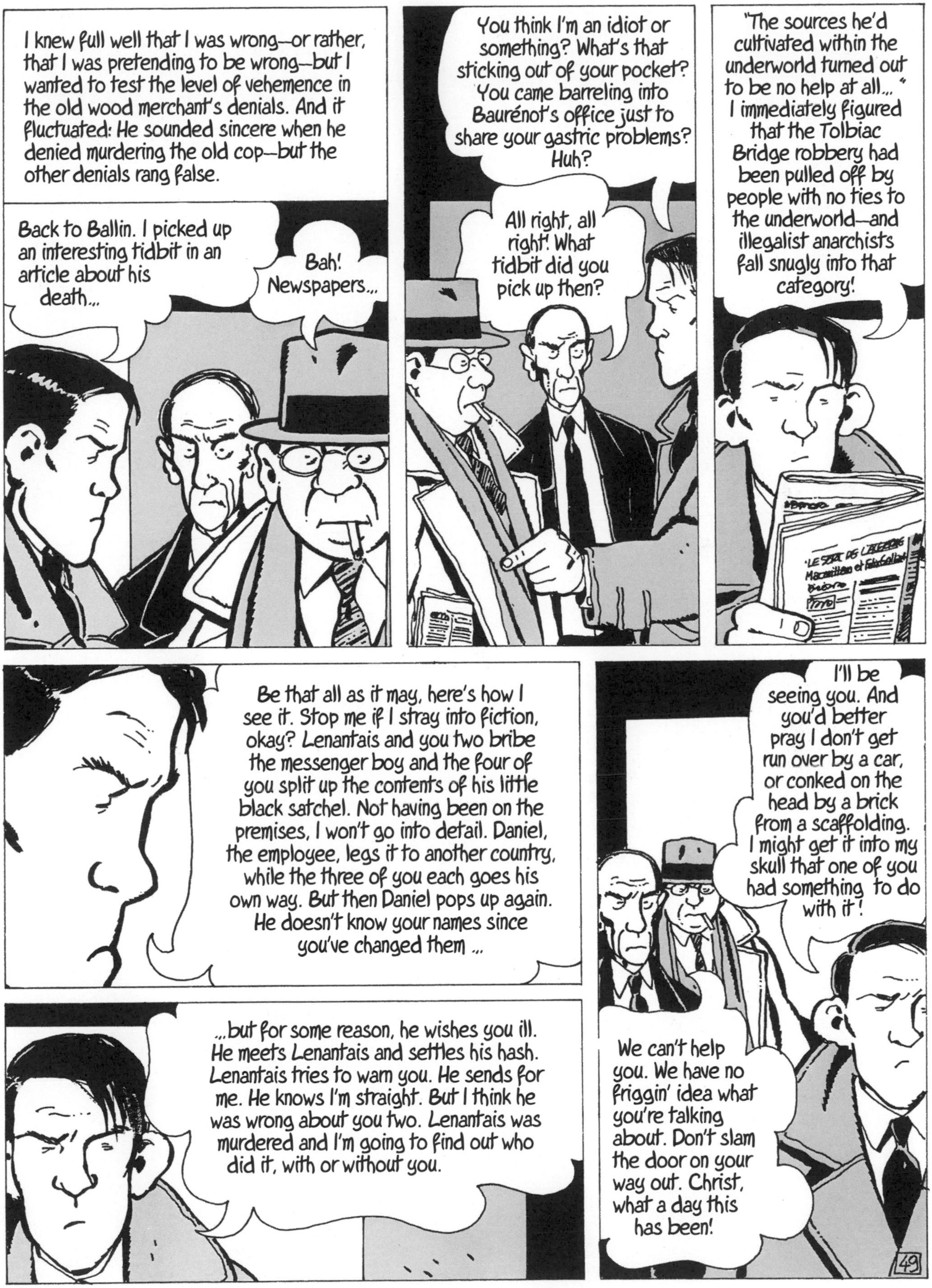

I knew full well that I was wrong--or rather, that I was pretending to be wrong--but I wanted to test the level of vehemence in the old wood merchant's denials. And it fluctuated: He sounded sincere when he denied murdering the old cop--but the other denials rang false.
Back to Ballin. I picked up an interesting tidbit in an article about his death...
Bah! Newspapers...
You think I'm an idiot or something? What's that sticking out of your pocket? You came barreling into Baurénot's office just to share your gastric problems? Huh?
All right, all right! What tidbit did you pick up then?
"The sources he'd cultivated within the underworld turned out to be no help at all..." I immediately figured that the Tolbiac Bridge robbery had been pulled off by people with no ties to the underworld--and illegalist anarchists fall snugly into that category!
Be that all as it may, here's how I see it. Stop me if I stray into fiction, okay? Lenantais and you two bribe the messenger boy and the four of you split up the contents of his little black satchel. Not having been on the premises, I won't go into detail. Daniel, the employee, legs it to another country, while the three of you each goes his own way. But then Daniel pops up again. He doesn't know your names since you've changed them ...
...but for some reason, he wishes you ill. He meets Lenantais and settles his hash. Lenantais tries to warn you. He sends for me. He knows I'm straight. But I think he was wrong about you two. Lenantais was murdered and I'm going to find out who did it, with or without you.
I'll be seeing you. And you'd better pray I don't get run over by a car, or conked on the head by a brick from a scaffolding. I might get it into my skull that one of you had something to do with it!
We can't help you. We have no friggin' idea what you're talking about. Don't slam the door on your way out. Christ, what a day this has been!

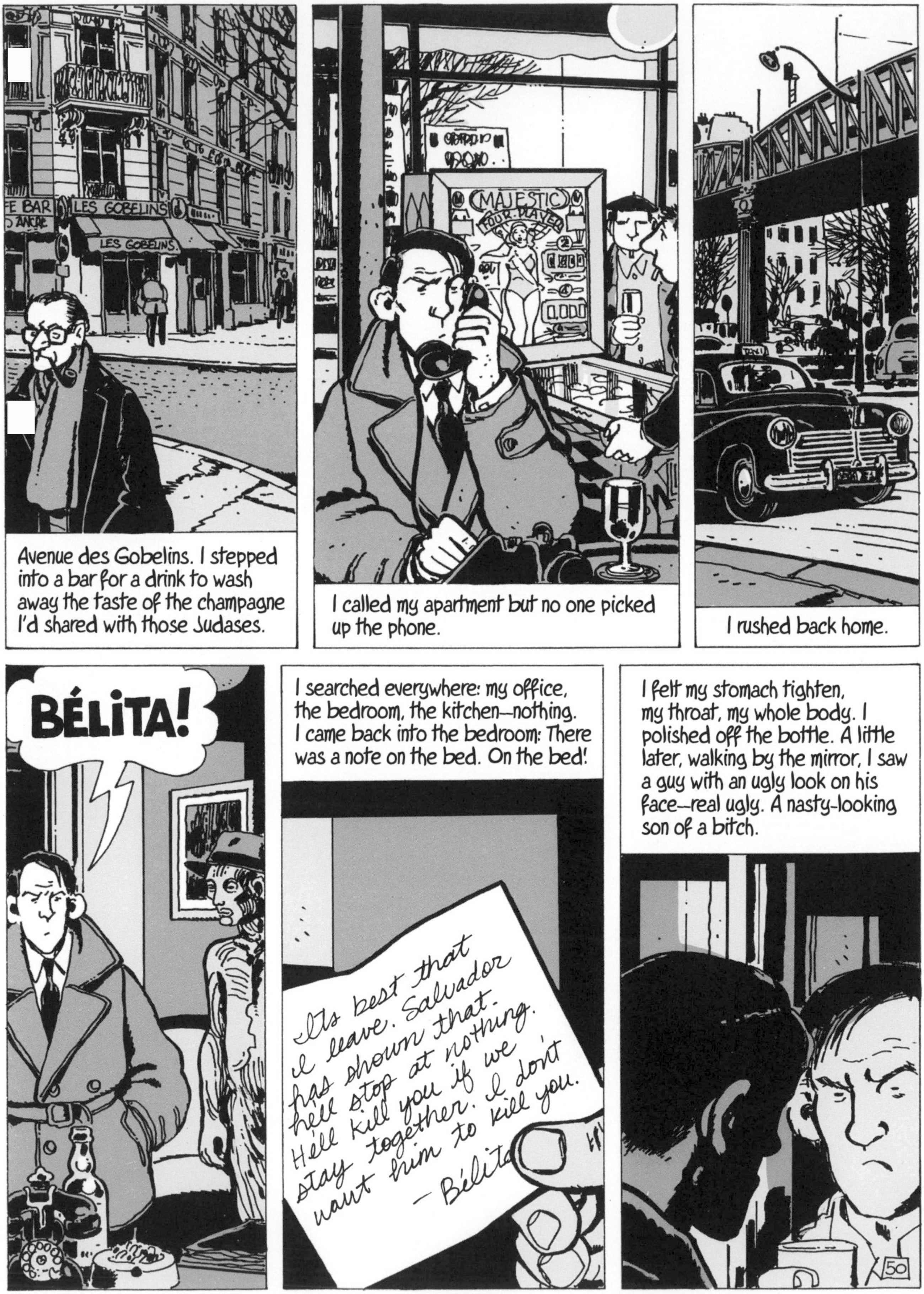
FE BAR
LES GOBELINS
LES GOBELINS
Avenue des Gobelins. I stepped into a bar for a drink to wash away the taste of the champagne I'd shared with those Judases.
MAJESTIC
FOUR-PLAYER
I called my apartment but no one picked up the phone.
I rushed back home.
BÉLITA!
I searched everywhere: my office, the bedroom, the kitchen—nothing. I came back into the bedroom: There was a note on the bed. On the bed!
It's best that I leave. Salvador has shown that he'll stop at nothing. He'll kill you if we stay together. I don't want him to kill you.
— Bélita
I felt my stomach tighten, my throat, my whole body. I polished off the bottle. A little later, walking by the mirror, I saw a guy with an ugly look on his face—real ugly. A nasty-looking son of a bitch.
50

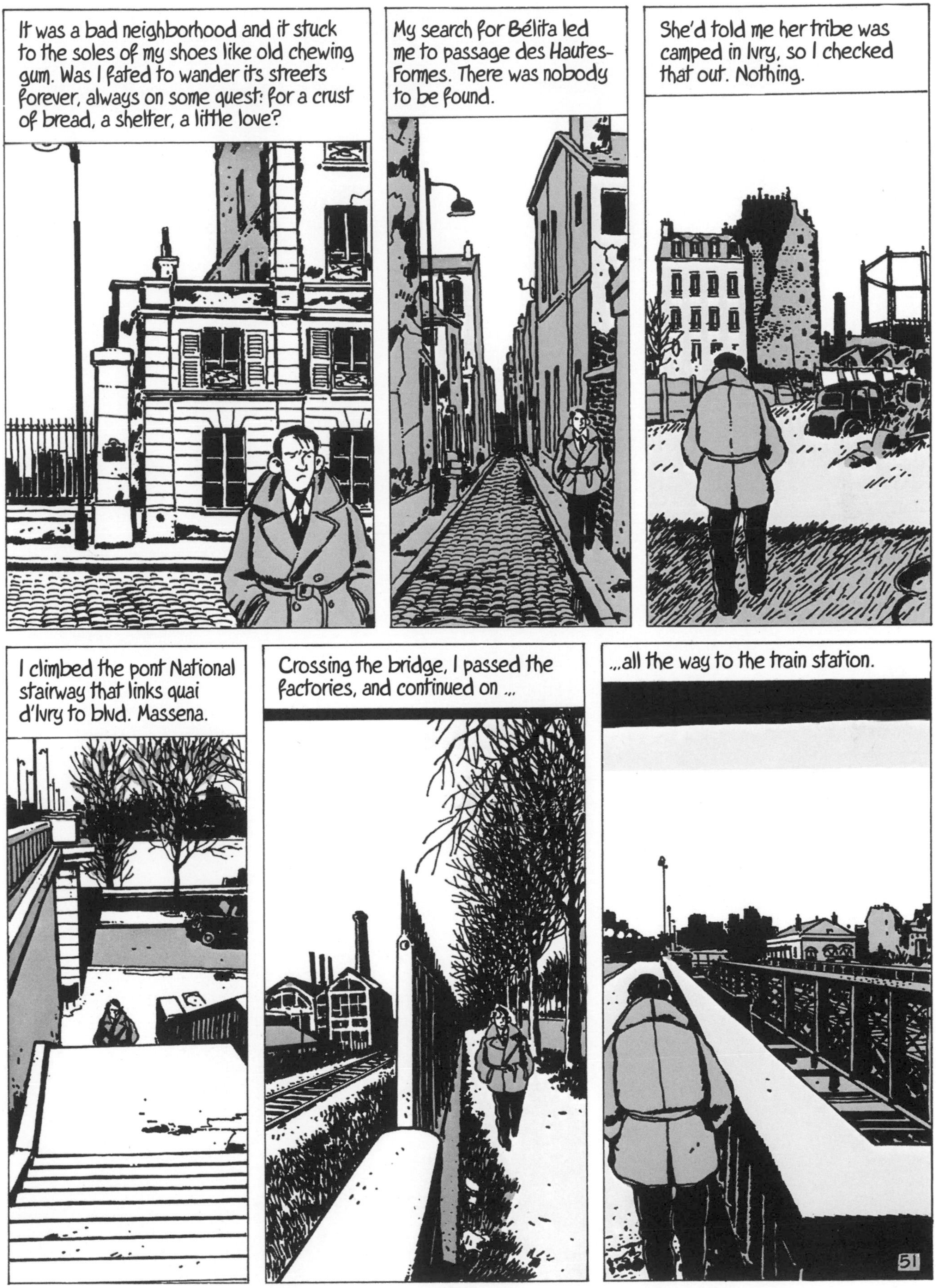
It was a bad neighborhood and it stuck to the soles of my shoes like old chewing gum. Was I fated to wander its streets forever, always on some quest: for a crust of bread, a shelter, a little love?
My search for Bélita led me to passage des Hautes-Formes. There was nobody to be found.
She'd told me her tribe was camped in Ivry, so I checked that out. Nothing.
I climbed the pont National stairway that links quai d'Ivry to blvd. Massena.
Crossing the bridge, I passed the factories, and continued on ...
...all the way to the train station.
51

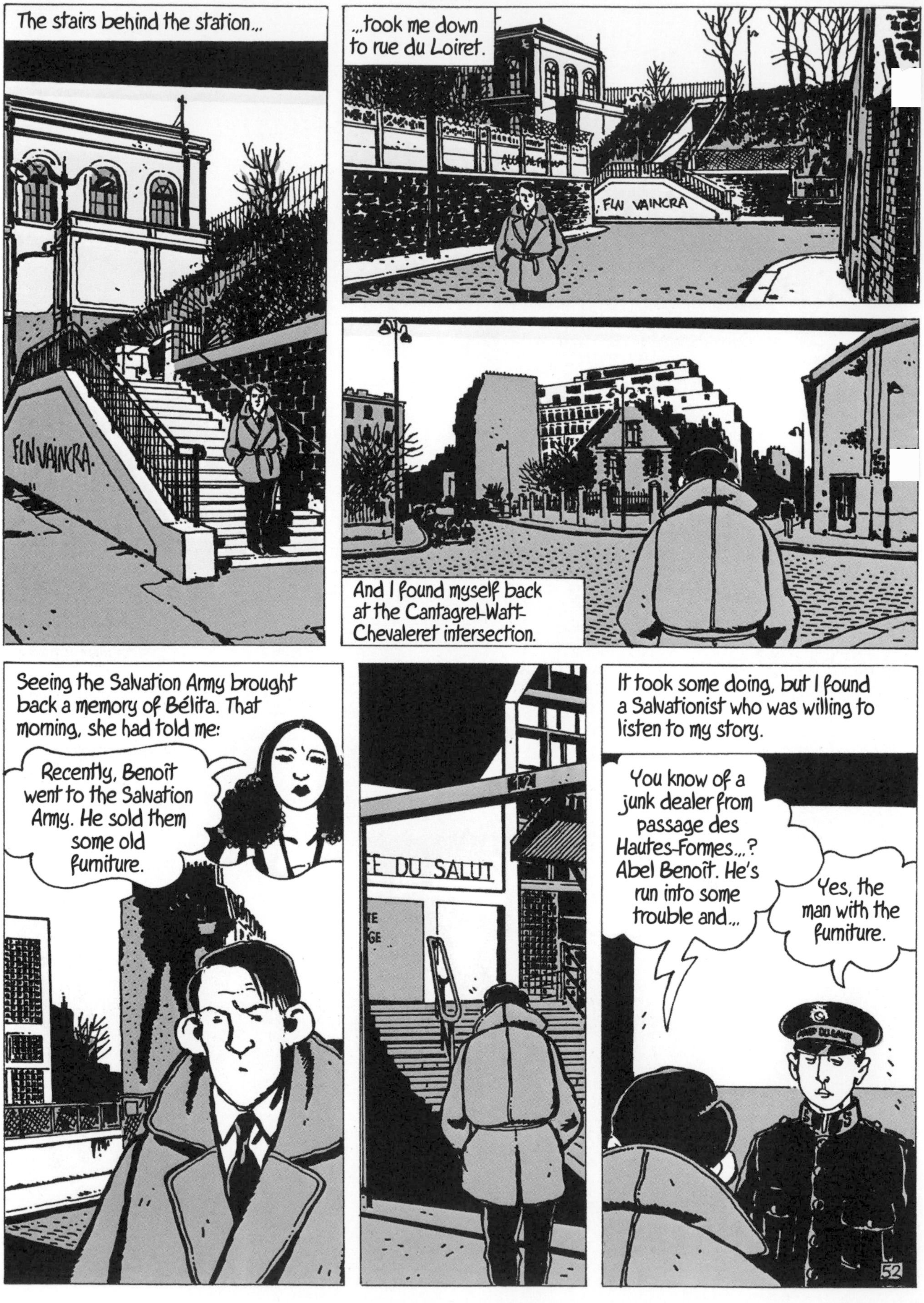
The stairs behind the station...
FLN VAINCRA.
...took me down to rue du Loiret.
FLN VAINCRA
And I found myself back at the Cantagrel-Watt-Chevaleret intersection.
Seeing the Salvation Army brought back a memory of Bélita. That morning, she had told me:
Recently, Benoît went to the Salvation Army. He sold them some old furniture.
EE DU SALUT
It took some doing, but I found a Salvationist who was willing to listen to my story.
You know of a junk dealer from passage des Hautes-Formes...? Abel Benoît. He's run into some trouble and...
Yes, the man with the furniture.

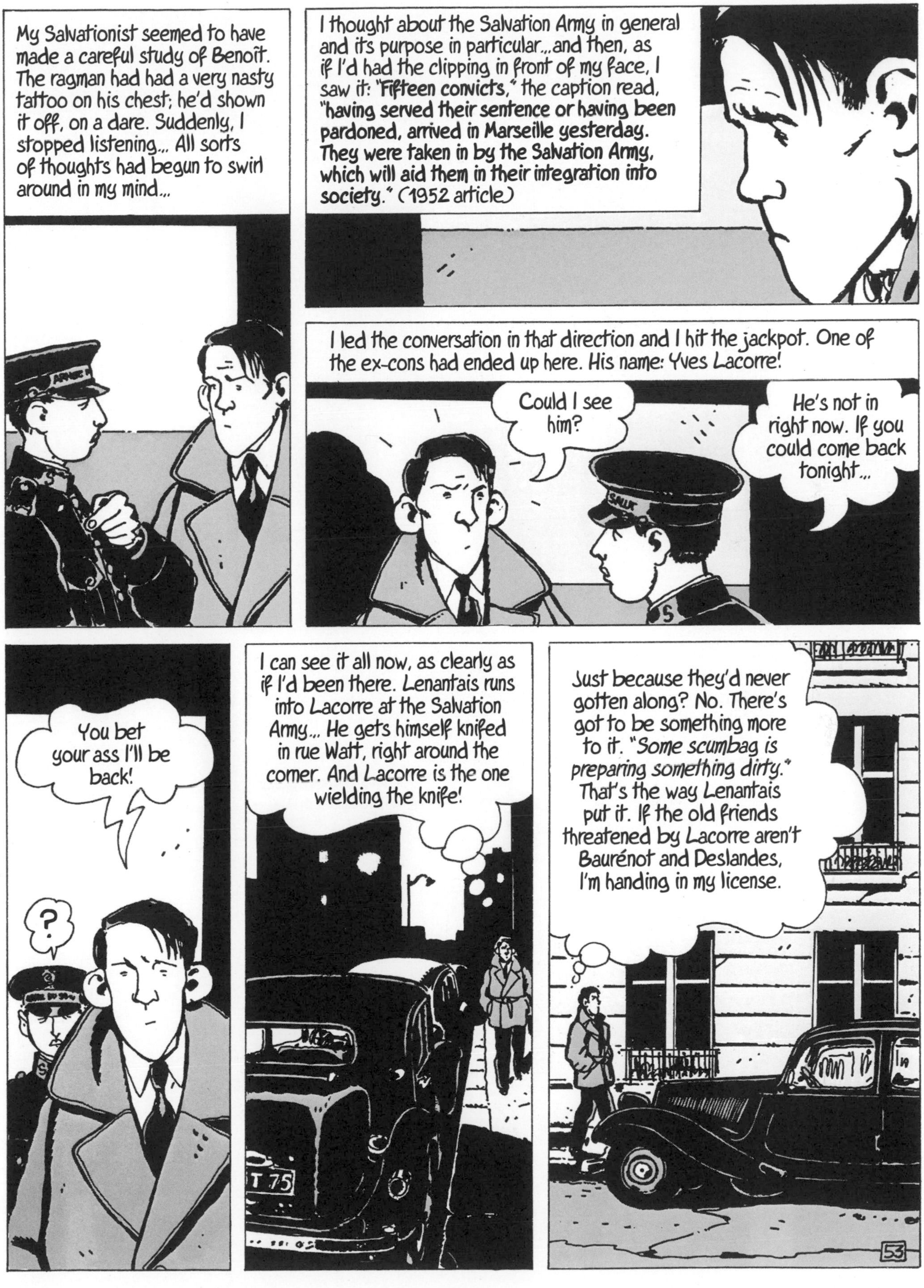
My Salvationist seemed to have made a careful study of Benoît. The ragman had had a very nasty tattoo on his chest; he'd shown it off, on a dare. Suddenly, I stopped listening... All sorts of thoughts had begun to swirl around in my mind...
I thought about the Salvation Army in general and its purpose in particular... and then, as if I'd had the clipping in front of my face, I saw it: "Fifteen convicts," the caption read, "having served their sentence or having been pardoned, arrived in Marseille yesterday. They were taken in by the Salvation Army, which will aid them in their integration into society." (1952 article)
I led the conversation in that direction and I hit the jackpot. One of the ex-cons had ended up here. His name: Yves Lacorre!
Could I see him?
He's not in right now. If you could come back tonight...
You bet your ass I'll be back!
?
I can see it all now, as clearly as if I'd been there. Lenantais runs into Lacorre at the Salvation Army... He gets himself knifed in rue Watt, right around the corner. And Lacorre is the one wielding the knife!
Just because they'd never gotten along? No. There's got to be something more to it. "Some scumbag is preparing something dirty." That's the way Lenantais put it. If the old friends threatened by Lacorre aren't Baurénot and Deslandes, I'm handing in my license.
T 75
53

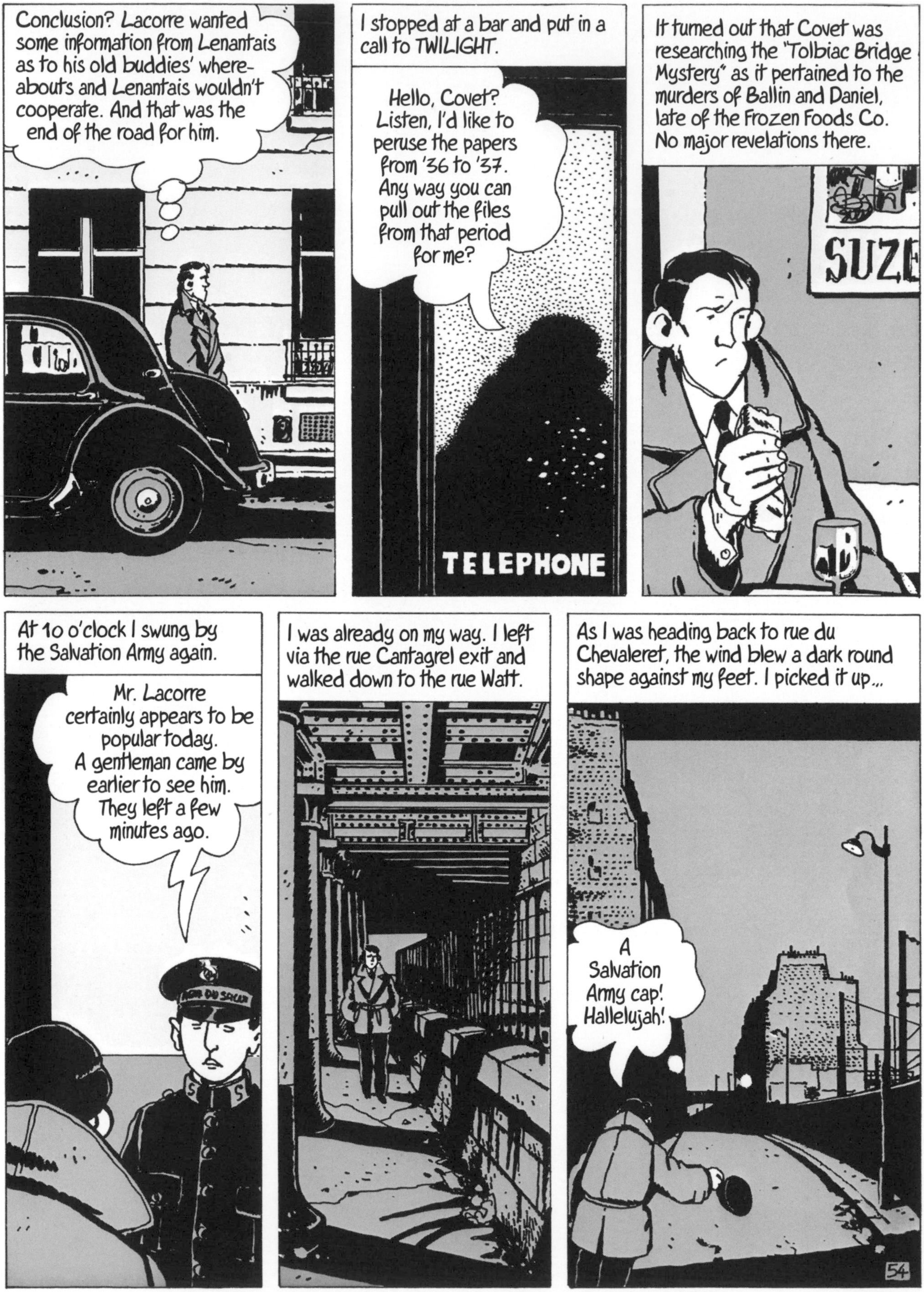

Conclusion? Lacorre wanted some information from Lenantais as to his old buddies' whereabouts and Lenantais wouldn't cooperate. And that was the end of the road for him.
I stopped at a bar and put in a call to TWILIGHT.
Hello, Covet? Listen, I'd like to peruse the papers from '36 to '37. Any way you can pull out the files from that period for me?
TELEPHONE
It turned out that Covet was researching the "Tolbiac Bridge Mystery" as it pertained to the murders of Ballin and Daniel, late of the Frozen Foods Co. No major revelations there.
SUZE
At 10 o'clock I swung by the Salvation Army again.
Mr. Lacorre certainly appears to be popular today. A gentleman came by earlier to see him. They left a few minutes ago.
I was already on my way. I left via the rue Cantagrel exit and walked down to the rue Watt.
As I was heading back to rue du Chevaleret, the wind blew a dark round shape against my feet. I picked it up...
A Salvation Army cap! Hallelujah!

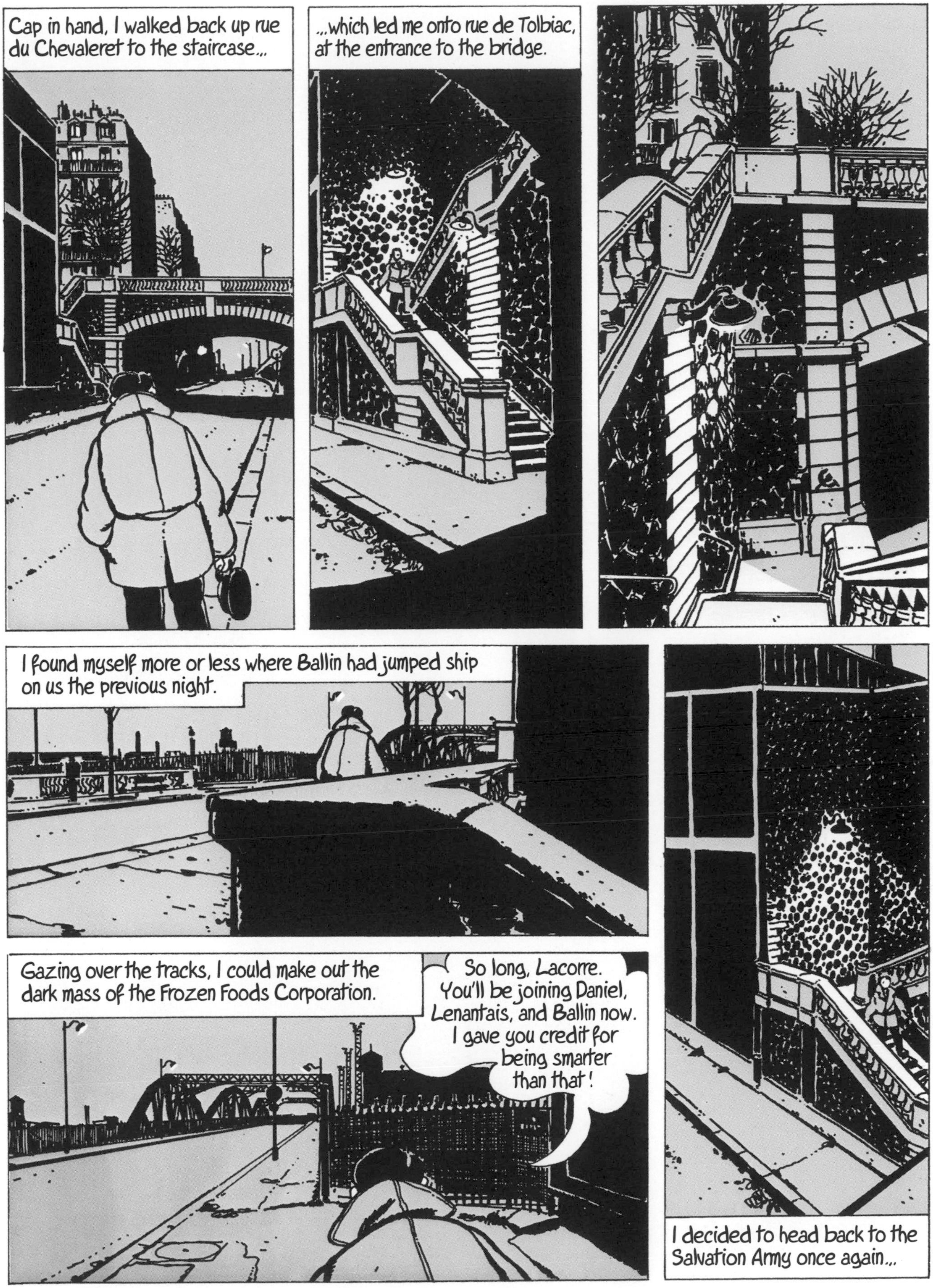
Cap in hand, I walked back up rue du Chevaleret to the staircase...
...which led me onto rue de Tolbiac, at the entrance to the bridge.
I found myself more or less where Ballin had jumped ship on us the previous night.
Gazing over the tracks, I could make out the dark mass of the Frozen Foods Corporation.
So long, Lacorre. You'll be joining Daniel, Lenantais, and Ballin now. I gave you credit for being smarter than that!
I decided to head back to the Salvation Army once again...

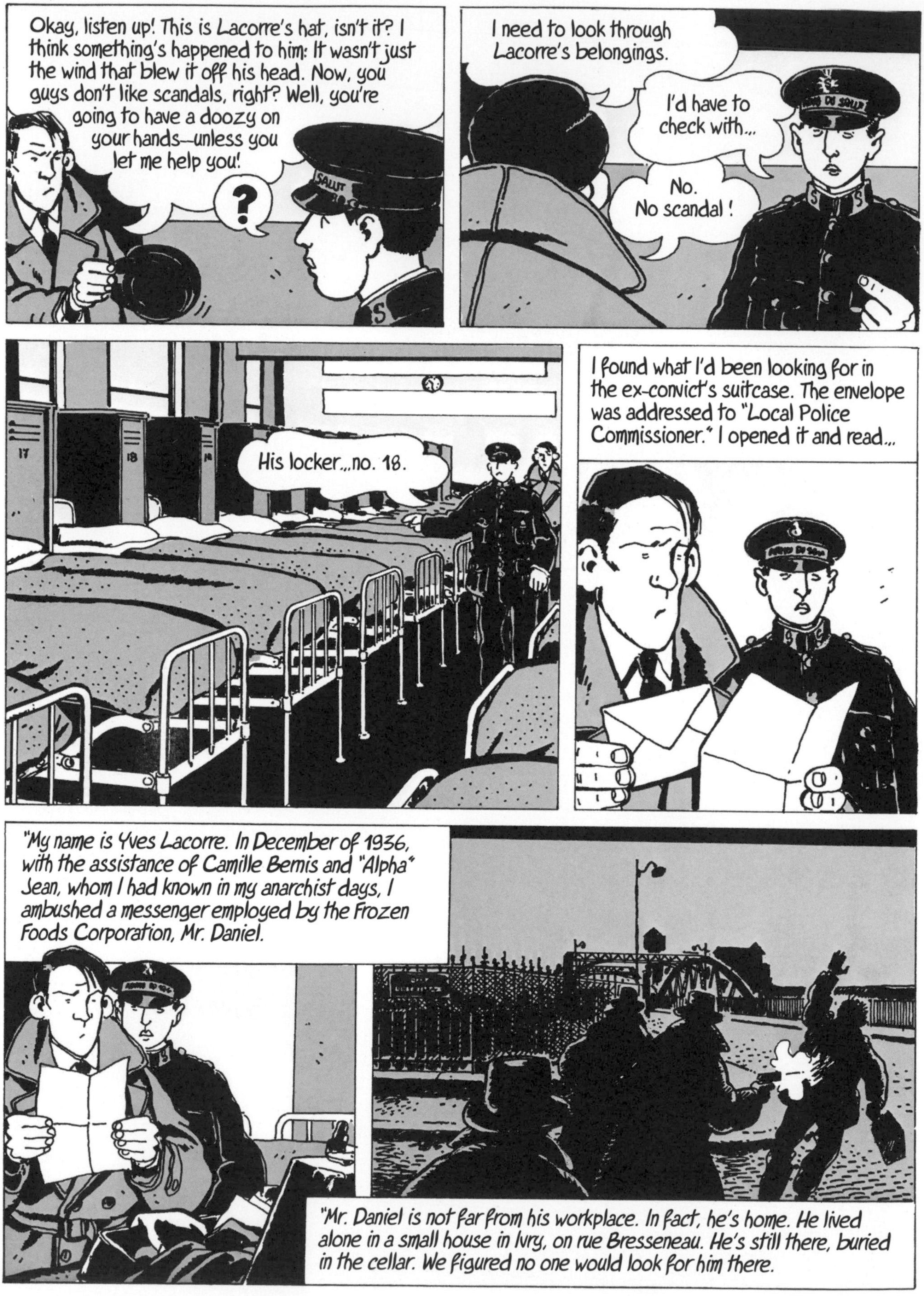
Okay, listen up! This is Lacorre's hat, isn't it? I think something's happened to him: It wasn't just the wind that blew it off his head. Now, you guys don't like scandals, right? Well, you're going to have a doozy on your hands--unless you let me help you!
?
I need to look through Lacorre's belongings.
I'd have to check with...
No. No scandal!
His locker... no. 18.
I found what I'd been looking for in the ex-convict's suitcase. The envelope was addressed to "Local Police Commissioner." I opened it and read...
"My name is Yves Lacorre. In December of 1936, with the assistance of Camille Bemis and "Alpha" Jean, whom I had known in my anarchist days, I ambushed a messenger employed by the Frozen Foods Corporation, Mr. Daniel.
"Mr. Daniel is not far from his workplace. In fact, he's home. He lived alone in a small house in Ivry, on rue Bresseneau. He's still there, buried in the cellar. We figured no one would look for him there.

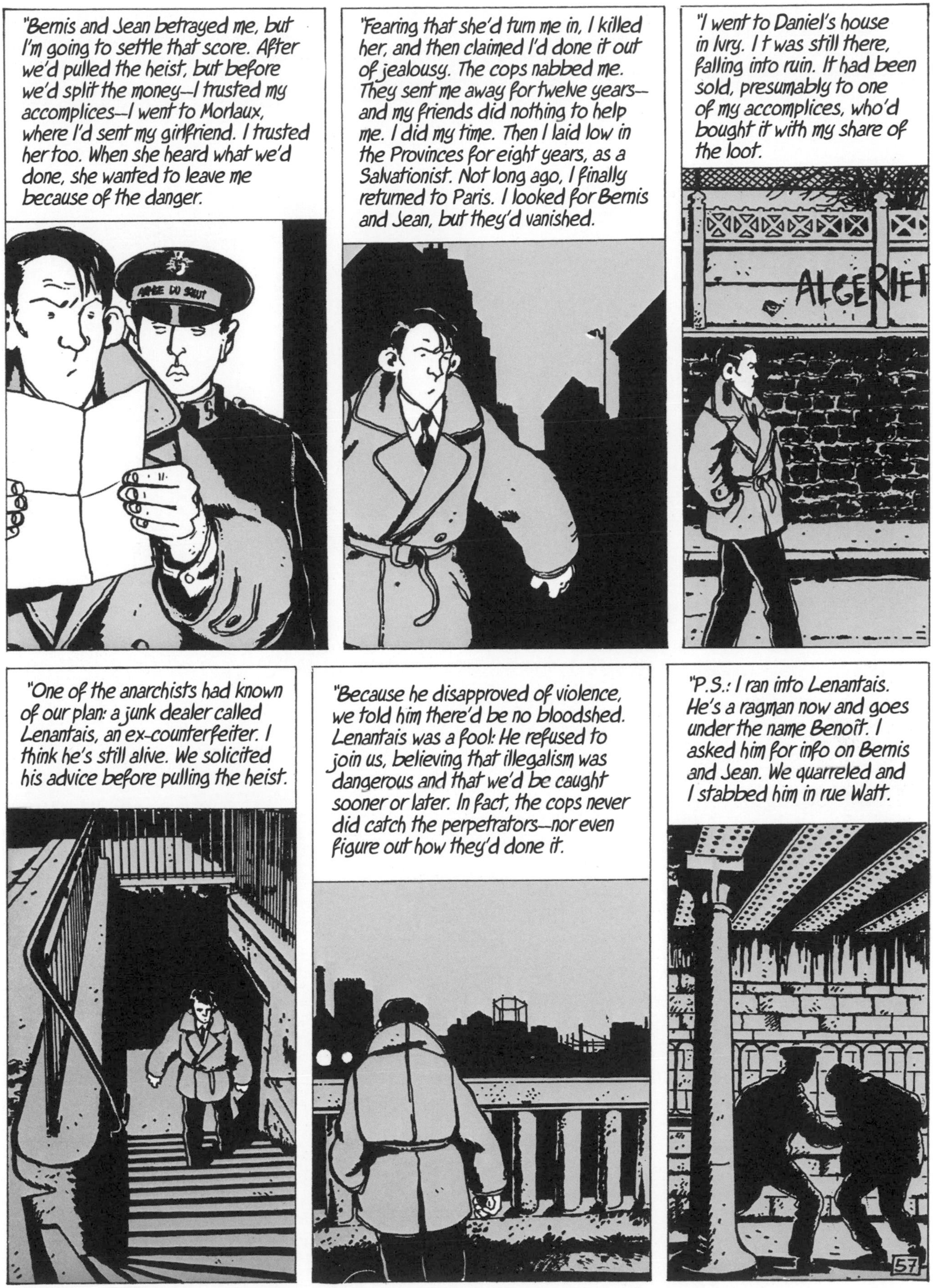
"Bernis and Jean betrayed me, but I'm going to settle that score. After we'd pulled the heist, but before we'd split the money—I trusted my accomplices—I went to Morlaux, where I'd sent my girlfriend. I trusted her too. When she heard what we'd done, she wanted to leave me because of the danger.
ARMÉE DU SALUT
"Fearing that she'd turn me in, I killed her, and then claimed I'd done it out of jealousy. The cops nabbed me. They sent me away for twelve years—and my friends did nothing to help me. I did my time. Then I laid low in the Provinces for eight years, as a Salvationist. Not long ago, I finally returned to Paris. I looked for Bernis and Jean, but they'd vanished.
"I went to Daniel's house in Ivry. It was still there, falling into ruin. It had been sold, presumably to one of my accomplices, who'd bought it with my share of the loot.
ALGERIE
"One of the anarchists had known of our plan: a junk dealer called Lenantais, an ex-counterfeiter. I think he's still alive. We solicited his advice before pulling the heist.
"Because he disapproved of violence, we told him there'd be no bloodshed. Lenantais was a fool: He refused to join us, believing that illegalism was dangerous and that we'd be caught sooner or later. In fact, the cops never did catch the perpetrators—nor even figure out how they'd done it.
"P.S.: I ran into Lenantais. He's a ragman now and goes under the name Benoît. I asked him for info on Bernis and Jean. We quarreled and I stabbed him in rue Watt.
57

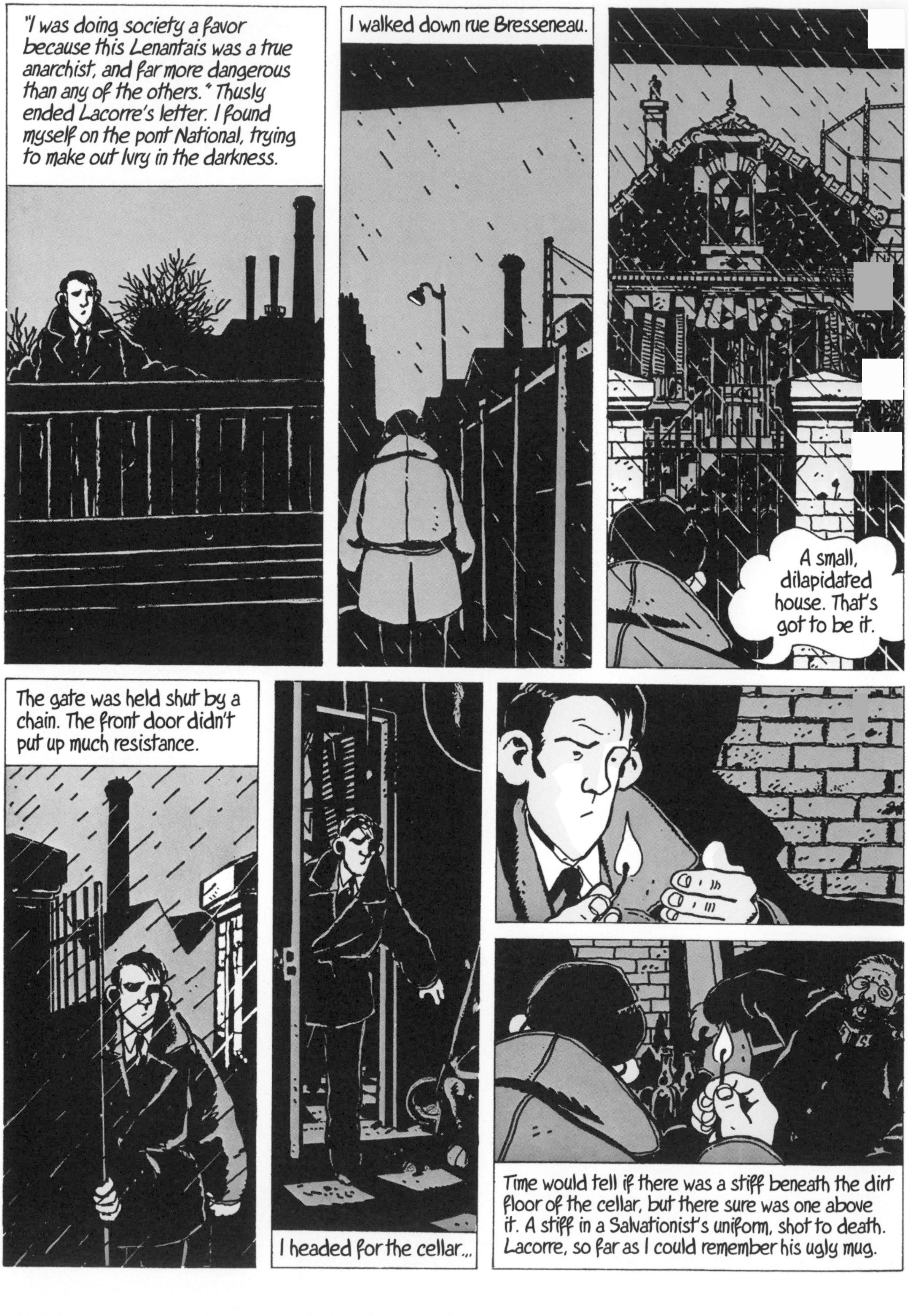
"I was doing society a favor because this Lenantais was a true anarchist, and far more dangerous than any of the others." Thusly ended Lacorre's letter. I found myself on the pont National, trying to make out Ivry in the darkness.
I walked down rue Bresseneau.
A small, dilapidated house. That's got to be it.
The gate was held shut by a chain. The front door didn't put up much resistance.
I headed for the cellar...
Time would tell if there was a stiff beneath the dirt floor of the cellar, but there sure was one above it. A stiff in a Salvationist's uniform, shot to death. Lacorre, so far as I could remember his ugly mug.

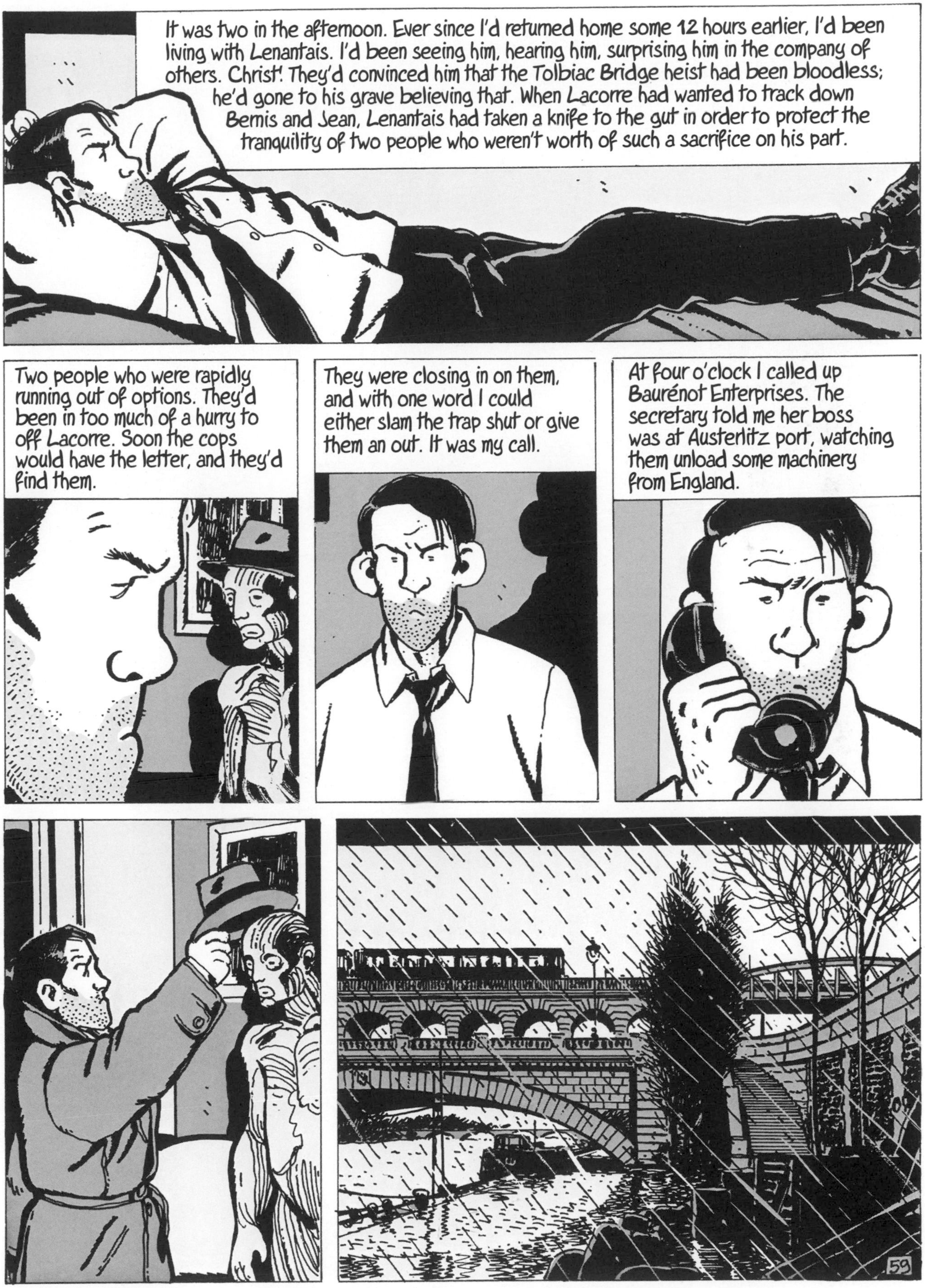
It was two in the afternoon. Ever since I'd returned home some 12 hours earlier, I'd been living with Lenantais. I'd been seeing him, hearing him, surprising him in the company of others. Christ! They'd convinced him that the Tolbiac Bridge heist had been bloodless; he'd gone to his grave believing that. When Lacorre had wanted to track down Bernis and Jean, Lenantais had taken a knife to the gut in order to protect the tranquility of two people who weren't worth of such a sacrifice on his part.
Two people who were rapidly running out of options. They'd been in too much of a hurry to off Lacorre. Soon the cops would have the letter, and they'd find them.
They were closing in on them, and with one word I could either slam the trap shut or give them an out. It was my call.
At four o'clock I called up Baurénot Enterprises. The secretary told me her boss was at Austerlitz port, watching them unload some machinery from England.
59

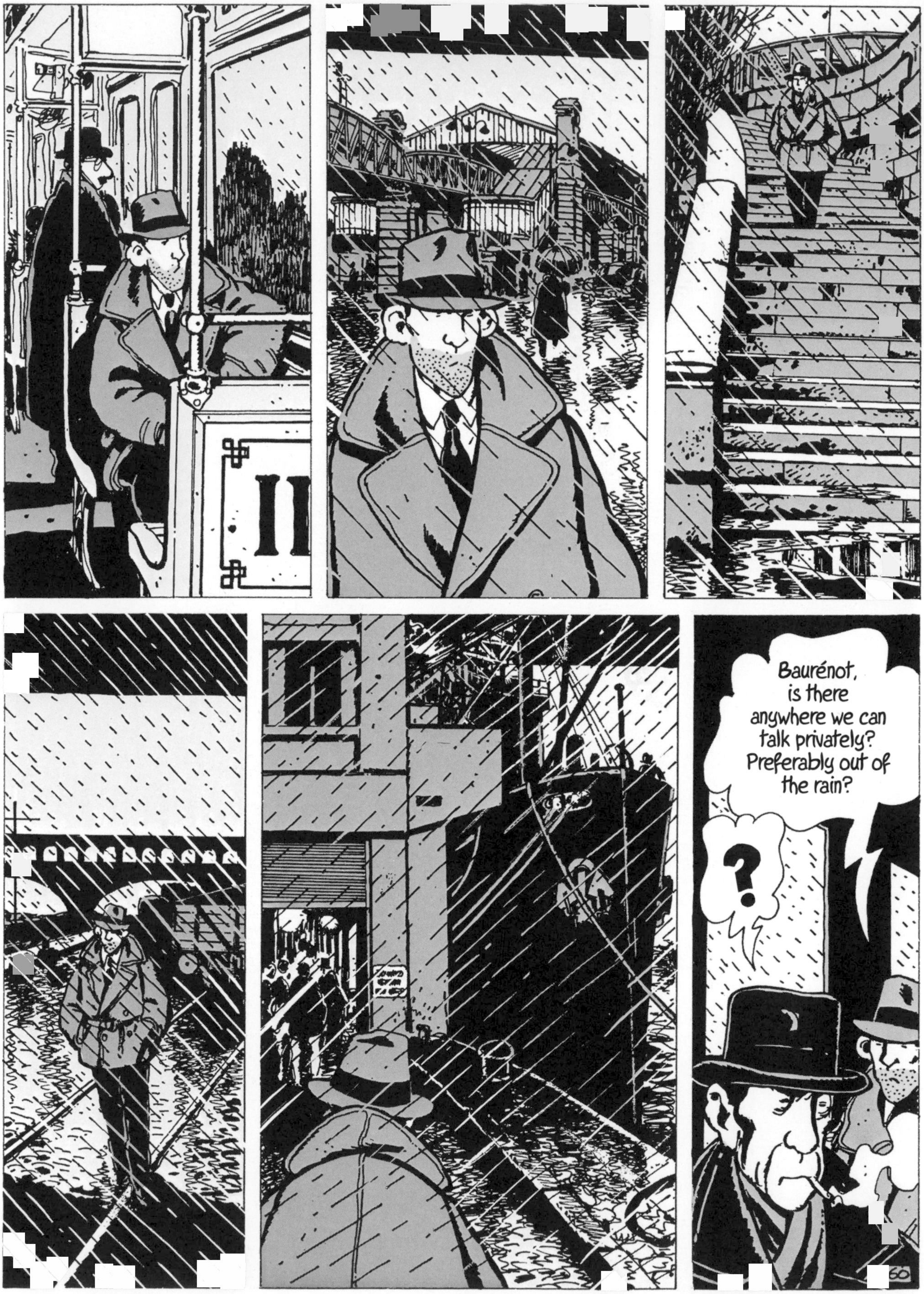

II
Bauránot, is there anywhere we can talk privately? Preferably out of the rain?
?

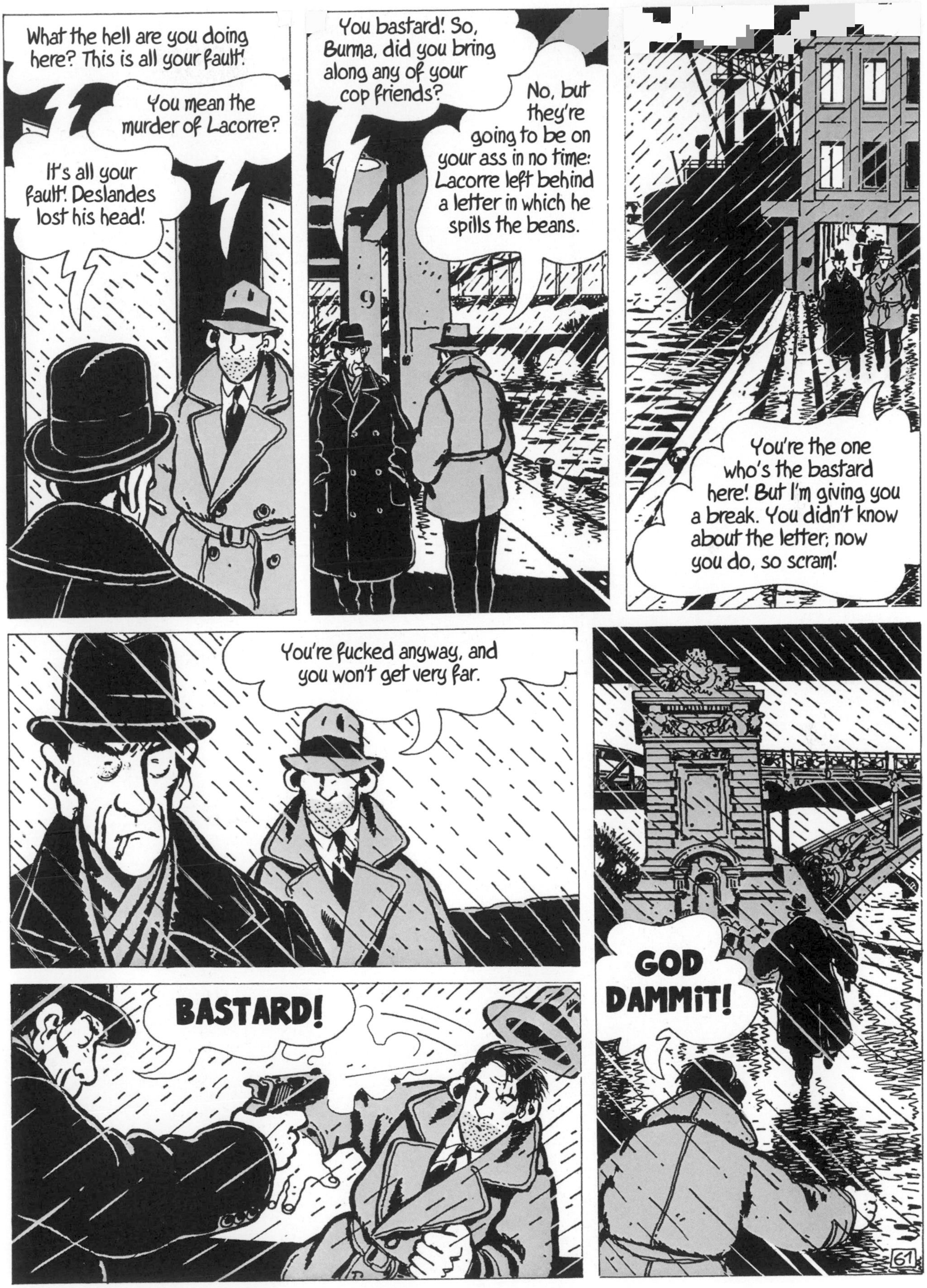

What the hell are you doing here? This is all your fault!
You mean the murder of Lacorre?
It's all your fault! Deslandes lost his head!
You bastard! So, Burma, did you bring along any of your cop friends?
No, but they're going to be on your ass in no time: Lacorre left behind a letter in which he spills the beans.
You're the one who's the bastard here! But I'm giving you a break. You didn't know about the letter; now you do, so scram!
You're fucked anyway, and you won't get very far.
BASTARD!
GOD DAMMIT!
61

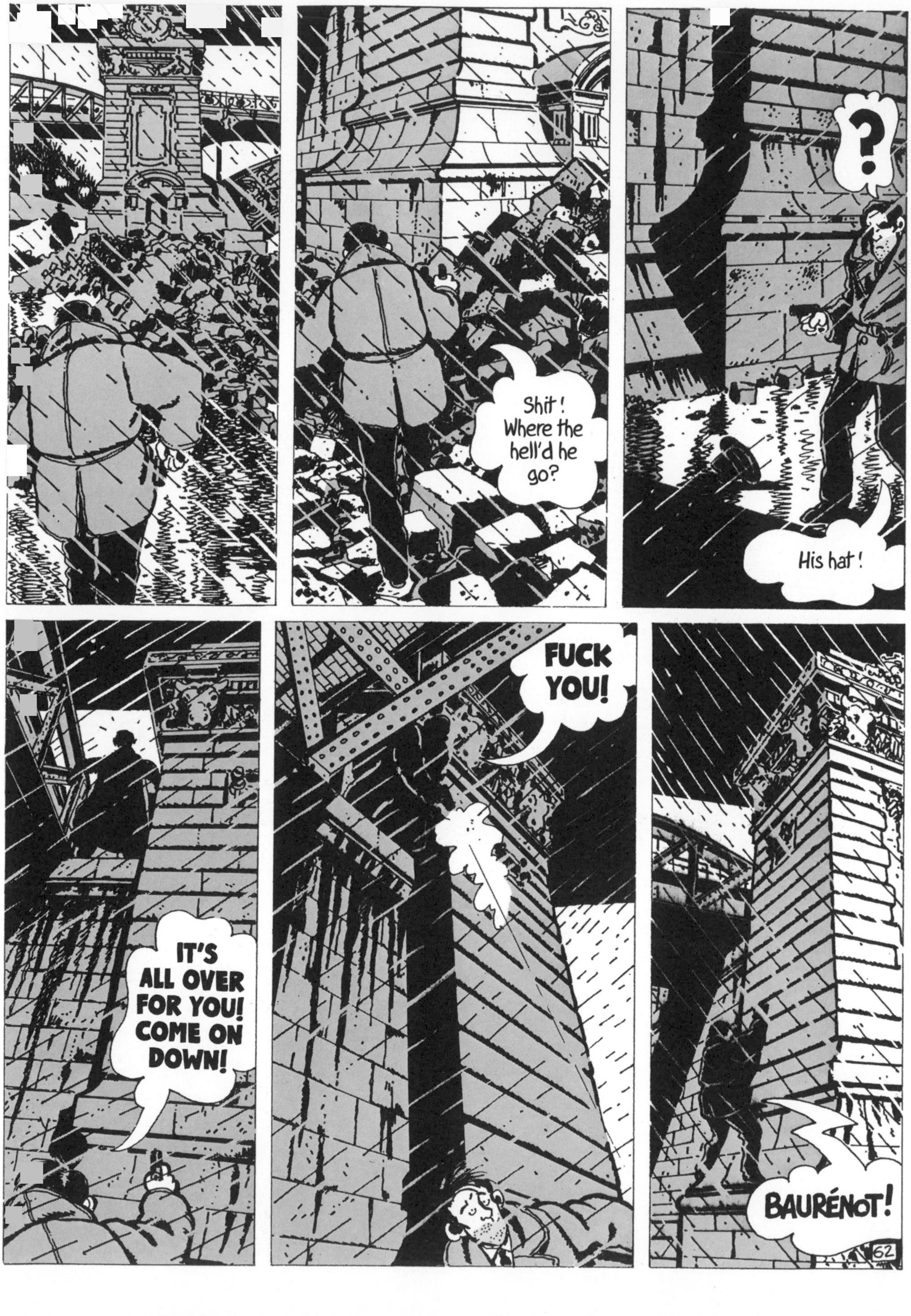
Shit! Where the hell'd he go?
?
His hat!
IT'S ALL OVER FOR YOU! COME ON DOWN!
FUCK YOU!
BAURÉNOT!
62

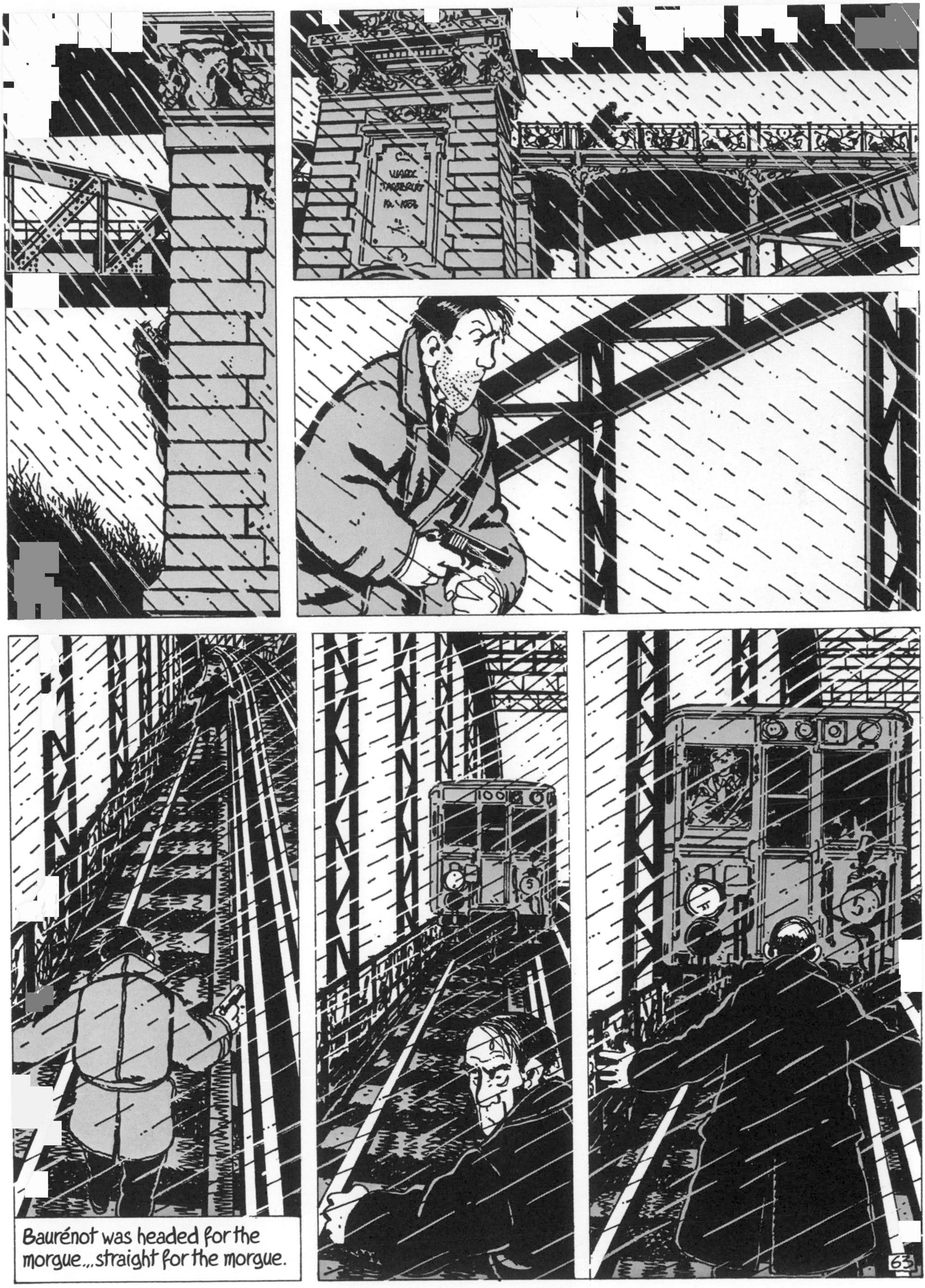
Baurénot was headed for the morgue... straight for the morgue.

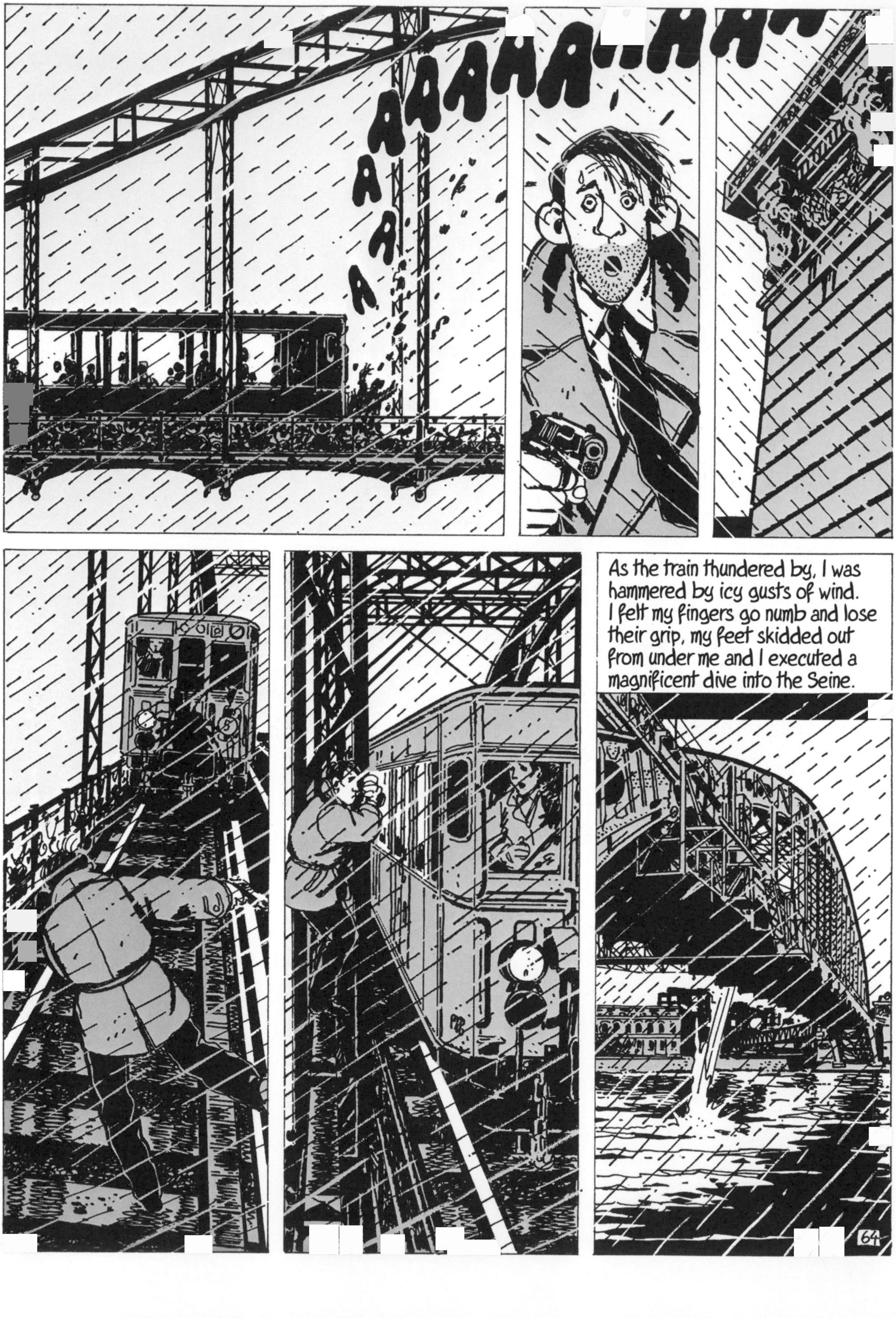
AAAAAAAAA!!AAA
As the train thundered by, I was hammered by icy gusts of wind. I felt my fingers go numb and lose their grip, my feet skidded out from under me and I executed a magnificent dive into the Seine.
64

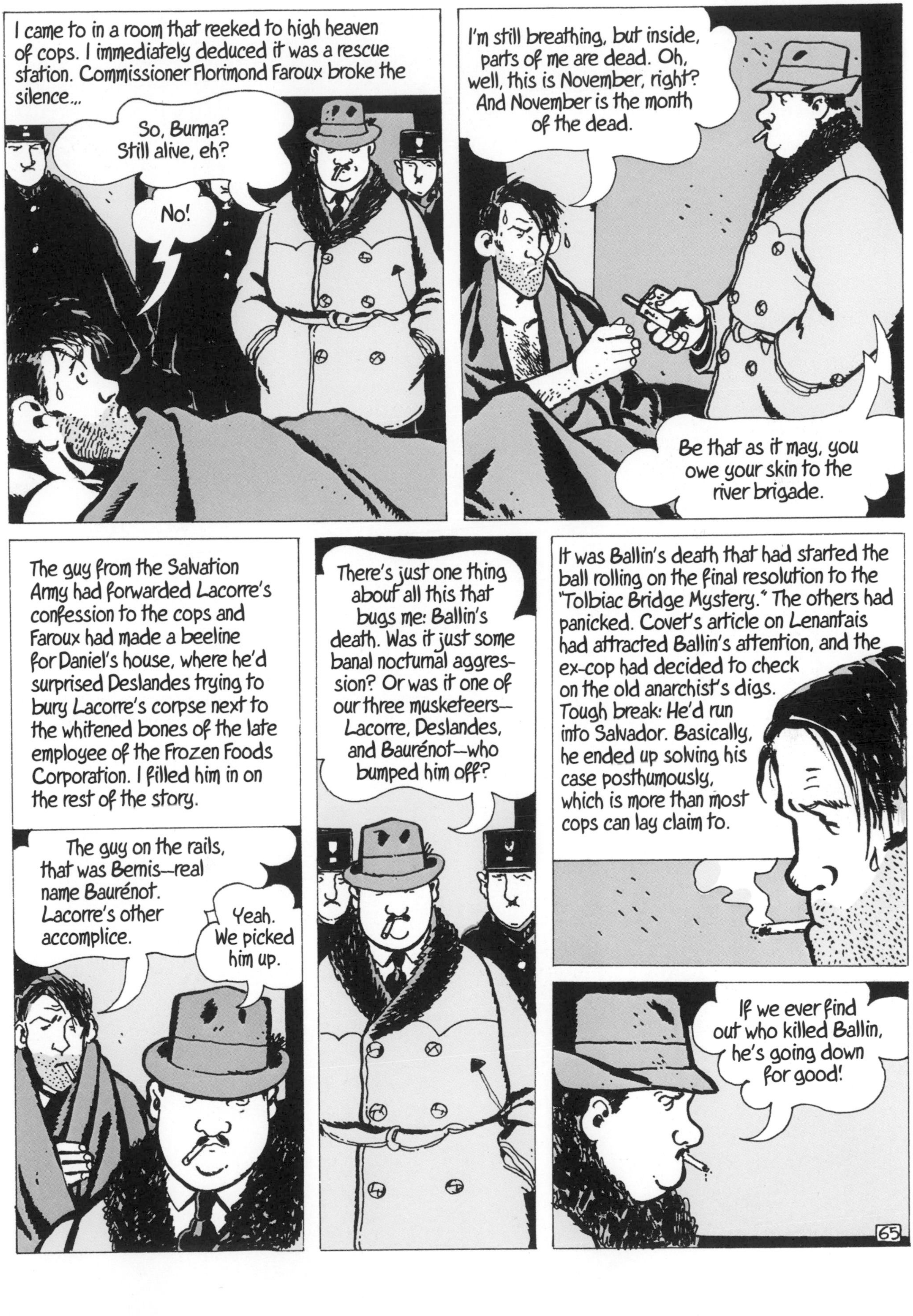
I came to in a room that reeked to high heaven of cops. I immediately deduced it was a rescue station. Commissioner Florimond Faroux broke the silence...
So, Burma? Still alive, eh?
No!
I'm still breathing, but inside, parts of me are dead. Oh, well, this is November, right? And November is the month of the dead.
Be that as it may, you owe your skin to the river brigade.
The guy from the Salvation Army had forwarded Lacorre's confession to the cops and Faroux had made a beeline for Daniel's house, where he'd surprised Deslandes trying to bury Lacorre's corpse next to the whitened bones of the late employee of the Frozen Foods Corporation. I filled him in on the rest of the story.
The guy on the rails, that was Bernis--real name Baurénot. Lacorre's other accomplice.
Yeah. We picked him up.
There's just one thing about all this that bugs me: Ballin's death. Was it just some banal nocturnal aggression? Or was it one of our three musketeers-- Lacorre, Deslandes, and Baurénot--who bumped him off?
It was Ballin's death that had started the ball rolling on the final resolution to the "Tolbiac Bridge Mystery." The others had panicked. Covet's article on Lenantais had attracted Ballin's attention, and the ex-cop had decided to check on the old anarchist's digs. Tough break: He'd run into Salvador. Basically, he ended up solving his case posthumously, which is more than most cops can lay claim to.
If we ever find out who killed Ballin, he's going down for good!

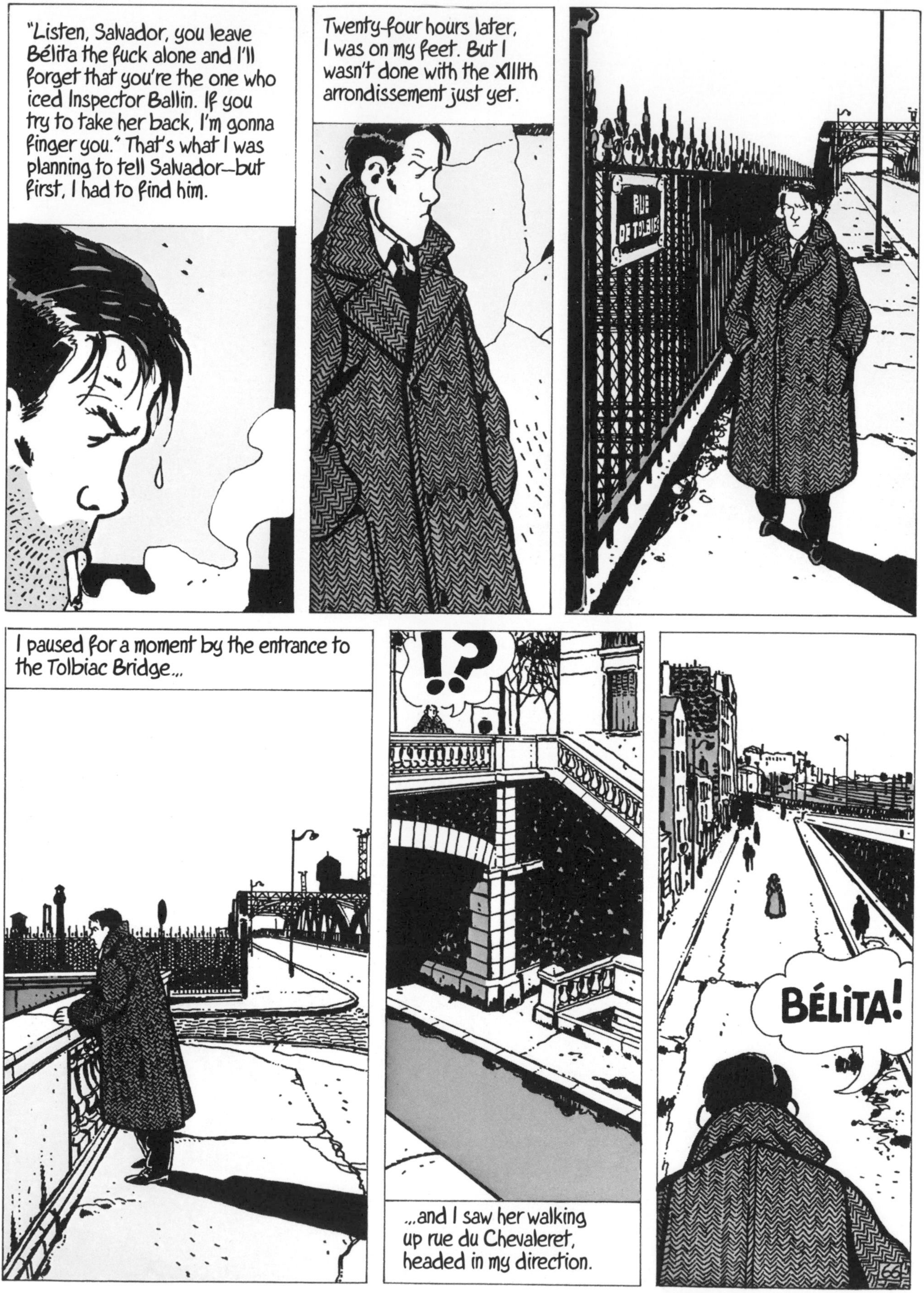
"Listen, Salvador, you leave Bélita the fuck alone and I'll forget that you're the one who iced Inspector Ballin. If you try to take her back, I'm gonna finger you." That's what I was planning to tell Salvador—but first, I had to find him.
Twenty-four hours later, I was on my feet. But I wasn't done with the XIIIth arrondissement just yet.
I paused for a moment by the entrance to the Tolbiac Bridge...
!?
...and I saw her walking up rue du Chevaleret, headed in my direction.
BÉLITA!
66

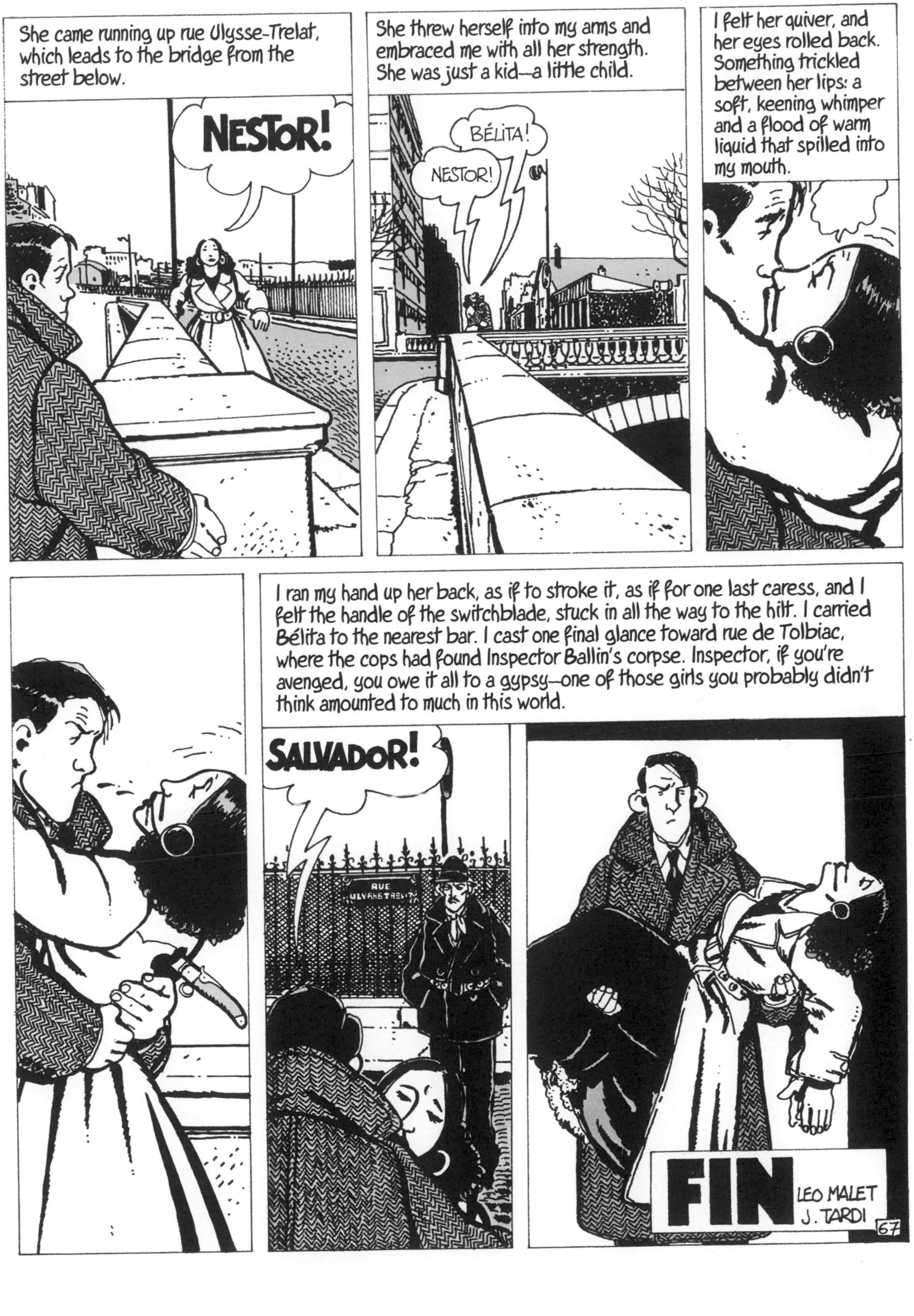

She came running up rue Ulysse-Trelat, which leads to the bridge from the street below.
NESTOR!
She threw herself into my arms and embraced me with all her strength. She was just a kid—a little child.
BÉLITA!
NESTOR!
I felt her quiver, and her eyes rolled back. Something trickled between her lips: a soft, keening whimper and a flood of warm liquid that spilled into my mouth.
I ran my hand up her back, as if to stroke it, as if for one last caress, and I felt the handle of the switchblade, stuck in all the way to the hilt. I carried Bélita to the nearest bar. I cast one final glance toward rue de Tolbiac, where the cops had found Inspector Ballin's corpse. Inspector, if you're avenged, you owe it all to a gypsy—one of those girls you probably didn't think amounted to much in this world.
SALVADOR!
FIN
LEO MALET
J. TARDI

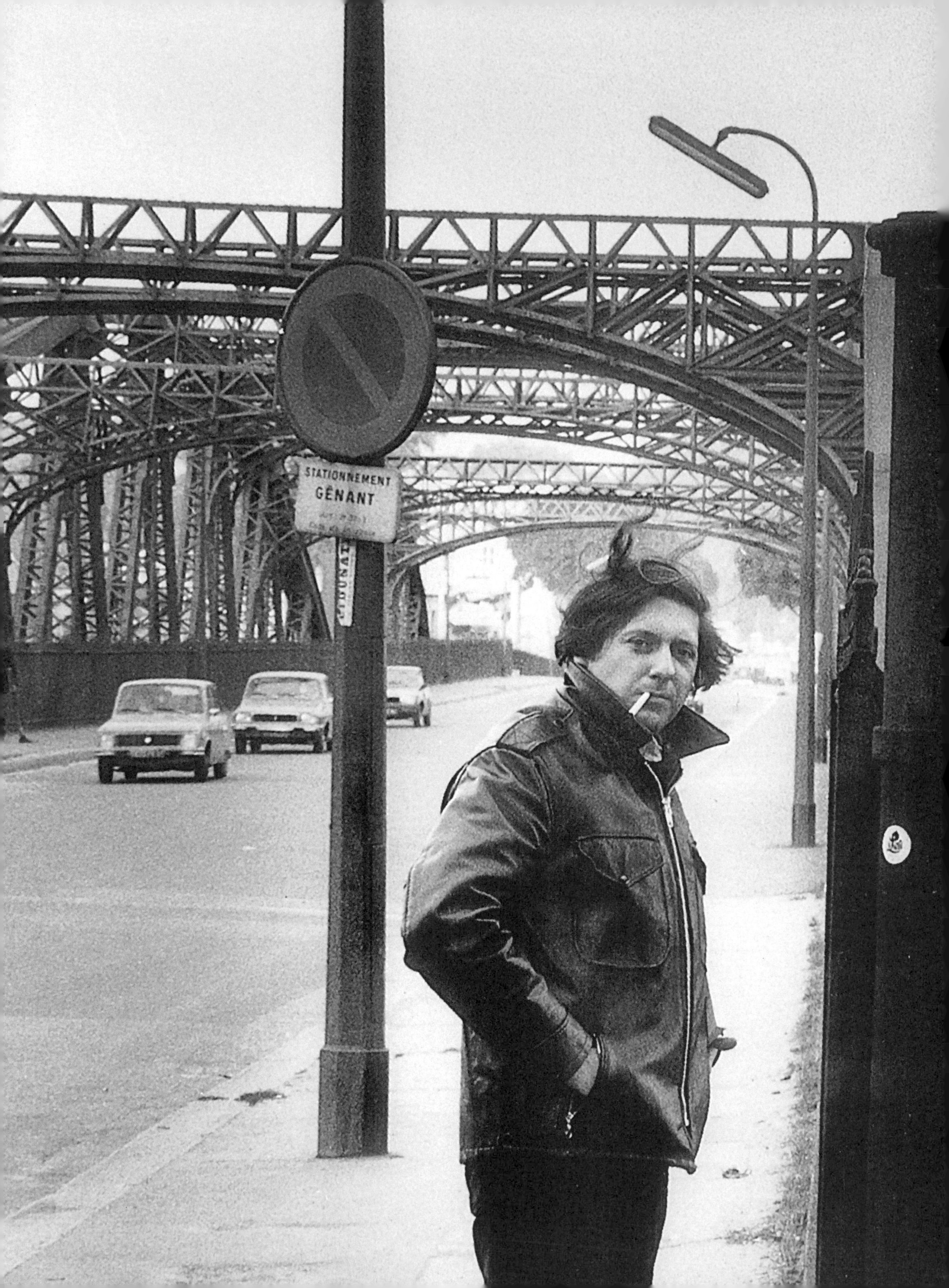
STATIONNEMENT
GÊNANT

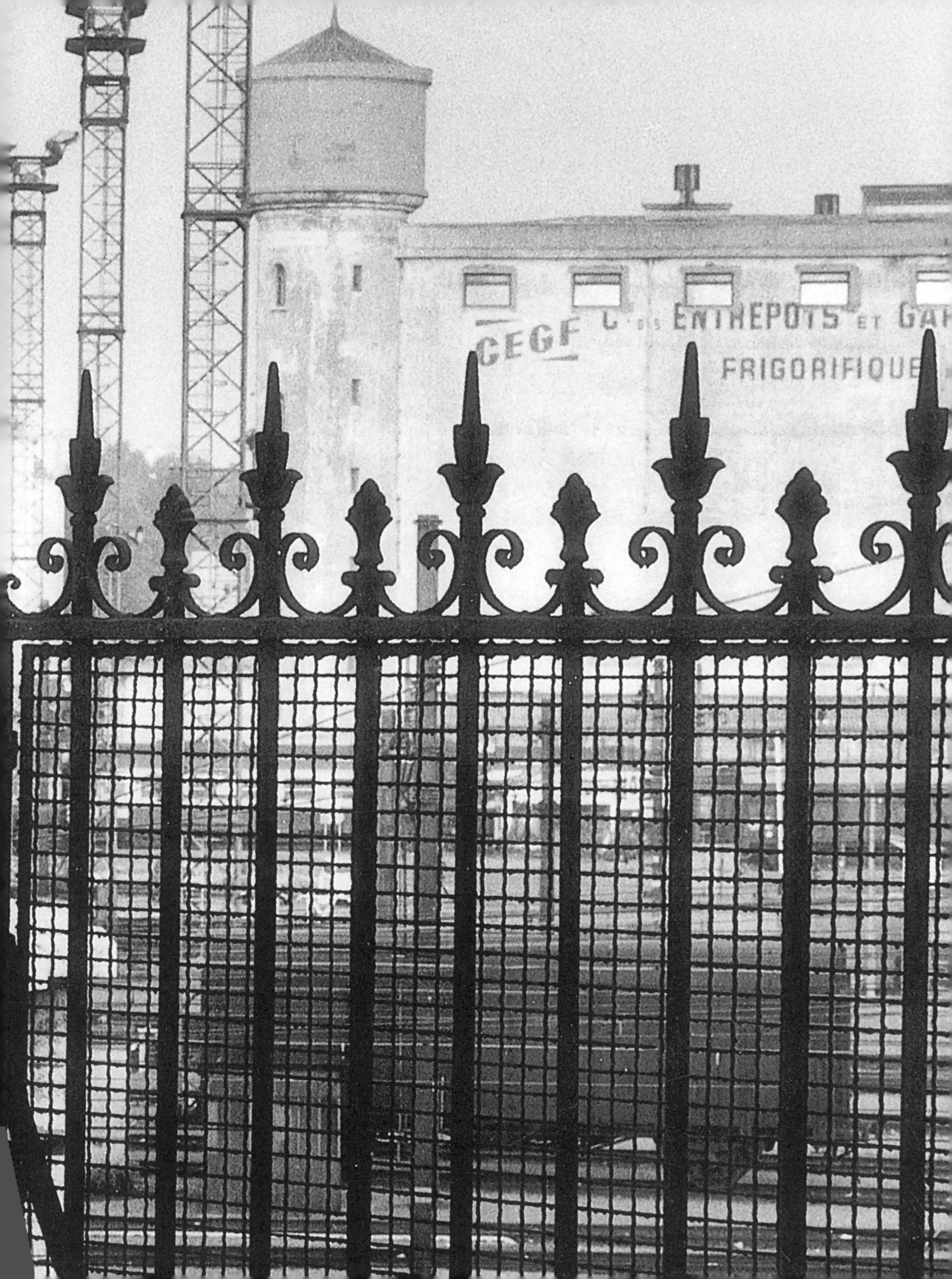
CEGF
ENTREPOTS ET GA
FRIGORIFIQUE

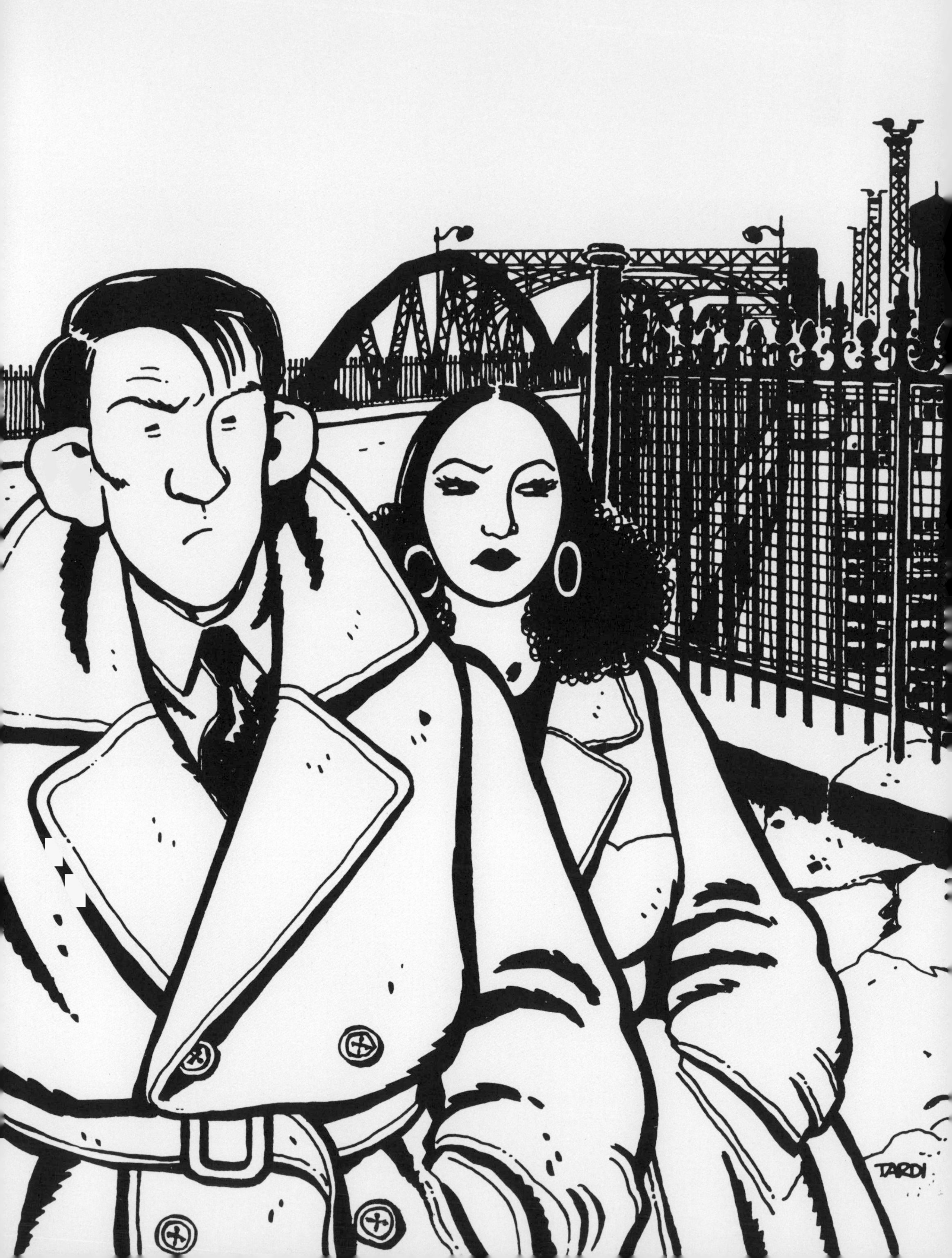
TARDI

LIGHT REMARKS WITH HISTORIC PRETENTIONS ON A RESILIENT CORPSE AND A MORE-OR-LESS LIFTED FOG

DEAD WOMEN ARE HARD TO KILL. Namely, the one I will speak of here: Bélita Morales. "The Morales girl," as the police report says.

It was one day in 1956, in the cold and dreary early morning hours of an executioner's dawn, when I cut down the young gypsy with the knife of her brother-gypsy. Afterward, feeling satisfied, the moment of emotion past, I was reeling slightly and yawning so widely as to unhinge my jaw—I had been typing on my Underwood for more than thirty hours. I scrawled "The End" with a soft-lead pencil after the last line, and went down to Felix's, a former taxi driver who ran a bistro beneath my apartment. I sipped coffee while smoking yet another pipe that tasted of ash.

Then, at a suitable hour, I took the sixty or seventy last pages of the manuscript to my publisher at Robert Laffont, and went home to sleep. I forgot Bélita Morales completely—in favor of, a few weeks later, Jeanne Marigny, who was more or less the central female protagonist in my next story.

Out of the fifteen novels I published in the incomplete New Mysteries of Paris series, *Fog on the Tolbiac Bridge* was written without a plan—only a vague idea like all the others. But with *Fog*, there was no possibility to return to earlier chapters and make things consistent; for example, correcting continuity between an earlier chapter and a later chapter because something had happened during the action of the story that necessitated these modifications, adjustments. That was how I usually worked.

But with *Fog*, it was another story. I was always late in delivering my work (those who asked me to write this know something about this), and the publisher was losing patience. I had been obliged to give him the first hundred pages, which had gone directly to the printer. I was cornered.

I had to hold to what I had already written and I was allowed no deviation. "Art is born from constraints," said someone with whom I do not agree.

But, on this rare occasion, I had to make this maxim my own, and it turned out to be beneficial for *Fog*. If I tell you all this a bit tangentially, it's not to fill space on a page, as you may believe; but because *Fog*, which was not written like my other novels, revealed itself also to be different than the others in another way.

It enjoyed much more success with the public; personally, I held it among my favorites for imprecise reasons. For, I believed I wrote a novel *attacking* the XIIIth arrondissement (I had an old score to settle with the neighborhood), but in the end the novel defended it.

I received several letters on this topic, notably from my old "comrade" Georges Vidal, who wrote: "it is a fog alive with countless tiny lights rising in the distance."

Georges Vidal was at twenty the manager of the anarchist newspaper *Le Libertaire*. On a foggy day at his offices in November 1923, he received a visit from an adolescent who would become the unhappy hero of the most mysterious and foggiest case of the century: the Philippe Daudet Affair.

Fog was subject to multiple new editions, and that is how the successive resurrections of Bélita Morales began.

There were serials in the weekly papers: the one from Club du Livre Policier, the one from François

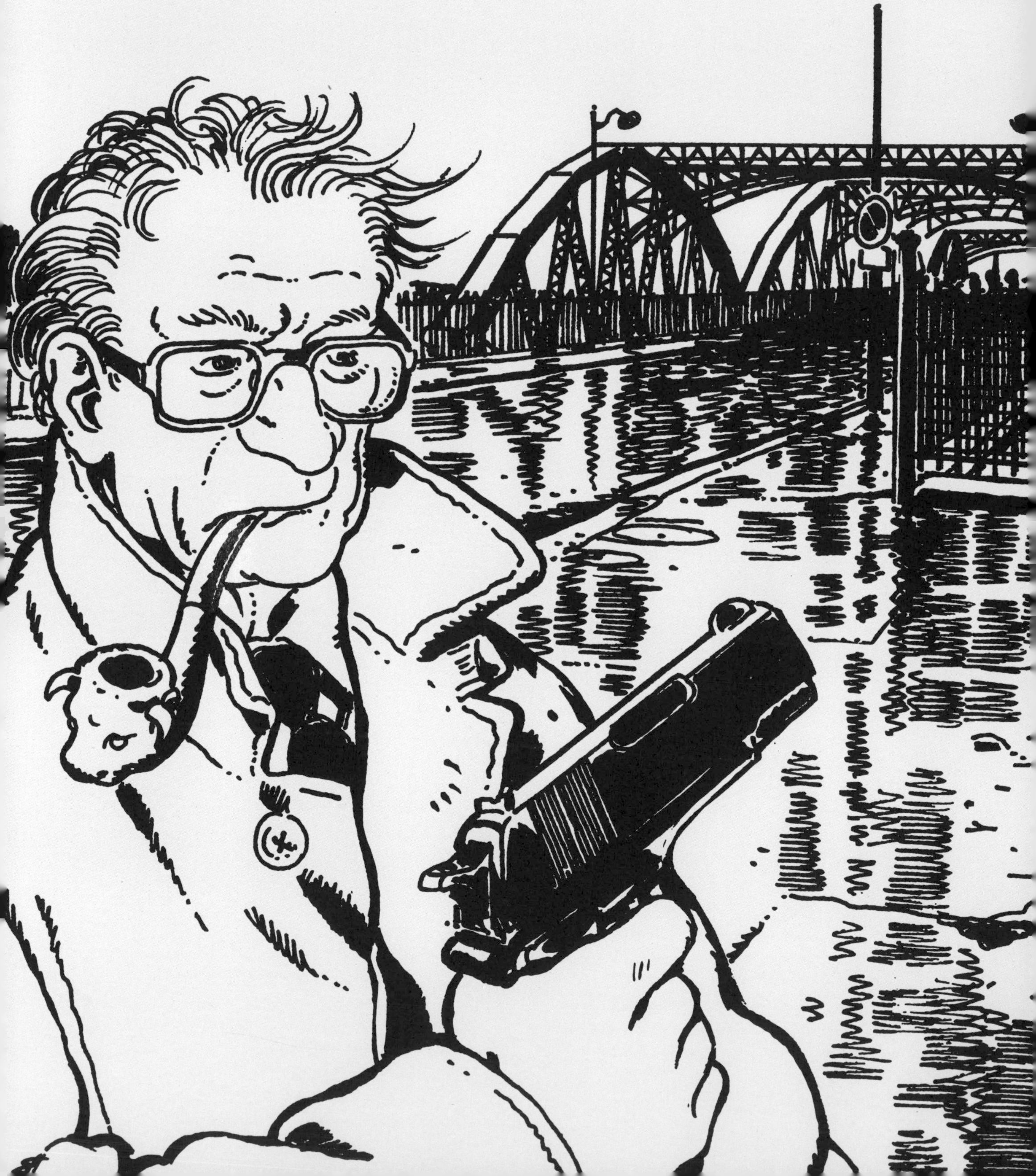

Beauval, the Livre de Poche, etc. The gypsy girl came back to life again and again.

But she had never been represented visually, with the exception of the original cover. And that is when, at last, Tardi came in.

Fans and lovers of comics, you're going to flip. Your Ninth Art has never thrilled me. I must confess that I am more or less against comics. (We'll save the debate for another day.)

Nevertheless, one day, walking past the Casterman bookshop on rue Bonaparte, I was struck by the comic books in the window. I, who had never bought such a thing, quickly purchased (as quick as Adèle Blanc-Sec) the extraordinary adventures of that young lady.

The strength and charm of the drawings; the nostalgic poetry of the setting whose realism paradoxically heightened the fantasy; the atmosphere on the whole; everything convinced me that Tardi was an artist after my own heart and that he would have made an excellent illustrator, if only. . . . Why not? We can always dream. I spend my life doing it. The case presented itself.

From our first conversations, Tardi seemed to me a sensitive and generous person of great politeness and great modesty.*

As for the vegan hostel, on which he requested information, Tardi was able to translate my memories with a remarkable fidelity and, with a few details, his vegan hostel is the one I knew in 1925–'26. I will say nothing of other settings. No one but Tardi can execute them with such exactitude.

No one else can so perfectly enshroud the setting with such a dampness and thickness. No one else can bring the underlying depression to the surface. As for the characters. . . .

When *Fog* appeared as a serial in *À Suivre* magazine, I received from my former readers a few critiques addressing the physical appearances of Burma, Faroux, Bélita, etc., and Tardi's interpretation of them.

Since I had never known exactly what appearance Nestor Burma took, it is difficult for me to judge. It is Tardi's cinematic interpretation.

On the screen, Burma was successively incarnated by René Dary (1946), Michel Galabru (1977), and Michel Serrault (1982). These three actors look very little alike. Who comes closest to my hero? They all have some aspect of him, but also enormous dissimilarities.

Tardi behaved as a film director does. He translated the characters in the novel (whom he knew, I realized with astonishment, better than I did) such as he saw them. Tardi adapted the book—he was not confined to simply being its brilliant illustrator. I would have liked to have seen *Fog* brought to the screen. There were attempts, but they failed.

In place of a film version, there is Tardi's comic.

More improved by Tardi's pencil than the magic lantern, the ephemeral Bélita Morales will not return any time soon to the realm of shadows. As I said before, this dead woman is hard to kill.

Léo Malet
February 19, 1982 (on a foggy day)

(*) A modesty I will qualify as shameful, but which is to his credit, because it is exercised in a world of swamps teeming with so many plagiarists of low caliber; all individuals who blow hot air in inverse proportion to their smallness. Hot air? We'll call them farts: foul-smelling, by definition.

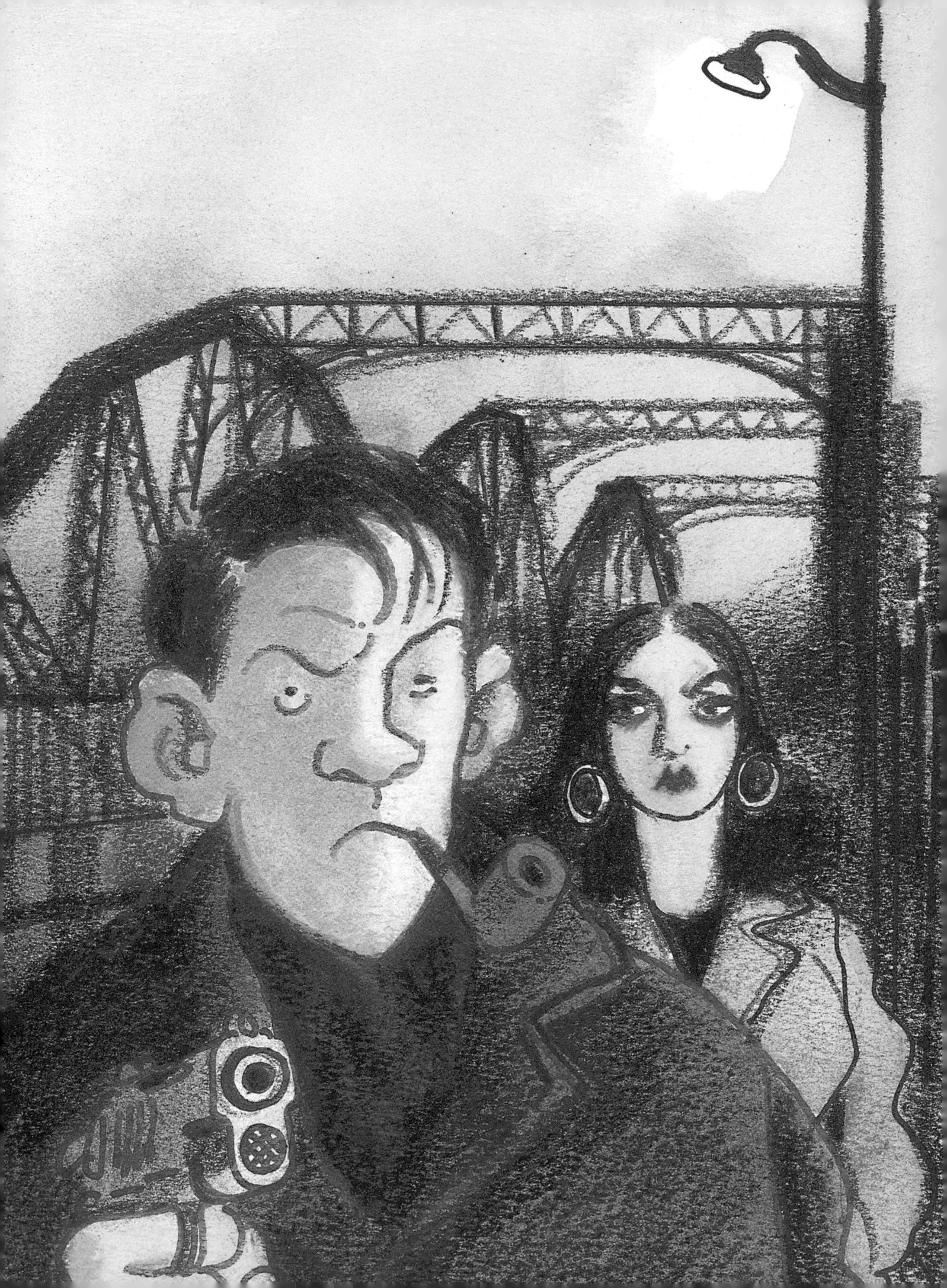

FANTAGRAPHICS BOOKS

TRANSLATOR Kim Thompson
EDITOR Kristy Valenti
DESIGNED BY Jacob Covey
SUPERVISING EDITOR Gary Groth
PRODUCTION Paul Baresh
FONT DESIGNED BY Allan Haverholm
PROVIDED BY Christopher Ouzman of Faraos Cigarer
ADDITIONAL LETTERING Keeli McCarthy
EDITORIAL ASSISTANTS RJ Casey, Reed Draper, Sharon Frajlich,
Mackenzie Pitcock, and Heidi Swenson
ASSOCIATE PUBLISHER Eric Reynolds
PUBLISHER Gary Groth

 Fantagraphics Books, Inc. 7563 Lake City Way NE, Seattle, WA 98115(800) 657-1100 www.fantagraphics.com. Follow us on Twitter @fantagraphics and on Facebook at Facebook.com/Fantagraphics.

ISBN: 978-1-60699-705-5
Library of Congress Control Number: 2016961053
First Printing: July 2017
Printed In China

Image credits:
PAGE 68 Tardi photo © J. M. Gerber
PAGE 72 Tardi drew this 1983 Malet portrait for a magazine.
PAGE 74 Tardi's cover for Malet's novel.

Léo Malet wrote thirty-eight Nestor Burma tales (five short stories and thirty-three novels). Eighteen of these, the "New Mystery of Paris" series, take place in a specific, numbered administrative district (arrondissement). In 1956, Malet wrote the novel *Brouillard au pont de Tolbiac*, set in the XIIIth arrondissement, where the River Seine's left bank is located. It was the first Nestor Burma book cartoonist Tardi adapted in the 1980s; he went on to write and draw four more. In the 2000s, other artists began to contribute to the Burma graphic novel series.

TARDI is a European writer-artist who helped pioneer the graphic novel. Born in Valence, France, in 1946, he broke into the comics magazine *Pilote* in 1969. The animated film *April and the Extraordinary World* was based on his work, and, in 2010, Luc Besson adapted his Adele Blanc-Sec series into a feature film. An author of, and collaborator on, more than thirty genre-spanning works (noir, war, steampunk), he's won every major and minor European cartooning award and is in the Will Eisner Hall of Fame (and has collected two of that institution's trophies). His studio is in Paris.

LÉO MALET (1909–1996, Montpellier) was a French crime novelist, surrealist poet, and singer. His Nestor Burma series has been adapted into film and television, and commemorated on a French postage stamp.

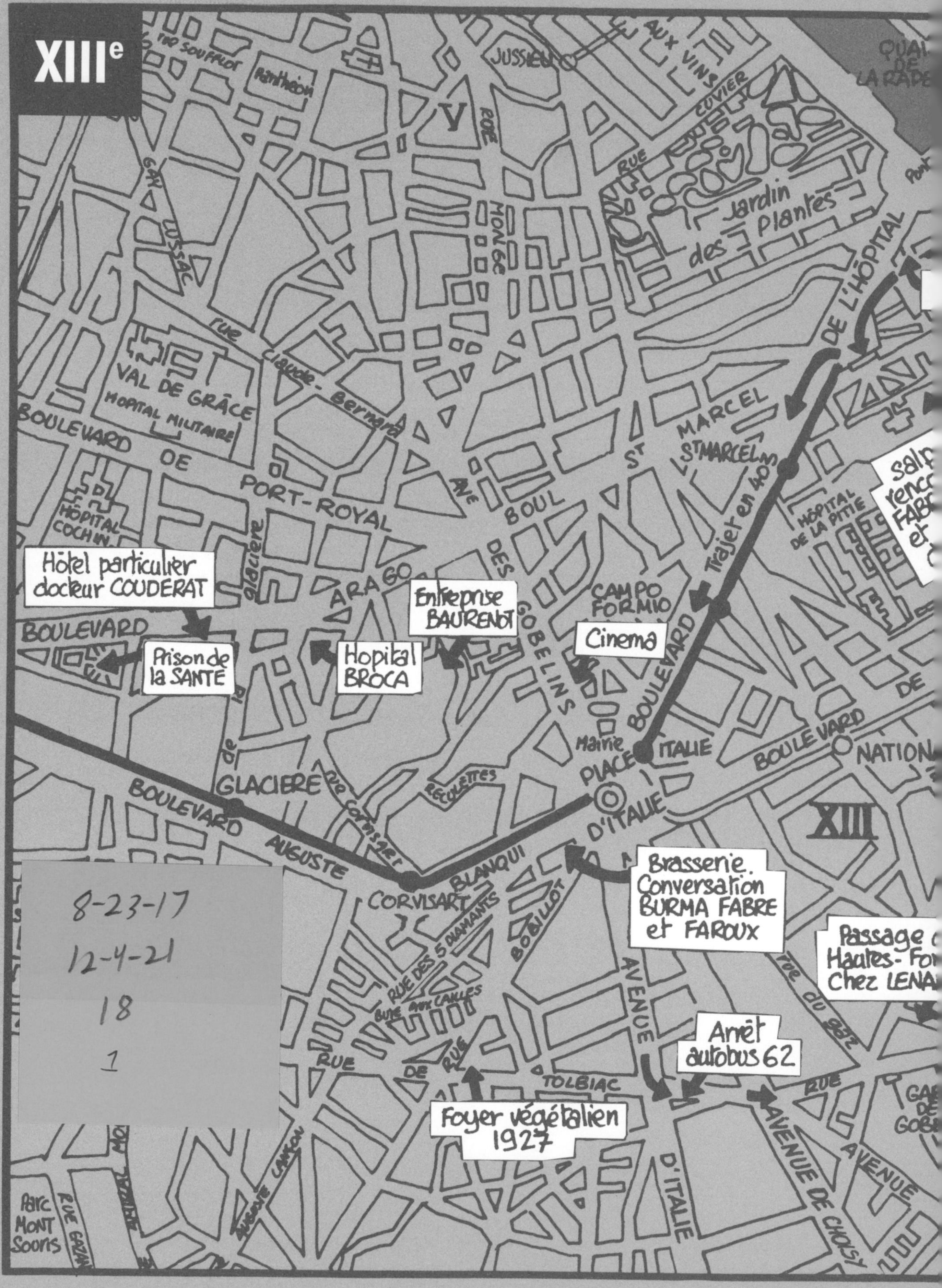
XIIIe
Hôtel particulier docteur COUDERAT
Prison de la SANTÉ
Hopital BROCA
Entreprise BAURENOT
Cinema
Brasserie. Conversation BURMA FABRE et FAROUX
Arrêt autobus 62
Foyer végétalien 1927
Trajet en 40
Jardin des Plantes
VAL DE GRÂCE
HOPITAL MILITAIRE
HÔPITAL COCHIN
HÔPITAL DE LA PITIÉ
BOULEVARD DE PORT-ROYAL
BOULEVARD ARAGO
BOULEVARD AUGUSTE BLANQUI
BOUL DES GOBELINS
BOULEVARD ST MARCEL
BOULEVARD DE L'HÔPITAL
BOULEVARD DE L'HÔPITAL
PLACE D'ITALIE
AVENUE D'ITALIE
AVENUE DE CHOISY
RUE DE TOLBIAC
RUE CLAUDE-BERNARD
RUE MONGE
RUE CUVIER
RUE DES 5 DIAMANTS
BUTTE AUX CAILLES
RUE GAY LUSSAC
JUSSIEU
CAMPO FORMIO
GLACIERE
CORVISART
Mairie
Panthéon
V
XIII
Parc MONT Souris